Cougar

She likes her men rough, tough...and two at a time.

Shannon Tally's heart has been broken one too many times, but it hasn't put a damper on her sex drive. If guys can play the field, so can she. And the two hot, sweaty ranch hands she spots "in the field" at her cousin's ranch will do nicely to play out her wildest fantasy: to tame not just one hunky cowboy, but two. At the same time.

Humans are a mystery to cougar shifter Chase Reya. They invade his home, threatening the animals and his solitude. That's why his leader sent him to the Tally ranch, to learn how to get along with humans. Or at least not to slice and dice them.

He never expected Shannon to stir a whirlwind of heat. And when the alluring female shares her affections with a werewolf, the combined sexual desire erupts even hotter. Only one person can generate this kind of passion—but can his lifelong mate be a *human?* For Shannon, a self-proclaimed lady "cougar", fidelity could be a tall order. Not to mention accepting his true nature...

Warning: Contains animals who are armed and dangerous and find a whole new use for spurs. If you like undomesticated pets, light bondage and m/f/m sex as graphic as it can get, then take a trip into these wilds...but be careful. With more than one animal after your hide, you may end up in bed with more than you can handle.

Wild Cat

She's a real wild cat...in and out of bed.

Alexandra's brother has changed since his mate's death, but she's certain he's no cattle killer. When she gets the chance to track down the real culprit, she jumps at the opportunity to clear the suspicions hovering over his head. And maybe ease her own grief.

Connor would do anything for Alex—even be her mate if she would only ask. Instead he settles for coming with her, ready to protect her from the rogue as well as human hunters. When another tracker shows up accusing them of the crime, though, there's no stopping Alex's instant attraction to the lone werewolf.

Dirk is on the same mission, but for a different reason: His pack owes one of the ranchers a favor. Once he finds Alex examining the latest bovine victim, though, he shifts his goals to include her mile-long legs wrapped around his waist. If only he can get past her interfering friend.

Trigger-happy hunters send them all into hiding, where huddling for warmth turns hotter than expected. The heat burns away any pretense that this is a sexual romp. It's a destined love that a killer could destroy...unless Alex makes a heartbreaking choice.

Warning: Beware of claws, fangs and weapons of a very personal nature. The sex is hot and raw, including the kind of threesome you'd love to have. Oh, yeah, and a heart-wrenching plot.

Look for these titles by *Beverly Rae*

Now Available:

Touch Me
Wailing for Love
To Fat and Back

Cannon Pack
Howling for My Baby
Dance on the Wilde Side
Running with the Pack

Para-Mates
I Married a Demon
I Married a Dragon

Wild Things
Cougar
Wild Cat
Clawed

Magical Sisters
Magical Sex

Wild Things

Beverly Rae

SAMHAIN
PUBLISHING

Samhain Publishing, Ltd.
11821 Mason Montgomery Rd., 4B
Cincinnati, OH 45249
www.samhainpublishing.com

Wild Things
Print ISBN: 978-1-60928-297-4
Cougar Copyright © 2011 by Beverly Rae
Wild Cat Copyright © 2011 by Beverly Rae

Editing by Jennifer Miller
Cover by Kanaxa

Cougar, ISBN 978-1-60504-945-8
First Samhain Publishing, Ltd. electronic publication: March 2010
Wild Cat, ISBN 978-1-60928-244-8
First Samhain Publishing, Ltd. electronic publication: November 2010
First Samhain Publishing, Ltd. print publication: September 2011

Contents

Cougar

Dedication

To all the strong, beautiful women in the world, whatever their age.

Chapter One

"Damn it all, Chase, you know you can't rip into a couple of campers up from Colorado Springs and expect no one to notice," Haken snarled, his eyes sparkling with anger.

"I suppose you wouldn't have done anything?"

Haken averted his gaze for a moment and Chase knew the truth. "I'd have found a less violent way to solve the situation."

Yeah, right. Chase remembered how easily his claws had slid through their soft white skin and smothered the self-satisfied feeling that their scars would serve as reminders not to mess with poor defenseless animals again.

"I get it. I really do. And I'm not saying I don't understand why you did it." Chase opened his mouth to speak, but Haken lifted a hand to cut him off. "But just because the council may sympathize with your intentions doesn't mean we agree with how you handled it."

Chase stood his ground, a cool mountain breeze feathering over his nude body, ready for whatever punishment the council gave him. The other werecats milled around the two men, unwilling to join in the discussion yet too curious not to show up at the rare group gathering. *Curiosity may have killed the cat, but these wimps are just plain pussies.*

Haken stalked to the other side of the small bare patch of land, startling the two cubs wrestling nearby. The boys shifted quickly, returning to their human forms before scampering out of the way. "You need to learn how to deal with humans on their level."

"I don't like humans and I mix with them only when I have to." Chase, like most werecats, preferred a solitary life in the woods, living in his cat form, staying as far from human civilization as possible. Those who liked living in their human forms provided the clan with what few outside provisions they needed.

"Times are changing. It's growing more difficult to stay away from them. When we come in contact with humans, we have to know how to act. Behaving oddly, much less attacking them, only draws unwanted attention." Haken narrowed his eyes, his lips drawing back in a snarl. The only difference between Haken's human and cat displays of anger was the laid-back ears of the predator currently hidden inside the man. "The elders and I have decided you need to learn a lesson."

He growled at the female gliding too close to Chase, an obvious gesture of attraction. She purred, her yellow gaze fixing on Chase a second more before heeding the leader's warning.

"Therefore, we're *asking* you—" Haken locked eyes with Chase, "—to spend time with the humans. Get to know them. Learn to resolve issues without shifting and tearing them apart."

Asking, my ass. He could refuse, but to do so would insult the leader who had helped him avoid punishment in the past. *Aw, shit. I know I'm going to hate what he's got planned.* "What does the council want me to do?"

"The human owner of Shiloh Hills Ranch, Bob Tally, knows about us and has agreed to set you up with a job as a ranch hand." Haken recognized the revulsion in Chase's expression. "That's right. Human ranch hands. You can learn how to deal with humans while you're working alongside them."

"And if I don't?"

"Let's not go down that road yet. Just go and talk to Tally. Then decide."

He studied the pride leader's determined yet hopeful face. "Fine. I'll go. But only to talk."

"Good." With the council's message delivered, Haken turned on his heel and strode out of the clearing. The other cats followed his unspoken direction and hurried into the darkness of the surrounding forest.

Rage flowed through Chase, followed swiftly by disgust. *Spend time among humans? Learn how to interact with them? The idea is ludicrous, not to mention insulting. Hell, I'd rather spend time with a wolf pack.*

Okay, maybe not. But almost. Tired of standing on two legs, he tucked his chin and shifted, dropping to all fours. With a swish of his tail, he darted down the hillside, rushing as though he could outrun the ridiculous sentence.

"So you're Chase Reya."

Chase didn't bother answering since the question sounded more like a statement. Instead, he coolly regarded the seasoned cowboy standing behind the contemporary glass-topped desk that was out of place with the rest of the rustic furnishings in the Shiloh Hills Ranch office. Mounted animal heads—deer, elk, bear but thankfully no pumas—decorated the cabin's walls. A gun cabinet boasted shotguns and rifles along with one ancient pistol, a collector's item. If he had to talk to this human, then he'd let the man speak and get the ordeal over with as quickly as possible.

Dressed in jeans and a button-down plaid shirt, Bob Tally was the perfect image of an old-time cowboy. Unlike his movie-star counterparts with their perfect smiles and manicured nails, he was wiry and weather-beaten, with scars marking his hands from years of wrangling cattle and horses. Gray streaked his once-coal-black hair, while wrinkles aged by the sun and laughter framed the intelligent blue eyes scanning him from top to bottom. "Not much on talking, huh?"

When Chase merely lifted an eyebrow, he chuckled and reached out his hand. Chase eyed the outstretched hand and fought the urge to ignore it. He knew a handshake was the acceptable human method of greeting. Reluctantly, he grasped Bob's hand, gripping it with a firm hold. Bob held on, keeping his grip longer than was necessary until Chase brought his eyes up to meet the older man's.

"Look, son, I know you don't want to be here, but I owe Haken—and your kind—a favor. So let's make this easy on both of us. Agreed?" Bob finally released his hand. "Yeah, I know what you are, but the others don't. So no going down on all fours around here, is that clear?"

"Clear." *Not that it matters since I'm not staying.*

Bob leaned over the desk, palms flat on the smudged surface. "Good. We'll get you settled in the bunkhouse with the rest of the hands." His body language sent the unmistakable message that he'd brook no arguments. "You shouldn't have any problems...if you give it a real chance."

Chase caught the underlying warning in the man's tone and let it roll off his back. "Hold up. I haven't decided if I'm taking this job."

Surprise flickered across Bob's features. "I thought this had already been decided."

"No one decides for me."

The cowboy took his full measure. "I see. Well, it's no skin off my nose but, if you do stay, I don't want any trouble. Understood?"

"I won't start any trouble. *If* I stay."

Bob was a smart one, finishing the thought for Chase. "But you won't run from trouble, either, I bet."

"What's that about trouble, Cousin Bob?"

The older man's mouth fell open, dropping the toothpick he'd balanced between his teeth. Chase pivoted, uneasy that someone had sneaked up behind him, and drew in a sharp breath at the beautiful woman standing in the doorway.

The female grinned first at Bob, then shifted her mocha-colored eyes toward Chase. His body tingled in instinctive sexual recognition, disturbing his calm demeanor. Curly honey-blonde hair framed the sweet face. Full pink lips betrayed the angelic roundness of her features, and Chase wanted nothing more than to take them between his teeth and nibble on the kissable, plump flesh. Soft curves accented her smallish breasts and hips, hips that were perfect for a man to hang on to, and that begged him to force her legs wide to thrust inside her and take a leisurely ride. Saliva flooded his mouth while the material of his jeans pushed back at his cock straining beneath.

"Well, I'll be damned. Shannon, girl, what the hell are you doing here?" Skirting the desk and meeting her halfway, Bob bear-hugged the woman, pressing her arms to her sides and lifting her off her feet. "Figures you'd walk in right when I was talking about trouble. You, my dear cousin, are trouble with a capital *T*. But you're the kind of trouble worth having around."

Let her go. The strange thought hit Chase, unnerving him in its intensity. Although Bob's embrace was not at all sexual in nature, Chase clenched his fists to keep from yanking her out of his hold. *What the hell is wrong with me? She's nothing, no one to me. A human.*

At last Bob released her and they kissed each other on the cheeks. Chase found he could breathe again. Or at least until she turned her attention to him. He struggled to stone-face his expression.

"I'm sorry, Bob. I didn't mean to interrupt." She spoke to her cousin, but her eyes were all for Chase.

He heard the alluring call of her sexuality in her dulcet tone and frowned as the heat flushed from his face down to tantalize his testicles. *Who is this female?*

"Don't you worry about that. We were just finishing up." Bob barely acknowledged Chase with a tilt of his head. "Chase Reya, this is my cousin and reigning cougar, Shannon Tally."

"And damn proud of it, too."

Cougar? Chase sniffed, trying to catch the shifter scent on her. *She's no shifter. So what can he mean?*

Bob hugged her again. "Tell me what you're doing here all the way from Georgia."

Shannon—even her name made his desire for her grow—smiled, keeping her gaze squarely on Chase. "I decided it was high time to visit my favorite cousin." She dropped her eyes, not in the least way demurely, and scanned him from head to toe. "I'd heard Colorado had some amazing sights and I wanted to see them." A pink tongue peeked out between the ruby lips, enthralling in its brief appearance. "And what I've seen so far makes me want to see more."

Is she coming on to me? Although werecat females tended to be aggressive in attracting sexual partners, Chase wasn't sure if human females were the same. *Should I ask? Am I supposed to respond in a certain way?* He'd never considered sex with a human female, but this one had him ready to rut her up, down and every way in between.

"I'm glad you're here. How about I show you the guest room and let Chase find his own way to the bunkhouse?" Bob lifted an eyebrow at him. "*If* you're signing on."

"Yeah. I'm staying." The words were out of his mouth in an instant. No way could he walk away from this female. At least not until he'd gotten inside her. His cock twitched, already feeling her warmth wrapped around him.

"Good. Then head on out and let the boys fix you up." Bob pulled Shannon around, breaking her visual lock on Chase. He jerked, physically thrown by the loss of her attention. He followed the pair, silently watching her delectable behind sway as the older man led her out of the office and up the stairs to the second floor.

He tilted his head, still watching them until they turned the corner on the second story and disappeared down the long hallway. His mouth dried up and he gripped the stair railing for support. *I have to have her. One way or another, I have to have her.*

Please be outside. Shannon rushed to the guest bedroom window, hoping Bob hadn't delayed her too long. *If he'd yakked at me any longer, my ear would've fallen off.* At last she'd complained of needing a rest. But maybe she hadn't gotten away fast enough. Granted, she would still find Chase around the ranch during the next few days, but she needed to see that animal of a man right now. Otherwise she might think she'd dreamed their meeting. Throwing the curtains aside, she pressed her nose against the window pane and scanned the yard below. Ranch hands milled around, hurrying to do whatever ranch hands did.

Where is he? She bit her lip, nerves threatening to take over, and searched the area between the main house and the bunkhouse. *There he is.* His yellow hair shone in the bright light, setting him apart from the other men. But if his hair hadn't marked him, she would've noticed him simply from his confident, powerful swagger. He stopped for a moment, listening as another hand spoke to him.

The flutter in her abdomen signaled another wave of excitement. *Shannon, girl, you've got to get yourself some of that.*

17

She'd come to visit Bob with the single-minded purpose of screwing as many hunky cowboys as she could get between the sheets and anywhere else she could fuck them. But she'd never expected to run into a man like Chase. He was different from the others, wilder than any man she'd ever met. He was everything she'd fantasized in a cowboy—young, tall, tanned and sporting a major bulge in his jeans.

Be careful. The familiar warning sounded in her mind yet, unlike all the times before, she pushed it aside and allowed the dangerous thought entry. *This man could be more than just an amazing hunk of sexuality.* She hadn't felt that particular type of yearning since Jarrod had left her alone and sobbing in front of all her family and friends. A lump formed in her throat and she resolutely swallowed. *I will never let any man hurt me again. Men are for sex and only for sex.*

And she could feel the sexual attraction in her gut. Her body was ready for a hot time in the not-so-old west. One way or another, she'd have him riding her long and hard.

She closed her eyes and imagined how it would be. She lay on the soft grass, enjoying the sun warming her naked body. Chase, nude and glistening with a healthy sheen, lowered his body over hers, the muscles in his arms bulging as he supported himself with his hands next to her head. Rising up, she ran her tongue over the granite-hard pecs, drinking the perspiration off them before it could drip onto her body.

With a quick glance at the real prize, she twisted and cupped his balls in her palm. "Fuck me, cowboy. Try and break me. If you dare."

He groaned and slipped his scorching gaze from her face, over her ready-to-be-sucked nipples and down her flat stomach to the curly blonde patch below. "I don't want to break your spirit, sweet filly. I just want to ride you until you won't ever want anyone else on top of you."

Shannon rocked her hips forward, tempting him to move

against her. Adopting a horrible imitation of John Wayne, she quipped, "Cowboy, get ready to get bucked off." *Not that I really want to win this little contest.*

He chuckled, then suddenly grew very intense. Taking her mouth with his, he scraped his teeth against her lips. Slowly, teasingly, he first tugged her upper lip into his mouth, then nibbled on her bottom lip. She slid her hands along his arms, over the mountainous shoulders and clutched him behind his neck. *I'm never letting you go, cowboy.*

He feathered kisses along her jaw, down her neck and onto her shoulder in a wild race. He nipped at her, licked at her, making her breaths come quicker, faster. Kissing her, he traveled his way between her breasts, along the soft swell of her belly, to pause for a dip into her belly button. The move, surprisingly sensual, made her twitch.

"Shit, Chase. Don't go swimming in the pond when you can dive into the ocean."

He cast her a quizzical expression before realization hit. "Don't worry. I know how to swim really good."

Scooting back to sit on his legs, he slicked his palms down her side, following the bend of her waist. Pushing her legs apart, he raked his tongue along the curve between her leg and mons, blowing warm air against her skin. She shivered under the hot sun and grabbed his hair. "Lower, Chase. Go lower."

"Is this low enough?" Shoving his arms under her legs, he lifted her, bringing her bottom off the ground.

"Hey!"

With her buttocks held in the crook of his arms, he thumbed her folds aside and dove in. His mouth latched onto her clit and pulled—hard. Jolting upward, she grabbed his shoulders, but couldn't hang on. Not with all the shaking her body was doing.

Like a man forbidden to drink for centuries, Chase sucked,

tugged, bit and sucked again on her throbbing clit. Crying out, she fell back down and let him eat her up. Her body shook, orgasm after orgasm racing through her, her heart threatening to burst out of her chest. She clutched at the grass beside her, tearing out handfuls as she tried to find some way of surviving the ecstasy. Yet if she had to die, this would be her choice of demise.

Just when she didn't think she could handle the agonizing pleasure a second more, he tracked his hand up her side, over the curve of her breast to rub his thumb over her nipple. His hand traced a hot trail down to her buttocks again and fondled them. Fingering the crease between her cheeks, he latched onto her wet clit and lashed his tongue around the sensitive nub. The simple touch shot zings of desire into her already-tensed muscles.

"Chase. I'm so wet. Please. Fuck me."

He answered, his words smothered against her.

She squirmed, hoping to make him go deeper. Instead, he broke free from her. "No. I didn't want you to stop."

With a chuckle, he moved to her side and thrust his hand between her legs, his two fingers sliding easily into the wet cave. His thumb took up where his mouth had left off.

Hell, it's not what I'd asked for, but it's still good. Damn good. She arched her pelvis, pushing at him, drawing his fingers deep inside her pussy, clenching the walls of her core. A small wave rolled through her and she clutched at the grass beneath her.

"Oh, shit. I want you inside me. Fuck me, cowboy."

Shannon cried out and spread her legs wider, giving him more room. Room enough to place himself between her legs. His mouth took hers again, plunging his tongue inside her, giving her a taste of him, a taste of her. He moved, gliding over her body and she felt the heat of his erection forcing its way between her legs. No longer able to think, she let her instincts lead her and rubbed against him, urging him to sink his cock into her. The fire burned hotter and wilder inside her. Wrapping her legs around his waist, she thrust her pussy against his crotch and moaned an urgent plea.

Denying her still, he slipped his tongue from her mouth and scorched a path down to find her tits again. Shannon closed her eyes, enjoying the sensation of his teeth nipping at her as he tugged and teased her aching buds. She writhed against him, her nails digging marks into his back and, at last, he answered her call.

He entered her, hard and fast, the size of his shaft creating delicious friction within her vaginal walls. He kept thrusting into her, pounding into her, and she pushed back, urging him to go deeper, faster, harder.

"Shannon?"

"Yes." She squeezed her closed eyes tighter and concentrated on the delicious feel of him inside her. "Oh, yes."

"Shannon, girl, open up. It's me."

Shannon jerked her hand out of her jeans, whirled around and almost fell over in her hurry to the door. *Thank God I locked it. Otherwise, Bob probably would've barged right in.* "Y-yes?"

"If you're feeling up to it, I thought I'd show you around the ranch."

She grinned and sucked her come-slicked fingers clean. "No need, cuz. I know you have work to do. Don't worry about me. I can explore on my own."

"Name's Chase." Chase met the frank looks of the ranch hands with a hard one of his own and waited for someone to question his arrival. *Damn, I hate this.* Within a few moments, however, they'd grown uneasy with his defiant stare and dropped their gazes to continue doing whatever they'd been doing.

All of them except for one. The non-human one.

The werewolf in cowboy's clothing, his legs crossed at the ankles in a careless fashion, leaned against the wall next to a bunk bed and grinned at him. A grin that said, "I know what you are, too."

Chase smothered a low growl. *If he keeps grinning like that I'm gonna have to shove that smirk all the way down his throat.* When the wolf moved, slowly, deliberately, Chase paralleled him, keeping a safe distance between them. *Come on, wolfman, make the first move.*

"Where are you planning on sleeping, c—" Wolfman's grin grew wider. "Chase, was it?"

He started to call me cat. Chase fought the urge to tell him to go chase a car and never come back. Instead, he walked over to a different bunk bed and tossed his pack on the lower bed. "Here will do. If it's free."

Wolfman placed a hand on a young redheaded cowboy sitting at the table where five men were playing poker and acting as if they hadn't noticed Chase's arrival. "It's free. John won't mind using the top bunk from now on. Will you, John-boy?"

John, his Adam's apple bobbing with a swallow, nervously glanced between them, then agreed with a curt nod. He averted his gaze and returned to the game.

"You got a last name?"

This hound is getting under my nerves real fast. Even faster than a dog normally would. "Reya." He leaned over and tested the firmness of the mattress but kept his eyes on the werewolf. *Neither Haken or Bob mentioned a werewolf.* "And who are you?" *The humans' mascot?*

"Dirk Claxton from around Denver. Ever heard of the

Cannons of Denver?"

The Cannons as in Cannon wolf pack. Of course he had. Although he'd never met any of them, he knew their reputation. They were considered the ruling werewolf pack in the state. Maybe even the entire western half of the country.

The squeal of a chair's hind legs on tortured wood floor announced the departure of another cowhand. They'd started clearing out, alone or in small groups, a minute after Chase walked in. *Good noses can always smell a fight brewing and good brains know when to get out of the way.* "Yeah, I know of them. Never met any of them, though." He didn't like the way the wolf had edged toward him, almost as though sizing him up for an attack. *Figures. I haven't been here an hour before I get thrown out for fighting. But at least this time it's not with a human.* He took a deep breath, rose and got ready for whatever the shifter threw at him.

Even then he wasn't ready for Shannon Tally.

"Hi, guys." She scanned first Chase then Dirk, her eyes glistening with intense interest. "Or should I say *howdy* instead? Do ranch hands really speak cowboy like they do on television?"

The scent of lust filled the room. Chase closed his eyes and sniffed, taking in the heady aroma. Yet the scent wasn't purely hers. His instant reaction to Shannon's appearance was met in force by Dirk's. The werewolf's attraction to the female was so strong Chase could do more than merely smell it. He could feel it pressing against his skin. Yet, surprisingly, her scent filtered into the mix with as much passion as the combined weres' desires.

She smells hot and ready for fucking. Chase took in the easy seductive way she moved, obviously aware of their interest, yet accustomed to the admiration. *She's regal. Like a queen in her castle.* Maybe her carriage came with her age, since she was older. While she had the confidence of a woman well into her late thirties, she retained the vitality, the allure, the beauty of a young female. Her hips flared nicely in the skin-tight jeans while the vee of her blouse highlighted her small but perky chest. A knowing smile lifted the corners of her lips, highlighting the turned-up nose that crinkled when the smile turned into a grin.

Again the urge hit him, making him momentarily forget about the werewolf. *I have to have her. And once I do, I can get the hell out of this place.*

"What's wrong, boys?" Shannon paused, dragging their attention to her and only her. "Did I interrupt a little male bonding?" She smothered the urge to giggle. Why weren't these two talking? Sure, she was used to having a strong effect on the opposite sex, but this was ridiculous. *Hell, their tongues are almost hanging out of their mouths. Yep, this is gonna be fun.*

Of course, she'd known that the second she'd laid eyes on delectable Chase. Although finding him alone with another hunk had thrown her for a moment, she'd recovered quickly. *Please, God, tell me they're not gay.* Not that she had anything against players from the other team, but she so wanted a good long taste of Chase. And the second cowboy, too.

Nope. No maybe about it. She wanted them both. Preferably together. All she had to do was make it happen.

Her gaze drifted back to Chase. *Maybe I'll play with him more than the other... Nope, girl, keep it fun and free. No attachments—other than the physical ones tenting up their jeans.* She dropped her attention to their crotches, focusing on the goal in mind.

She moved a little closer to the shorter, stockier man. He was the exact opposite of Chase but just as yummy. Where Chase was lean, he was broad. Where Chase radiated a cheetah-like smoothness, a sleek animal ready to spring at her in the next second, this one exuded a slow but steady brute-like quality. Just as she'd hoped, the ripples of tension wafting off Chase hyped up.

"Hi, I'm Shannon Tally. Bob's cousin from the South." Giving him an ooh-you-are-so-yummy look, she imagined the tall lanky cowboy naked and positioned between her legs while the other sucked on her tits. Or maybe they'd stand, with one nailing her from the front and the other from the back. "And you are...?"

"No one. He's no one."

Ooh, jealous already? Very juicy. "Wow, Chase, talk about rude." She flattened her palm on the other man's chest and delighted in the way his heart picked up speed. "And you're wrong. I'm sure he's someone. Someone very special." She met the shorter man's sky-blue eyes and held on. "Tell me your name, cowboy."

"Dirk. Dirk Claxton, sugar."

Sugar. How cute. She lowered her gaze to slide over his slightly opened mouth then back to his eyes. "I'm happy to meet you, Dirk, Dirk Claxton." *Did his eyes change color? Naw, couldn't have. But I would've sworn...*

A low rumble from Chase interrupted her thoughts. *How odd. Did Chase just growl? And he'd moved closer. Sweet.* She placed her other palm on his chest, holding back both men. His heart, just like Dirk's, raced against her skin.

Slowly, seductively, she ran her palms in circles around their chests, delighting in the rugged firmness of each man. *I wonder if they're both as hard down there?* She let her hands skim down their shirts, enjoying the way their abs tightened beneath the thick material, and stopped an inch above the waistlines of their jeans. *Easy, Shannon. Take your time.* She paused, giving them a chance to back away, take her hand—

something.

But neither man moved, neither one giving an inch to the other. She dropped her hands to her side, closed her eyes and took a breath to enjoy the palpable sexual awareness between the cowboys. *Holy shit. I do believe I've won the horny sweepstakes with these two.*

Without warning, she pushed against Dirk, pressing her breasts against his chest. He stiffened, but in a good way. She ran her hands along his arms until she took his face in her hands. *I bet Chase is watching this big-time. Are you jealous, Chase?*

Dirk exhaled the moment their lips touched, breathing warm air into her mouth. She took his breath inside her. Sticking her tongue in his mouth, she lapped up the taste of him. His hands gripped her ass, thrusting her pelvis against his bulging crotch. The flame of her desire surprised her and, for a moment, she was tempted—hell, more than tempted—to push her jeans down and beg him to eat her. She teetered on the brink, closer than she'd ever expected to come and pushed against him. Dirk, however, kept her there and nibbled on her lips.

Damn. What have I started? I don't want Chase to think I've chosen Dirk over him. She nipped him back and struggled between what she knew she should do and what she wanted to do. *Oh, screw it. Screw me. Even with Chase standing by, watching. Hell, especially with Chase watching.*

Suddenly, Dirk wrenched away from her, leaving her bereft and unsatisfied. *What the hell?* A furious Dirk pulled Chase's hand off his arm, then stood chest to chest with the angry man.

"Back the hell up, cat-man. In fact, why don't you scat and leave us alone?"

Cat-man? But Shannon didn't have time to wonder about the odd name. *Forget that. Check out the expression on Chase's face. Jealous doesn't remotely cover it.*

Chase chest-bumped Dirk, his hands clenched at his side. "Leave her alone, dog face."

What is it with these two and their weird name-calling? Shannon could almost see the steam radiating from the men. Any other woman would try and cool them down. Or run away. But she wasn't any other woman. Instead, she stepped between them, getting squashed against them.

"Settle down, boys. No harm done. In fact..." she turned to confront the tawny-headed hunk, "...if you'd waited another minute or two, I'd have had time to do this."

Grabbing him by the shirt, she tugged Chase forward and slammed her mouth on his. He beat her to the punch, however, by getting his tongue into her mouth first. She fought to keep her triumph from showing on her face. She fondled the firm roundness of his ass and groaned into his kiss. He tasted musky, like Dirk had, yet different. His kiss had something else. A tangy indefinable something, reminding her of the untamed outdoors she longed to explore. He took her breast and rubbed his thumb over her already-taut nipple. A soft mew escaped her. Covering his hand with hers, she encouraged him to do more, take more. Where Dirk had excited her, Chase drove her crazy. *Fuck me. Fuck me hard over and over again. Damn, how I want to make my fantasy come true.*

Without warning, the kiss ended, making her gasp in surprise and disappointment. She stepped away, unsteady on her feet, turning her head to try and hide her emotions.

Shit. When did I lose control of the situation? I was supposed to be the tease, not them. Pulling herself together, she got ready for their gloating. After all, they'd taken control and used her horniness against her. What she saw on their faces, however, nearly buckled her knees.

Chapter Two

Chase and Dirk stood shoulder to shoulder, staring at her. Each man's gaze bore into her, yet she no longer saw the men inside those eyes. Instead, they looked at her like she was game to be eaten, a deer caught in the hunt, ready to be played with, then slaughtered.

She gritted her teeth, gathered her last bit of strength and smiled. "Whew. I have to admit, guys, I didn't expect that." She struggled to even out her breathing before she took the next step. "But I enjoyed every bit of it. With both of you." Tossing her head to make her curls bounce, she swayed provocatively to the door, paused with her hand on the doorknob, then glanced back over her shoulder. "I'm definitely going to enjoy playing with both you boys." With a wink, she opened the door and walked out.

Once the door closed behind her, Shannon released the pent-up air she'd held and tried to steady her nerves. Both men exuded an extra animal-like sexuality, but she knew she'd come face-to-face with something more, something she'd tried to protect herself from for the past ten years. Mentally she strengthened the emotional wall she'd built the day Jarrod had dumped her at the altar, lifted her chin in defiance and strode back to the house.

Seeing Shannon kiss the wolf churned Chase's insides into a volcanic boil. Dirk's hands on her ass drove him to the brink of insanity, obsessing with the need to take the shifter by his hair and toss him through the wall. Although tormented by the sight of his female—because she would be his one way or another—he kept his hands fisted at his side and didn't wrap them around the canine's throat. Instead, he held his fury in check and did the only thing he could do. He pulled them apart. Then she kissed him back, unleashing every ounce of passion he'd tried to contain.

He thrust his tongue into her mouth, wished he was thrusting his shaft inside her instead, and soaked up all her flavors. Swishing his tongue around, he swept away the werewolf's saliva, literally cleansing her with his own. Yet the kiss, instead of cooling the boil of the lava roiling within him, stirred the heat, sending the burn to a higher, hotter level. He gripped her breast, contenting himself with rubbing her tit instead of ripping her clothes off and sucking her nipple. When she covered his hand with hers, he silently shouted victory and then quietly died inside.

He had no choice but to break free. No choice unless he wanted to push her over the edge of the table and ram her from behind. But he wouldn't do that with the werewolf watching. Instead, he released her, then watched her stride in that sexy walk of hers right out of the room. He bit back the words to beg her to stay.

I don't know what just happened, but I'm damn sure going to find out. In the same moment, Chase and Dirk glared at each other, then turned in opposite directions. Chase was determined not to show the wolfman how much she unsettled him, no matter how much he ached for her. After all, she'd kissed the damn dog first. He couldn't help but wonder which kiss she'd enjoyed more.

The two men studiously ignored each other, saying

nothing. Chase attempted to think of other things—how long he'd have to stay at the ranch, how he would deal with humans—but every thought came back to the curly-locked blonde who'd awakened a primal need he hadn't known existed.

Shit, I never counted on this. Being with humans and now a werewolf is going to be hard enough. But seeing her every day, wanting her every second... Chase drew in a ragged breath. *Damn.* He lifted his gaze toward the door but, instead, found the wolf staring at him. "What the fuck are you looking at?"

Dirk remained stoic, his features blank. Yet Chase could sense his underlying bemusement. "She's something, isn't she?"

"Yeah, you could say so." *And she's mine. Or will be if I have anything to say about it.*

Dirk chuckled, finally letting the humor hidden beneath show on his face. "You do have a way of understating things, kitty."

Chase was beside him before Dirk made it to the door. "I'm no kitty and you'd do well to keep that in mind." *Come on, dog breath, let's get this on, fang to fang. Right now a fight would do me good.*

Irritatingly, however, Dirk ignored the warning and looked out the window. Chase followed his lead to see Shannon talking with her cousin on the wraparound porch of the white country-style main house. The wind buffeted her curls, blowing them into her face. Brushing them back, she shook her head and laughed. Bob pointed at the corral and she turned, giving Chase an even more delectable view.

She's beautiful. Chase took her in, devouring every inch of her rounded curves, the tightness of her jeans accentuating the cleft between her legs, the rise of her breasts. Although he'd heard of other weres taking human females—sometimes even for their mates—he'd never considered the idea of fucking one. Until now. *Shit.*

"You want her."

Chase ignored Dirk's comment, keeping his attention on Shannon. *Go away, little doggie.*

"Well, that's just too damn bad."

Figures he'd say so. Chase shifted far enough to change the shape of his eyes, letting them narrow into slits. "Is that so?"

"Yeah, it is."

Although he knew where the conversation was headed, he had to go with it. To blow it off would be too much like backing down. No way would he back down to some mangy-haired mutt. "How so?"

"Because she's mine."

Chase resisted the urge to snarl. Instead, he crossed his arms—as much to act nonchalantly as to keep from breaking the dog's back—and focused on Shannon's movements while keeping Dirk in his peripheral vision. "Hmm. So, you've marked her? Fast work, pup. Especially since you two just met."

Dirk tensed, a slight change in his demeanor, but nonetheless, Chase caught it. "Who said anything about marking her?"

Why did my thoughts go in that direction? As though the werewolf would take her as his mate. Chase snorted at Dirk's questioning look. "Don't you hounds always stick with one bitch for life?"

"After we're finished nailing every other bitch we want first. Trust me, cat-man, I'll have that pretty little thing sucking my dick before the week's out."

Not if I can help it. Chase shot the man a challenging smirk. "If it's going to take you that long, then you'd better forget it. She'll be flat on her back with her legs wrapped around me before the sun comes up tomorrow."

"Seriously, man. I know cats think they rule the world and

everything in it, but are all you guys so delusional?"

"Not delusional. Justifiably confident."

"Then it sounds like we have a problem."

"Really?" Chase pulled the door open and paused. "No problem here that I can see. Aside from having to worry about catching fleas." Enjoying the annoyed expression on Dirk's face, Chase stepped into the bright sunlight.

"Dang, did you see the honkers on that woman?"

Honkers? Chase rolled from his back to sit on the edge of the bunk bed. The ranch hands sitting around the table took turns tossing coins and cards to the center in yet another game of poker. The way Chase figured it, humans enjoyed wasting time doing trivial things. So far he'd managed to get along with most of the hands mainly because he kept to himself and stayed out of the way. But this new topic of conversation caught his attention.

"Yep, she may be a little long in the tooth, but she's still got a smokin' bod. Man, those legs go all the way to her chin." The cowboy called Mick bumped his fists against the first man's. "Plus, I heard from one of the men at the tack store that she's ready to ride any young stud that'll give her a good bucking. Emphasis on the young part."

The men chuckled, adding lecherous murmurs of agreement that rankled Chase's nerves. Although they hadn't mentioned Shannon by name, he knew they were talking about her and their talk both irritated and confused him. What was it about humans and sex? In his world, sex was shared freely and openly between one or more partners. Humans, from what he'd observed, had too many rules and taboos about the natural act. In fact, he was thankful that Shannon's attitude about sex was more shifter-like than human. But it didn't make it any easier to hear them talk disrespectfully about her.

Mick flipped his cards toward the middle of the table and took a swig of his beer. "Yes, sir, boys. Shannon Tally is a real live cougar."

Cougar again? Don't humans know what a cougar is? Or does this word mean something different in human-speak? He muttered a curse and decided he had to know. "What do you mean she's a cougar?"

All the cowhands stared at him as though he'd asked if they could shift into two-headed birds. Mick snorted and let out a raucous laugh. "You're shitting me. You don't know what a cougar is?"

Keep cool, Chase. Don't let this worthless human get to you. "The only cougars I know are mountain lions."

Mick pushed back his chair, tilting it on the back legs so he could lean perilously backward. His wide smirk grew bigger. "Where the fuck were you raised? With wolves?"

Dirk, who had remained silent until now, sputtered his beer. "Like hell he did. Wolves would've had him for a snack. A tough, tasteless snack. Watch how you talk about wolves, Mick."

The cowboy paused to consider Dirk's strange remark, then let it drop to turn back to Chase. "A cougar is an older woman who still has a hot bod and likes fucking younger men. She's in her prime."

"Her prime what?" Chase hated asking this jerk, but he had no choice. He had to know.

Another round of laughter circled the table. "Her sexual peak, of course. That's why a cougar woman wants to have sex with younger men. Older dudes can't keep up with her." Mick eyed Chase suspiciously. "Are you planning on taking our little Shannon for a ride? Because if you do, then be sure to get in line fast. Otherwise, you'll get stuck with sloppy seconds."

Chase was on his feet, killing the raucous laughter of the men and bunching Mick's shirt in a tight grip. He wasn't sure what sloppy seconds meant, but he sensed it was a derogatory term. And he'd be damned if he'd let this human talk about Shannon that way. "Why you lousy hu—" Without wanting to, he shifted, allowing his eyes to change and his teeth to grow. Mick's eyes grew wide and he sensed the man's heartbeat beating faster.

"Hey, Chase old boy, take it down a notch, will ya? After all, we wouldn't want anyone to get hurt, right?" Dirk wrenched him away from a very scared and cowed Mick. Leaning in, Dirk warned, "Careful, puddy-cat. You're about to show your claws."

Chase closed his eyes, forcing his inner animal back into submission.

Coughing, Mick stumbled to the opposite side of the room, nearly bumping into the door Bob stepped through. Bob surveyed the room, taking in the now-very-quiet Mick and then landing his gaze on Chase and Dirk. "What's going on?"

Chase knocked Dirk's hand away and slid back onto his bunk bed. "Nothing."

Dirk shot him a warning glance. "That's right. Nothing at all."

But Bob didn't buy it. "That true, Chase? Mick?" Neither man answered. "Dirk, how's our new hand getting along?"

Chase bristled. *Why the hell is he asking that mutt? Like he's my master or something.* He bit back a snarl.

"Not bad." Dirk didn't bother covering his smirk. "He needs to learn how we do things around here is all. But don't worry. I'll be happy to give him the benefit of my experience."

Chase nearly choked on the thought. *Why that skuzzy hound!*

"Good. Just make sure no one—" he sent Chase a pointed look, "—causes any trouble. Every hand's part of a working crew and I expect all of you to get along."

Getting along in the human world obviously means taking a certain amount of shit from another hand without tearing his heart out. Chase leaned on the wall behind his bunk and glared at the worn comforter. *I'd better go back to avoiding the rest of them until I get out of this place.* He bit back a growl. *Unless Shannon's involved.*

Shannon ran her gaze over the shirtless man shoving a pitchfork into the hay. He worked with his back to her, muscles rippling in his broad shoulders, highlighting the bulge of each tendon as he lifted load after load of hay from the stack over to the floor of the horse pen. Perspiration glistened on his body, showing off more of his fine definition. Worn jeans, frayed at the bottom where the cuffs met scuffed boots, settled an inch or so below his lean waist, tempting her to push them even lower. His thick blond hair lay at the back of his neck, wrapping around to fall in front of him whenever he bent over.

And oh, when he bent over! She tilted her head, zoning in on the firm round ass pushed her way with each forward thrust of the pitchfork.

He'd taken his sweet time, but she was glad she'd waited for Chase to find his way to the stables. After giving him thirty minutes inside, she'd slipped across the yard toward the barn. "Fancy meeting you here, cowboy."

Chase rested the pitchfork against the stall. A smile flashed across his face before being replaced by a somber, uninterested expression.

Yeah, right. Like I really believe you're not happy to see me.

Making sure she moved her hips in a practiced way meant to allure even the most resistant of men, Shannon crossed over to him, getting close. Very close. She could smell the sweat mixed with another aroma, his personal scent of desire. *I wonder what he smells like in bed? During sex? After sex?* An image of Chase strapped to her bed flashed through her mind. *Fantasies, like wishes, can come true. If you're willing to make them come true. And I'm more than willing.*

"Pretty corny line."

Again, she studied his expression. Or rather the lack of one. *Don't even try to hide your feelings, big guy. No one can kiss me the way you did and then pretend he's not ready to kiss me again. Kiss me and more.* She tossed her curls and sidled over to him. "Yeah, I know. But I like the old-fashioned pickup lines."

He narrowed his eyes and a slight edge of smugness played at the corners of his lips, betraying his aloofness. "Does that mean you're trying to, uh, pick me up?"

He sounded unsure of the phrase which only made him that much sweeter. Taking his hands, she pulled on the fingers of his work gloves, slowly removing them and letting them fall to the ground.

"Trying? Oh, honey hunk, I never simply try." She looked at him—*oh, how I love a tall man*—and tiptoed her way up to plant a peck on his lips. "I just do it."

He licked his lips, tasting the chaste kiss. With a flicker of emotion across his face, he finally let go of his pretence. "Then just do it."

He reached for her, but she slipped out of his grasp and walked toward the back of the stable. She suddenly felt like the cat teasingly playing with a mouse. A very delectable masculine mouse. "You know, I've always wondered if I'd enjoy a roll in the hay. Seems to me hay would make for an itchy bed." *Good. He's following. As if there was ever any doubt.*

"You're right. Hay is itchy. But if you're getting fucked the right way, you won't notice."

She arched an eyebrow in silent question. "And you would know, right? Having had lots of willing fillies in the hay?"

He didn't answer, instead letting her figure it out on her own. At the back wall, in the dim light sneaking through the boards, she unbuttoned the first button on her blouse. When he didn't say anything, she undid the next one, continuing until her shirt lay open to her waist to reveal the swell of her breasts. He blinked, his eyes altering somehow.

Wider? No, narrower. I wish I could see his pupils right now. I bet they're as big as all of Colorado.

"Chase." Saying his name was all she needed to do. He was by her side, faster than she'd have thought possible. But the end result was all that mattered.

And yet he didn't touch her. She frowned, unable to believe he hadn't pulled her into his arms. But he wanted her, she had no doubt. His breathing came in shallow puffs, his mouth slightly parted in invitation while his gaze slid from her throat to the valley between her breasts.

At last, he reached out, using only his index finger to lightly graze over her breast. She inhaled, stunned at the response that small touch sent through her body. If one finger could heat her up that much, his cock would likely burn her alive. She'd gladly die in that fire.

Intrigued, she kept her hands at her side and waited for his next move. Dragging his fingertip along the curve of her breast, he paused at the edge of her blouse. She heard the ragged intake of his breath and matched it with one of her own, then held her breath. *Shit, don't stop now.*

He let out a burst of air and slipped his fingers under the blouse until finally his hand hid under the loose material. And still he hadn't touched her nipple. She straightened, wanting to force him to feel her until she either exploded or pushed his hand where she wanted it.

At last, he continued the torturously slow path toward her aching tit. His fingers finally slid over her taut nub, burning the nipple as though he'd lit a match to her skin. She arched, unable to do anything else.

"Look at me."

She did as he commanded and lost herself in the conflicted expression on his face. "Yes?" She hadn't meant to whisper, but her voice had suddenly lost its strength. *Tell me anything. Tell me everything.* Without warning, she realized she wanted more from him. But more than sex? She hadn't wanted more from any man in a very long time.

"If I go on, I won't stop."

His hand closed over her breast and her knees almost buckled. "If you stop, I'll kill you."

Surprise burst into his eyes, soon replaced with amusement. "What if someone comes in? What about your cousin?"

"He's off running an errand. As for the others...I don't mind putting on a show if you don't." *Not as long as you're my costar.*

He considered her explanation, then slid his other hand under her shirt and cupped both breasts. Pushing the blouse aside, he tugged it from her jeans then shoved it off her shoulders, down her arms to slide to the ground.

She shivered under his frank appraisal, confused at her shy response. *After all the lovers I've had, why am I acting like a timid virgin?*

Chase growled, a low, slow rumble in his throat that sent a different kind of shiver through her. He angled his head and enclosed her mouth with his. Hot musk filled her mouth, spicier than she remembered from the earlier kiss. Sucking on her tongue, he followed with not-so-tender bites to her lips, sweeping along her lips to flick his tongue in the corners. She moaned, wanting more with each nibble.

Yet he still hadn't touched her anywhere else. As though he'd read her mind, he suddenly grabbed her butt, pressing her breasts to his chest. Her firm tits flattened against the unyielding expanse and she arched backward to push her tits harder against him. Her hands slid behind him, becoming slick with his sweat. Running over the contours that were so like the rugged hills surrounding the ranch, she dug her fingernails into him, wanting to leave her mark.

This man is dangerous. Physically, and even more frighteningly, emotionally. Part of her, the part that kept her invisible wall fortified, warned her to stay away from him while another side, the side she hadn't heard from in years, called to her, urging her to take another chance.

He hissed in pain and broke their kiss. Yet he didn't appear angry. Instead, he looked pleased. "Using your claws already?"

Claws? As in nails? She tilted her head to study him. "I don't mind a little pain. Do you?"

"Not that kind of pain."

That kind? She dove into his eyes, searching. *Does he know the same type of pain I know? The kind that leaves scars on the inside?* She tried to calm down, returning to the guarded persona she knew so well.

His eyes glowed, the hazel giving way to the growing golden flecks and becoming more slanted than she remembered. "So are you up for a little fun?"

"Little?" She dropped her gaze to his crotch. "I sure hope not."

"Don't worry about that. Let's get you naked." He made that growling sound again, reached for her and yanked her jeans and thong down her legs, almost knocking her to the ground. He lifted her legs one by one, like he was shoeing a horse, and jerked her boots off.

"Hey, I'm not going to be the only one playing nudist. Drop

39

'em, handsome."

He hurriedly shucked his boots and jeans. The lean waist that had hinted at the sizable package under the jeans hadn't lied. Tawny hair, not unlike her own golden curls, framed his dick, already oozing with his pre-come. She took in every inch of him—every *horny* inch—and licked her lips.

"Oh, man." Her pussy flooded with cream, her nipples hardened and she ached for his touch. "I can't wait for you to fuck me."

"First things first." Chase took her by the arms, stared at her for a moment, then turned her around. "I want to see your ass."

"My ass?" *Ah, he's a tush man.*

"You've teased me long enough with that sexy walk of yours. I want to see what drives it."

Placing a hand between her shoulder blades, he bent her forward. She placed her hands flat against the wall and spread her legs, sticking out her buttocks for him.

"So? What do you think? Is it everything you imagined?"

"And more."

"Sheesh. I hope not too much more."

He knelt, taking her cheeks and squeezing them. "I've wanted to squeeze these ever since I watched you walk up the stairs with Bob."

The slap on her rump startled her. "Ow."

"I thought you could take a little pain."

"I can. When I'm expecting it."

"With me, sugar, you'd better expect anything."

A second slap smarted her right cheek, stinging into her backside. She dropped her head and watched her boobs jiggle from the strike. "Spank me again. I've been a bad, bad girl."

"And I bet you're very good at being bad."

"Cowboy, you have no idea." She wiggled her ass at him, challenging him to strike her one more time.

"Then you deserve this." He smacked her a third time, slightly harder than the others, but she was ready for it.

"Damn, how I love a nice rosy ass. So round and pink. In fact, I want to take a bite out of it." He grazed his teeth from the middle of her butt, over the still-stinging flesh and into the cleft between them. Taking her by the legs, he swept his tongue from the top of the crevice down and then back up.

The wetness between her legs grew to a flood. She moaned, closed her eyes and bent even lower, opening herself to him. "Ram your cock into me, cowboy. I need you to shove it deep inside me."

"In time. Let's not rush a good thing." He skated his hand between her legs and she shifted, placing her feet farther apart. Gliding his fingers between her folds, he caught her throbbing nub between his thumb and finger—and twisted.

Shannon yelped in pain and bolted upward.

He stopped her, pushing her back into position. "All you have to do is say the word and I'll stop."

Although he'd surprised her again, she couldn't stand the thought of his not touching her. "Don't you dare." She reached between her legs, found his hand resting on the curve of her leg and covered her pussy with it. "Rub me, Chase. Rub me while you bite me."

"You want me to *bite* you?"

The way he said the word alarmed her, but not as much as it excited her. "Yeah, bite me. Bite me like you mean it."

He moved his fingers, rubbing, stroking, pinching her clit. Her come burst from her, her breath coming in ragged pants, her mind growing fuzzier while her body grew more alive.

Supporting herself with one hand, she fondled her tit, rubbing her palm against her nipple.

Floating little bites along the line of her buttocks—*harder!*—Chase worked his way from one cheek to the other. Moving back toward the center, he paused, sucked her flesh into his mouth, then let go. He nipped her tender clit between his fingers, massaging it, tweaking it until, at last, he bit her, sinking his teeth into the fleshy roundness of her butt.

"Argh!" The climax erupted deep within her pussy, shooting outward in shockwaves. Her legs trembled with the effort to stand. "Oh, shit. You really bit me. And hard." Her warm blood trickled over her bottom and slid down her leg.

"You told me to." His voice grew gruffer, harsher. "I couldn't stop myself. But I didn't bite deep enough to—"

"It's okay." *Hell, it's more than okay. I want him to bite me again. Either that or...* "Oh, shit, Chase." Another smaller climax sent aftershocks along her legs. "You've got me so hot. Fuck me now before I can't stand up any longer."

Chase rose, turning her toward him. He latched onto one tit with his hand and the other with his mouth. His tongue battered her nub and she clutched his hair to keep him close. Taking turns with each nipple, he ran his other hand between her legs and thrust a finger inside her aching pussy.

"Damn it. Fuck me," she panted, even though his fingers were doing a great job of fucking her. Still, she wanted more.

He popped her tit out of his mouth and chuckled, tickling the moist tip with his warm breath. "Are you always this impatient?"

"Only when I want something as much as I want this." *As much as I want you.*

"You're so damn wet. So hot." He nuzzled his face into her breast. "Get on your knees." Placing his hands on her shoulders, he guided her to the ground. Hay tickled her legs, but she soon forgot that when she came level with the wavy patch surrounding the long, thick shaft. "Suck me, Shannon. Suck me first. Then I'll fuck you until your legs give out."

She took him in her hand, thrilling at how soft the tip felt. Gently squeezing him, she wrapped her hand around him and tentatively slid her palm from the tip to the base. His impressive shaft curved ever so slightly, purplish-blue veins running the entire length of it to meet together at the large mushroom cap. *If ever there was a perfect cock, this is it.*

A thunderous roll of lust whipped through her and her pussy clenched in anticipation. *No man has every made me this hot without fucking me. Not this fast.* "I love your dick. It's thick, warm and juicy. Hell, all I need is mustard to top off this hot dog."

He tensed up and went still.

"Did I say something wrong?"

Chase relaxed, then caressed her hair and tweaked her nipple. "No, it's okay. Come on, baby. Stop talking and put your mouth to good use."

"Hey. Watch it, bub." Taking his joke in stride, she laid her palm against his flat abdomen and circled her tongue around the weeping tip. Even that small touch burst a myriad of flavors into her mouth. *Yummy.* Chase tasted salty, musky, with a hint of something untamed. His dick jerked in response and she felt more than heard the rumble of his moan. The river between her legs boiled with heat.

Unable to wait another second, she dragged him into her mouth. He tensed, gripping her hair until it hurt, but she didn't care. Tasting his cock was the only thing that mattered. She slurped him inside, released him and did it again. He groaned and spread his legs wider. Sliding one hand to cover his taut butt cheek, she brushed the head of his dick across her lips, making a sexual lip gloss from his wet come.

"You taste sinfully good." Judging from the rise and fall of his stomach, she figured he couldn't respond. Satisfied with the control she had over him, she slipped him back into her mouth and tracked her tongue around his length, sucking whenever she needed to rest her tongue.

Taking her curls in both hands, he tugged her forward, driving his shaft deeper into her mouth. She choked but didn't resist. She'd take every inch of him, no matter what. Her pulsating pussy wouldn't let her do anything else. She slid her middle finger over her tender clit and rubbed. The instant she touched herself, another climax roared through her and she tightened her grip on him.

"That's it. Pull. Drag it back in. Don't be afraid of hurting me."

She glanced up, taking that second to flick her tongue over the tip before plunging him back inside. Chase locked his gaze on her, his eyes glazed over, his features hardening. She wiggled the tips of her fingers through the soft patch at the base and pushed against him, then released him inch by agonizing inch.

"Damn. Why didn't anyone tell me we had a show going on?"

Chapter Three

Chase yanked away from her, throwing her off balance and dropping her to her hands. He made a fierce feral sound and stumbled farther into the shadows, snatching up his clothes as he went. *He acts like a wild animal.* Shannon looked up, stunned and more than a little annoyed, to find Dirk leaning against the frame of a nearby stall. Wiping the hay from her hands and her legs, she rose on shaky legs and fisted her hands on her hips. "Hi, Dirk."

His eager gaze surveyed her, his eyes glowing with appreciation. "Evening, Shannon."

"What the fuck are you doing here?" A fully clothed and irritated Chase stepped in front of her and handed her shirt to her. She drew the shirt on and took her time buttoning it up. *Should I get Dirk to leave so I can finish with Chase? Or ask him to join us? Hell, I'm so horny I could split into hot little pieces.*

Dirk sported a sexy smirk. "Uh, looks like you're the one doing the fucking. Or at least *trying* to."

Until you interrupted us.

"Get out, dog."

The anger in Chase's voice was unmistakable. And a little disappointing. *No way is he ready for a threesome, which only leaves the choice of taking them one at a time. Unless I use this opportunity to ratchet up the tension between these two and make them want me any way they can get me—including sharing.*

Chase started forward, his coiled yet fluid movements reminding her of a predator ready to strike its victim. Shannon grabbed his arm, holding him back. "Hey, let's not make a big deal out of this." She tossed her hair, shaking it into place. "How long have you been standing there, Dirk? And more importantly, did you enjoy the show?"

"Long enough to know you like getting finger-fucked. Not to mention how my good buddy Chase likes to get blown." His lecherous grin answered the second question.

Again Chase broke free of Shannon's grip and lunged forward. She hurriedly took his arm with both hands this time.

Laughing, Dirk backpedaled, palms up. "Take it easy, man. No need to get so riled."

"Get the hell out before I throw you out."

"Sure, sure. Don't go sharpening your claws, you old tomcat."

Chase snarled at Dirk, pulling his lips back and showing his teeth.

Wow, he does sound like a tomcat. A really big, mean human tomcat with large eyeteeth. "Dirk, could you give us a moment? Or did you want something else?" Shannon kept her grip on the fuming man beside her. "Take it easy, Chase." Yet she had to admit, his jealousy made her feel sexy and wanted...and, surprisingly, safe.

Dirk's eyes looked different. More yellow? She squinted. *Naw. Chase's eyes look yellow, too. It's probably just the dimming light.*

"I sure do, sugar. I'd like to have some of your sweet lovin', too. 'Course, with the way Chase is acting you'll probably have to choose between us."

Probably? She studied him closer. *So Dirk is up for an orgy. Hmm.* "And you wouldn't mind getting in on a little three-way action?" She glanced at Chase and saw him grit his teeth. *Now if only I can talk him into doing a little two-on-one. The man's acting like we're a couple. A monogamous, one-man-one-woman couple.*

"As long as I get what I want, I could handle it. Even if it means having this alley cat around."

"I'm not sharing anything with this hound dog."

Again with the animal names? Confident that Chase wouldn't tear Dirk's head off, Shannon pulled on her boots and jeans, letting the two men stew while she decided what to do. Which did she want? A threesome or a fight? *Ooh, maybe a fight and then a threesome? Hmm, what a nice choice to have. Yep, things are definitely looking up.*

"Come on, old buddy." Dirk moved closer yet still kept his distance. "You can't tell me you wouldn't love seeing Ms. Thang here sucking me off while she spreads her firm round ass for you." He chuckled. "You may act like you wouldn't, but I saw your eyes spark up at the thought of it. So quit playing the she's-my-woman-and-I-ain't-sharing routine and let's get this party going."

Shannon studied Chase, the way he dodged her gaze by averting his own, and knew the big man wasn't telling the truth. *Dirk's right. But getting Chase to admit it is another matter.* "I tell you what, boys. Let's all sleep on the idea—especially you, Chase—and we'll talk again tomorrow. Until then, I've got a date with a vibrator."

Blowing them each a kiss, she sauntered out of the stable.

Shannon toweled her hair dry, then ran her fingers through the natural curls, staring at her reflection in the old mirror over the beat-up dresser. If she stayed here, she'd have to talk to her cousin about updating the furnishings in her room.

If I stay here? She passed the comb through her hair and questioned the Shannon in the mirror. "What the hell are you thinking? Why would you stay on a ranch away from your job, your friends, hell, your entire life?"

Chase's face flashed before her and she blinked, unsettled at his image's sudden appearance. *Pulease. Like I'd stick around for some sweaty cowboy. Wham, bam and thank ya, man. That's my motto.* A motto she was determined to keep. She *pffed* out her disbelief and continued getting ready.

But what if what she'd sensed from him was real? That he wanted her for more than a quick romp in the hay? After all, hadn't his jealousy toward Dirk gone above and beyond the normal male chest-beating she was used to when a couple of bucks had to share her? She bit her lip and, for a rare moment, allowed her defenses to fall. If she had another chance at happiness, at finding love, would she take it? Would the reward be worth risking another heartbreak? She caught herself smiling at the reflection and whirled away. *Knock it off, Shannon. Remember what happened.*

Jarrod's face, closed and unfeeling, rocked her, making her relive the embarrassment, the torture of his rejection. A small cry escaped her as the emotions of that day swept over her. Why hadn't she seen the signs before her wedding day? Why hadn't he told her that he didn't love her anymore before she'd walked down the rose-strewn aisle? How had she missed his affair with her best friend? She had believed in love and believed in him. No way would she ever make the same mistake again.

She snatched up her sundress, slipped it over her head and let it fall around her curves. No, she was mistaken about Chase. He'd turn out like every other man. All he wanted from her was sex, and once he got it, he'd toss her away.

She faced her other self again, fisted her hands on her hips and grinned. "Too bad for you, Mr. Reya, because once I get you fucked good and hard, I'll do the tossing."

r u ready for some action?

Shannon heeled the rocking chair into motion, checked her phone again and frowned. *Who's clax253?* Obviously it was someone who'd gotten hold of her cell phone number *and* knew she was horny as hell. *But then again, when aren't I horny as hell?* She giggled. Still she'd never received a text message from that address before. *Clax? Could it be Dirk Claxton?* She thumbed her response.

maybe. howd u get my #?

A few seconds later, her phone beeped, announcing a new message.

sources - let's do it in field.

Definitely a man who knew what he wanted and wasn't afraid to ask for it. Unlike Chase Reya who had yet to so much as say boo to her today. Was he bowing out and letting Dirk have her all to himself? If so, he wasn't the man she thought he was. Another beep brought the same message, repeated in caps.

"Patience, Dirk."

maybe, she texted.

She could use some fun in the sun. After a restless night filled with remembering Chase nude, his big cock ready to ram into her, she'd found that, for once, her ever-ready Standing O dual-action vibrator couldn't provide the necessary relief. Nothing and no one would satisfy her until she'd bedded that big hunk of a cowboy.

A horse's whinny brought her head up and her breath hitched in her throat. Chase stood at the entrance of the stable, his eyes locked on her while another man talked to him. She noticed, as she had before, how he'd interact with another hand, yet never get too involved with them. Almost as if he held them at a distance by being cordial, but not exactly friendly. He was aloof, reminding her of an independent, yet curious, alley cat.

God, he's sexy. Even from that distance she could see the yearning in his face. He might act aloof to the others, but he obviously wanted her in his space. *Good. It's about time you showed up.* She resisted smiling at him. He needed to be punished for making her wait most of the day before he acknowledged her presence.

how about sexting?

She uncrossed her legs, keeping part of her attention on Chase and his on her, then propped her bare feet on the railing. Her sundress floated around her, the blousy skirt billowing in the breeze. *That's right. Keep your eyes on the prize, Chase.*

Chase nodded at the man who then walked away. His gaze, however, stayed fixed on her.

sex texting? hell yes

Just as she'd thought, Dirk was up for anything.

im wearing a sundress no panties

hard alrdy

ull get harder

Shannon wiggled her fingers at Chase, then made a big show out of slipping her hand under her skirt. Startled, he quickly glanced around, checking to see if the other hands had seen. Licking his lips, he strode toward her. When he got close enough to see better, to see the expression on her face, she shook her head. *Uh-uh, Chase. Not too close.* Mimicking him, she licked her lips and saw him swallow.

more

more COMING, she typed quickly—*rubbing tits w phone—*

then pressed the hard metal to her breast and massaged her growing nipple. Chase followed her movements, reminding her again of a cat. This time, however, she was the mouse the cat wanted to pounce on and gobble up.

hot—more

She trailed her hand over her abdomen and under the strip of lace. Tunneling her fingers through the short curls covering her mound, she ran her middle finger between her folds. Chase, noticing the movement under her skirt, dropped his gaze to the slight hump formed by her hand. Spreading her feet wider, she slid lower in the chair and let her legs fall open.

A beep brought her back to Dirk.

finger-fucking

want to be ur finger

Talk about hot! Sexting for one man while she finger-fucked herself and another man watched was more than fun. *This is fantastic fuckin' fun.* She separated the folds and stroked her already throbbing clit. Good thing she was proficient at one-handed texting, not to mention one-handed masturbating.

im so wet

She closed her eyes, listened to her pounding heart and opened them to find Chase at the top of the steps, mere feet away from her. The raw sensuality filling his face sent a rush of wetness onto her finger. *Oh, Chase, how I wish you were the one finger-banging me.*

dick is out

Dirk's next message came right on the heels of the first.

beating off

Shannon closed her eyes again, this time imagining both Chase and Dirk standing over her, watching her pleasure herself while they pumped their engorged cocks. Knowing those two, they'd probably have a competition to see who could jerk off the longest. She sighed, again deciding that, one way or another, she'd have them both, two dicks at one time. Chase would come around. She'd make him want her enough to share her with Dirk. She moaned, not too loud, but just loud enough, then opened her eyes. Chase's attention darted between her face and her hidden hand.

Making sure he saw her, she thumbed another message, mouthing the words so Chase could follow along.

want NEED to fuck

The frown on Chase's face warred with the desire in his eyes.

come to me

where?

stable?

cabin

She hadn't expected the teasing game she played to be so rough on her. The churning in her abdomen needed release and she wanted someone to help her with it. "Chase, come here."

want u to eat me

ur driving me crzy

He moved to her side faster than she thought possible. *How does he do that?* Standing over her, his gaze fell to where her skirt had fallen between her legs. His lips parted and she smelled the lust oozing from him. Her eyes widened at the bulge in his jeans that was level with her head. *I remember it being big, but not that big.* She suddenly wished she had three hands.

going to explode

"Chase, stand so that you're blocking me from the others."

He repositioned his body, putting his back to the yard and shadowing her body.

Lowering her eyes, she ordered him, "Put your hand on my tit."

52

He hesitated, looked around once more, then slipped his hand beneath the top of her dress. The spaghetti strap fell off her shoulder, letting the bodice fall low enough to expose half of her breast. He cupped her, taking her nipple between his fingers and squeezing. Smothering a cry, she thrust two fingers into her pussy, using the upper part of her finger above her knuckle to press against her hot clit.

"Chase." She panted, her climax coming closer and taking her breath away.

He rubbed her tit, moving faster, pressing down so hard that it hurt. But she loved the pain and wanted more.

"Let's go somewhere private." His voice was dark, even threatening, yet seductive.

The twitch in his jaw echoed the excitement inside her. "Not right now."

"Why the hell not?"

She coughed out a short laugh. "I'm a little busy."

He squeezed her again, then ran his other hand through her hair. "I need you. I couldn't stop thinking about you all night. Let's finish what we started."

"I'd love to. But let me finish this first." Knowing it was a risk, but wanting to jolt him, she lifted the phone, making sure he could read the screen.

coming

I need to fuck you

"What the hell?"

His hand squeezed her breast and she climaxed in the same second, her body shaking, the surge rolling through her. Still, he didn't remove his hand. "Who are you texting?"

Once her climax ended and she could breathe evenly again, she withdrew her hand from under her skirt. Dropping the phone onto the table next to her, she placed her hand over her tit, over his hand, and kept him there. Anger, confusion and lust filled his face. "I was sexting Dirk." She batted her eyes and gently removed his hand from her breast. "But I'm so glad you came along when you did. Sexting is never as good as the real thing." Relishing her control over him, she stuck her wet-slickened fingers in her mouth and sucked.

He inhaled, following her every lick, every swirl of her tongue. "You were doing what?"

He's irritated but curious, too. "Sexting Dirk. You know. Doing dirty talk while texting. Like phone sex. And I like to pleasure myself at the same time."

His mouth dropped opened, ready to speak, then slammed shut.

Come on, Chase. Let your libido overrule your jealousy. "But I'd much rather have you between my legs instead of my hand."

"Me?" Furious or not, his gaze still wandered to the dress falling between her legs. "Or Dirk?" His jaw worked, either from anger or lust. Maybe both? "You mean I felt you up while you were talking to that w—guy?"

Ooh, something else is going on behind those dark eyes. As though he's imagining Dirk and me... Yes, there's definitely something more in his tone. He's confused. Wanting me for himself yet unable to resist the idea of watching me with another man. Maybe he's imagining all three of us, together, slick with each other's come. This is promising.

She ran her moist fingers along the waist of his jeans, noted his harsh breathing, then walked her fingers over his crotch. The spasm beneath his tight material gave her a glow of satisfaction. "Uh-huh. But you can't say you didn't enjoy it, too. The mountain in your jeans is evidence enough."

He stepped back, moving out of her reach. "You're driving me out of my mind."

You and Dirk both. Shannon readjusted her dress and

gracefully stood. "Just like the dream of you hammering into me drove me out of my mind." She leaned against him and rested her palm against his granite chest, watching her hand move with the rise and fall of his breaths. "Look, Chase, you want me and I want you. But I want Dirk, too. I want to feel his cock against my ass while you suck on my clit." Fascinated, she watched the struggle behind his eyes. Did they change color? *His eyes are very interesting.* "And I always get what I want."

He stood absolutely motionless. Motionless, except for the fire flashing in his eyes. *I've got you now, cowboy. Nothing brings a man around better than a challenge. Especially a challenge involving a man he doesn't like.* "So what do you say, Chase? Want to enjoy a ménage a trois?"

"No."

Did he hesitate? "Are you sure?"

"I said no."

She hadn't expected him to take her up on her offer, but she hadn't expected him to whirl around and stride down the steps so quickly either. Hell, instead of his one-word refusal, she thought she'd have time for more persuasion. She briefly considered following him and coaxing him into continuing yesterday's roll-in-the-hay-interruptus, then decided against the idea. *Shit. Let him stew awhile. The more torn up he is on the inside, the easier it'll be once I get those two hunks together.*

She sighed and picked up the phone again.

r u there?

yes - chase is here

A frowning emoticon blinked back at her. *him? why?*

i want him 2

r u sure? both?

both

now?

he said no

make him say yes

She laughed, delighted at Dirk's willingness to share her with another man. And since he was so willing, perhaps he could help her spring the trap that would finally catch the big cat. She frowned at the idea. *Weird. Now I'm using the dog and cat references.*

ideas?

maybe

let's talk—bhnd house

brt

Shannon stretched her arms, glanced at the stable where Chase had gone. *That man's harder than hell to get a grip on. I wonder, once we've gotten together, if he'll mellow. Hmm, he's going to get better looking with age, I bet.* She smiled, absently rubbing her ring finger. The implication of her thoughts and action struck her cold. *Why the hell am I thinking long-term? I'm not getting involved and I'm only going to be here a little while longer.* Still, she couldn't keep the twinge of regret from twisting her heart.

She returned to texting Dirk, squinting at the phone as she rounded the corner of the house. Suddenly, someone grabbed her from behind and clamped a hand over her mouth, stifling her scream.

Chapter Four

Chase should've known better than to give a human female a second look. But Shannon Tally had him wanting a second, a third look. Hell, even the idea of sharing her with Dirk was sounding better. What did it matter as long as he got what he wanted? But could he do a threesome with a werewolf?

He closed his eyes and let the vision take shape. Shannon, sandwiched between him and another man whose lowered face was hidden by fallen hair, clasped him around the neck. Swallowing, he could feel the heat of her breasts pressed against his chest, her legs wrapped around his waist as the unknown man slammed into her from behind. With every thrust, every grind, she made a soft grunting sound, a sound that only heightened his lust, thickened his shaft. He grew harder, longer, quickly coming to the brink. Her curly hair, damp with sweat, plastered to her face and her tongue, pink and oh-so delectable, flicked over her upper lip. Together the three of them moved, each man thrusting into her as she rode them to their ultimate releases. Her cry mixed with his howl.

Spent and using each other for support, the other man lifted his face and grinned. *Dirk!*

Frustrated, Chase tossed the bridle on the floor of the tack room, drawing the attention of two of the other hands.

"Hey, man, take it easy. If the boss man catches you mistreating his equipment that way, he'll tie you up by your tail." The cowboy scooped up the bridle Chase had tossed to the floor, shook it out and looped it over one of the hooks on the back wall. When the man turned around, ready to admonish him more, he stopped, his jaw hanging open.

Chase hadn't meant to shift as much as he had, but it felt good to throw some fear into the human. Besides, he'd only let his eyes narrow and his fangs grow a little. Keeping the sound low enough that the other cowboy wouldn't hear him, he bared his teeth and let a low mean growl roll off his tongue. The cowboy stiffened, took one last incredulous look at him and bolted from the room.

"Yo, Ben!" The second cowboy shot a questioning look at Chase, then hurried after the first. "What's the matter with you, man? Hold up."

Chase smothered his smile. Hopefully, Ben wouldn't run to Bob Tally and tell him his new hand had glowing eyes and deadly looking fangs. But if he did, it wasn't a big deal. The cowboys would make a joke out of Ben and his "monster". Only Bob would know the truth and Chase was fairly certain he'd overlook this one mistake. And if he didn't, well, then Chase could tell Haken he'd at least given this getting-to-know-humans thing a good try.

Besides, it wasn't as though he'd morphed all the way. What had Bob said? "No going down on all fours"? Well, he hadn't, had he? So, as far as he was concerned, he'd kept his end of the deal.

Although he hadn't been on the ranch very long, his patience with humans was already wearing thin. Or was it because a certain curly-headed blonde made him itch for a release of some kind, of any kind? He didn't know which and didn't care. If he had his way, he'd have two things happen. First, he'd have Shannon begging him for a real romp in the hay and then he'd get the hell back to the mountains. But how long would he stay to achieve his goal? The realization that he'd stay on the ranch until he'd had Shannon churned his gut. He no longer cared that she was human. All he cared about was getting inside her.

Would he fight Dirk for her? Not that he'd mind tearing the dog's throat out. Werewolves and werecats weren't sworn enemies, but they weren't bosom buddies, either. Normally, they stayed out of each other's way. But he wasn't about to let anything keep him from getting between Shannon's legs.

Still, if he couldn't have her alone, was he ready to do as she wanted? Was he ready to share her? Having had orgies with willing werecat females, Chase wasn't squeamish about group sex. But those orgies had always included two or more women. He'd never shared a female with another male—much less a werewolf. The closest he'd come was simply watching another threesome get it on. Hell, he would eagerly watch Shannon getting fucked by two werecats. Watching her go down on one man while the other screwed her in the ass would only increase his desire to have her. Once she'd finished with them, he could picture her striding toward him, wiping her mouth as she sent him a lustful smile. She'd lie down and spread her legs, opening her arms to him in invitation. Yeah, he could definitely watch her in a threesome. After all, his vision had made him hard—at least until he'd realized the other man was Dirk. But he'd never even given the idea of participating in a two-man, one-woman tryst a thought before now. Until Shannon.

Chase slapped his hands against his jeans, dust clouding the air around him. *So what's it going to be? Take Shannon with Dirk? Or don't take her at all?*

"Are you trying to give me a heart attack?" Shannon glared at Dirk who couldn't stop chuckling at his joke. "Sneaking up on someone isn't my idea of a joke, asshole."

"Aw, loosen up a bit, sugar. After all, it's not as if you didn't know I was coming." He winked at her and edged closer. "Besides, I was out to spook you, not scare you to death. Good thing I covered your mouth, though, or we'd have had the whole ranch down on us."

"On you, you mean." She scowled at him, but let him tug her closer. "Just don't do it again."

"Okay, okay." He snuggled against her, pressing his nose to her hair and inhaling long and slow. "Sugar, you sure do smell good."

"Which is more than I can say about you." She squirmed against him, yet not wiggling enough to actually make him let go. In reality, she liked his aroma. An aroma born of hard work and masculinity.

"Tell me more about this sex thing you want with me."

"With you and Chase."

"Yeah. Although why you want to fuck that old tomcat, I'll never know."

She leaned away to study him. "What is it with the cat references? And his calling you a dog? Are you guys into that scene? Because if you are, that's where I draw the line."

"Not in the way you're thinking."

Huh? She would've sworn his eyes flashed from blue to amber. Blinking, she again saw nothing but ocean-colored eyes. *The sexual frustration must be getting to me.* "What does that mean?"

"I'm joking. It's only our little way of playing with each other." He released her and held his palms up. "No, no. Not that way, either. Sugar, I am all heterosexual male." Taking her by the arms, he pulled her into an embrace and kissed her neck.

She relaxed, enjoying the feel of his lips on the slope of her neck and tilted her head. Pressing her breasts hard against his firm chest, she ran her hands along his back, tugging his shirt out of his jeans. His skin was solid under her fingers and she couldn't help squeezing the muscles in his back. Chase hadn't finished her off on the porch, so maybe Dirk could. After all, a woman like her couldn't survive on a few climaxes a day—especially self-induced ones. And what better way to get Chase out of her mind than to have Dirk inside her body?

Dirk slipped his hands under her dress, moaning when he found the lacy strip, the sole barrier keeping him from her treasure. With a yank, he freed her of her thong. "Spread 'em, sugar."

Her chest muffled his words, softening the tone, but she obeyed. Needing him to touch her breasts, she wiggled her shoulders, dropping the spaghetti straps down her arms.

"Mmm." He latched onto her tit, forcefully, dragging her hardened nub into his mouth. His hand found her snatch and she leaned against the wall of the house, whimpering in delight.

"Ohh."

"That feel good?"

She closed her eyes, letting the sun warm her from the outside as he warmed her insides. "Very good." *But not as good as Chase felt.* She tensed at the errant thought. Unwilling to let the thought take hold, she concentrated on the man loving her.

He plunged his fingers into her at the same instant he left one breast and caught the other nipple with his teeth. Fondling her other breast, he worked his fingers back and forth over her juicy clit.

"Damn, you're wet. Wet and ready." Grabbing her by the butt, he hoisted her up. She wrapped her legs around his waist, pushing her skirt out of the way.

He pinned her to the wall by pressing his body against hers, letting her support herself with her arms and legs. His hands brushed at her mons and he hurried to unbuckle and shuck his jeans. Using one hand to position her better, he pointed his cock against her throbbing clit and started to push in.

"Wait." The word exploded from her. She tried to clam up, but couldn't. "I can't."

"What the hell?"

Shannon forced his upper torso away, dropped her legs and slid to the ground.

"What'd'ya mean ya can't?" Dirk snarled his question through panted breaths. "What are you? A big tease?"

She struggled to find the right words. Although she'd been at the ranch a full two days and hadn't gotten laid once, no way was she a tease. She wanted Dirk. Of that she was sure. "No. But..."

"But what?" Seeing her smooth her dress, he started to zip his jeans. "You've put out enough messages for me to know I didn't misinterpret anything. So what's with all the flirting and sexting?"

I want Chase first. She swallowed the answer before it could slip out. "It's just that I want more time to really enjoy you. Anticipation is part of the fun. Besides, we're supposed to work on a scheme to get that threesome going."

He studied her and, for a moment, she was afraid he'd see through her excuse. "Sugar, I don't mind having you even while that c—Chase is around to share. But I don't see why we can't fuck first. Then I'll share."

She palmed his cheek and turned on all her charm. "Yeah. And it would be amazing." She dropped her gaze down to his crotch, then back up. "But I want the first time to be special. Besides, I get the impression that you'd like to needle him some. You know, like by getting your dick inside me first. And if that happens, he may give up and decide not to join us."

"At this point, with my dick aching like crazy, I don't much care about waiting for him."

"But think about how much better it would be if Chase watched. How hot that would be."

Dirk's eyes glittered with unhidden glee. "Ah, I see what you mean. Okay, then, let's put our heads together and figure out how to get the stubborn stick-up-the-butt where you, I mean we, want him."

I want him with his shaft buried so far inside me I can feel the tip poking out the top of my head. "Don't worry, I already have a plan. Just follow my lead and play along."

"The boss man wants you to muck out the stalls."

Chase closed his eyes, let the irritation from Dirk's voice flow out of his body, then glared at the werewolf. "And he sent you as his messenger?"

Dirk grinned that shit-eating grin he hated. "Yep. So you'd better get a move on. Daylight's burning."

Chase tossed his cards onto the table, folding his hand. Although he'd had a great hand and probably could've won the pot, he'd just as soon shovel manure rather than endure another minute playing poker with the ranch hands. An hour trying to relate to humans was long enough. Leaving his hat hanging on the bed frame—why humans liked wearing those things he'd never understand—he sauntered out of the bunkhouse.

He'd gone a few yards before he realized Dirk was at his heels. "Did you forget something, pup?"

Dirk kept going past him. "Nope."

Then why the hell is he heading for the stable, too? A low growl rumbled deep in his chest. Did Bob want them to work together? Would Bob do something that foolish to test his determination to get along? Even with the werewolf?

Once inside the dimly lit stable, Chase knew something

63

wasn't right. Dirk stood next to Shannon, his arm possessively wrapped around her waist. After the sexting incident, Chase had given her a wide berth, taking time to try and work her out of his system. Not that he'd been successful. He was as hot for her as ever. *Damn, she looks so good. Sexy, luscious and feisty. I bet she's already dripping with all the sweetness I'd love to lap up.* "What's going on?"

Dirk started to answer, but Shannon stopped him cold. "We're here to give you one more chance."

"One more chance at what?" He narrowed his eyes at Dirk, shifting slightly to increase his sense of smell. Did Dirk smell like deceit? He sniffed, catching the werewolf's scent, but not detecting any emotion other than his normal cockiness.

He'd forgotten, however, that he'd also catch Shannon's strong aroma of lust. He inhaled, drawing in her spicy fragrance. Her desire overwhelmed him and he struggled against throwing her to the ground and humping her. Even with Dirk standing nearby.

Hell, especially with Dirk standing nearby.

"Another chance at this." Shannon slipped the straps of the sundress off her shoulders to skim quickly down her arms, letting the garment fall to the ground and exposing her naked body.

"Holy shit."

For once Chase had to agree with Dirk. Suddenly, his throat closed up and his dick stood at attention. *Forget the damn dog. Trying to refuse her is like expecting a dying man to turn down immortality. I was stupid for even thinking I could forget about her. How can I turn down a female this hot even if it means sharing her with the werewolf?* "What are you doing, Shannon?" His voice came out forced and yet weak at the same time.

She moved closer, halving the distance between them.

Lifting her breasts, she kept her eyes on him and slowly, seductively licked each of her nipples. "Right now I'm doing what I want you to do." She spread her legs and slipped a hand between them. "Like I want you to do this."

Chase struggled to stay where he was. "And why's he here?"

The bouquet of lust grew stronger. Rubbing herself, she slid her middle finger through the patch of curls and between her folds. "Ooh. Dirk, give me a hand, won't you?" Dirk scooted up behind Shannon and bent to kiss her on the neck. His hands cupped her breasts and he rubbed his thumbs over her hard buds. She moaned, covering his hand with hers.

Is this a human way of torturing men? If so, she's doing a damn good job of it. Chase growled. "That doesn't answer my question." He didn't want to pull his gaze away from her breasts, away from Dirk's hands on her nipples. *Come on, Dirk, tweak them. Make her squeal.*

"I know you're no Einstein, but don't you get it? The lady wants both of us. Together." Dirk's eyes lost their blue and colored with an amber glow. "Beats the hell outta me what she sees in you, but I don't care. I'll screw a sexy bitch anytime, anyway—with anyone she wants."

Shannon pushed away the arm Dirk had crossed over her rounded tummy. "Watch who you're calling bitch."

"Sugar, bitch is an affectionate term where I come from." Dirk kneeled behind her.

Chase instantly hated himself. On the one hand, he wanted to stay exactly where he was. That way he couldn't see what the shifter was doing to her. On the other hand—*damn it*—he wanted nothing more than to watch him, join him. He remembered the feel of her buttocks and yearned to grasp the soft flesh, pulling her closer so he could drink in her sweet wetness as he spread her ample cheeks, opening her to Dirk's shaft. He groaned, thinking of how he'd lap her dry as Dirk pushed her against his face with every thrust.

God, how he could imagine it. She'd cry out, digging her nails into his shoulders, leaning forward for the werewolf. Then she'd fall to her knees and take him in her mouth, widening her opening for Dirk. He'd see everything the shifter did to her while enjoying how she stroked and pulled on his shaft.

Shannon giggled. "That tickles, Dirk." She smiled a knowing smile, almost as though she could see his vision, too. "Don't either one of you stop."

Grrrrr. Chase's growl reverberated around the stable.

"Sounds to me like someone's getting hot and bothered." Dirk ran his tongue along the side of her leg, his eyes glowing now.

"Wow, Chase. I think I just creamed. Make that sound again."

"I'll make that sound again, all right. When I'm between your legs."

"Then you'll join us?" Shannon reached behind her for Dirk's hands, then guided them around her hips and placed them over her curls. Dirk parted her folds and moaned.

"When I'm alone with you." Chase gritted his teeth and tried not to let what Dirk was doing turn him on even more. But he couldn't deny that it was. Watching someone else—even the werewolf—excite her was tearing him apart. Just not in the way he would've thought it would.

Shannon closed her eyes and leaned into Dirk for support. "That's it, Dirk. Rub right there. Oh, you're making me so horny."

Chase swallowed and took a step toward them. "Shannon." Her name came out hoarse, tense, needy. Was having multiple partners a human sex tradition? Was that why she wanted the threesome so much?

"Yes?" Shannon placed her hands over Dirk's and helped him keep her pussy lips apart.

"Fuck me." He didn't care how or when. All he knew was that he had to have her. Any way, anywhere, with anyone.

"I'd love to, Chase. Along with Dirk." She cocked an eyebrow at him, questioning him.

"Whatever." If the only way he could have her was to share her, then so be it. Whatever it took, he had to have her next to him, opening herself to him, fucking him.

She paused, searching him as though unsure that she'd heard him correctly. "Then we have our threesome?"

Dirk rubbed his fingers over her, spreading her wetness to her curls. Unable to find his voice, Chase nodded.

With a sigh, she removed Dirk's hands and motioned for him to stand. He skimmed his hands along the curve of her body and over her shoulders. Taking one of his hands, she licked his fingers. "Yummy. If I do say so myself."

Dirk chuckled behind her. "You sure are."

She tilted her head, letting him bite her along the shoulder. "Hmm, that's so good, Dirk. I wish you'd bite me. Hard."

"No!" Chase ran forward, stopping himself a few feet from her. "Don't say that to him." He glared at Dirk. "Don't even think about marking her."

Shannon and Dirk froze at the tone of his command. "Mark me? What does that mean? How would he mark me?"

Dirk pulled his lips into a silent, challenging snarl at Chase.

When neither Dirk nor Chase answered her, Shannon darted her gaze between them. "What are you two? Vampires?" She giggled and playfully slapped Dirk's arm. "I think both of you have seen way too many horror movies."

Chase was beside her in an instant. "Let's do this." He

reached out to take a breast, but Shannon swerved away, out of both of their grasps. He clenched his fists, fighting his ache for her.

"Not here. Not now." She retrieved her sundress and slipped it over her head. "This was just a preview of the fun to come."

Both men growled, then frowned at each other.

"Aw, that's cute how you both growled at the same time. But save it for the cabin, boys."

"The cabin?" Chase stared at the pert nipples pushing against the thin material. "So you got me ready to do this and now you're putting me off? No way."

"For once I have to agree with him. Forget the damn cabin. Let's do it now."

She placed a hand on each of their chests. "I know I've been testing your patience. But trust me, it'll be worth it." A mischievous expression softened her face. "Do you know where my cousin's hunting cabin is?" Chase nodded along with Dirk. "Good. Then meet me there later. Oh, and you'll have to walk. We wouldn't want anyone else noticing the horses hitched outside and wondering who's at the cabin, now, would we?"

"I still don't see why we can't do it here and now."

"Because Bob will be back in a little while and I won't risk him finding us. I don't mind putting on a show for others, but I draw the line at relatives." She took their hands and placed them on her breasts. Both men squeezed her, fondling her nipples. "You know the old saying, boys. 'Good things come to those who wait.' Seven o'clock at the cabin."

She brushed their hands off, tossed her hair and strolled out of the stable.

"I don't know about you, but I'll be at that cabin."

Chase scowled at Dirk. "Why don't you butt out for good?"

Surprise filtered across the werewolf's face. "Get over it, fuzz ball. Didn't your momma ever teach you to share your toys? Or has something else got you all twisted up inside?" He ran his gaze slowly from Chase's face to the floor and back again in an overt dare. "What's the matter? Cat got your tongue?"

Chase swallowed back another retort and instead focused on the odd twist in his gut. Something was definitely bothering him, but he couldn't get a hold on exactly what it was. Dirk laughed and strolled outside, finally leaving him alone with his thoughts.

Shannon. She's what's tearing me up. But why? She's just a human. Granted, she's the sexiest female I've ever met, but still only a human. The idea of the blonde vixen, her legs pushed over her head as he pounded into her, rocked him on his feet. *Damn, but I want her bad and I'll have her, too. But once I do, will I be able to forget her?*

Naked—except for the red cowboy boots and spurs jangling on her heels—Shannon paced the one-room cabin, looking out the front window every few minutes. *Sheesh, what the heck is wrong with me? I've had sex with more than one man before. This isn't any different than the other times.* Yet, try as she might to convince herself, she knew this time was very different. She couldn't shake the impression that something momentous was about to happen. *It's probably just my nerves.*

An image of Chase's face invaded her thoughts, pushing all others aside. *He makes it different, special. But why? Because he's such a hunk with an animal-like vibe?* She bit her lip and frowned. No. Dirk was just as delicious with his own wild side, but he didn't give her that incredible connected sensation every time he got near her. Chase was unlike anyone she'd ever met. *Or will meet.* "Argh!" She moved away from the window, although it was the unfamiliar thoughts she really wanted to get away from.

If only Chase shows up, that'll be... A warm feeling flowed through her and she smiled. *No.* She'd instigated this threesome. She was the one who wanted both men. Not just one. And certainly not one for more than just a fun time in the Old West. Resolutely, she forced away the vision of Chase and her, alone, making love in front of a roaring fire. Never mind that in that vision, she sensed a future, the same future she'd closed her heart to long ago. Hadn't she learned her lesson with Jarrod? No way would she let one man overwhelm her thoughts—much less her life. She was in control and determined to stay that way. *Then why do I feel so lost?*

"I must be getting old," she muttered. "Old and soft in the head." Shaking off the unwanted ideas, she concentrated on the reason she'd hiked the short distance to the cabin—good old two-on-one sex.

What if only Dirk shows up? Her chest tightened at the thought. *Then that lucky cowboy will have the best night of his life. Sex with Dirk will be great.* She frowned at the empty hole in her gut. *I really want Chase. I want him to be the first to fuck me. And the last.* "Damn, you'd think a monogamous-thinking alien has taken over my brain."

I am so not ready to settle down. Especially with a man I just met. The unruly part of her mind, however, wouldn't let her get away with the lie. *Unless Chase settled down with me.*

Stop it, girl. Get ready. They'll be here any second.

Blowing out an exasperated breath, she picked up the large bell, the one used to summon the ranch hands to the mess hall, and leaned against the wall next to the open window. Peeking around the frame, she waited for someone to arrive.

Oh, my God, there's Dirk.

Dirk stood at the top of a small rise, his thumbs hooked in

the front pockets of his jeans. Shannon scanned the area around him, searching for any sign of Chase—and came up empty. *Damn. Where is he?*

With a wicked grin on his face, Dirk started down the slope toward the cabin.

She sighed, then straightened up. *Well, no bother. If Dirk's the one who wants me, then Dirk's the one who gets me. At least for tonight.* She tossed her curls, ran a finger over her teeth and got ready to open the door.

"Hold up."

The all-too-familiar sexy voice sent a wave of excitement through her. *Chase.*

Chase's long, lanky legs chewed up the distance between him and Dirk.

"Shit, Mr. Kitty, I was hoping you'd lost my trail."

Chase cocked an eyebrow at Dirk. "With your smell? Hell, a bear with a bad cold could follow your stench." He glanced at the window.

Shannon darted back against the wall, waited a minute, then peered around the edge again. *He came. Chase came.* She pressed a hand to her chest and tried to calm her breathing. *Sheesh, I'm practically giddy with excitement.*

"Are you ready to join in? Or are you here to cause trouble?"

"Relax, dog face. I don't like you touching her, but if this is what she wants, this is what she gets. For now."

For now? Yet no matter what, Chase obviously meant something else would happen later. And if that meant he'd stick around, stick with her, then she couldn't help but thrill to the idea.

Finally! Time to get started. She took a breath, threw open the door and stepped inside the doorway, legs set wide apart, bell in one hand. With a fist on one hip, she clanged the bell loudly. "Hoo-wee! Hoo-wee! Supper is served." They stopped in their tracks, mouths parted slightly at her surprise entrance. She fought to keep from laughing and winked. "Come and get me, boys."

She pivoted slowly and seductively, then walked to the large wooden table, knowing they would follow her. She tossed the bell aside, letting it clatter to the floor. Hopping onto the end of the table, she set her boots on the two chairs she'd positioned there earlier, let her knees fall to the side and leaned back on her elbows, exposing everything and letting the two men get an eyeful.

Chapter Five

Chase stood in the doorway, the setting sun making a beautiful purple backdrop behind him. Her heart skipped a beat and she had to steady her nerves before she could speak. "Hiya, Chase."

"I'm first."

And you'll be the last. Damn it, Shannon, shut that stupid voice up! "We'll see."

"Hey, don't get your hopes up, man." Dirk nudged Chase to the side, taking his place in the doorway, and grinned. "Oh, honey, I'm home."

Shannon smiled, letting them think her reaction was to Dirk's joke. Chase would rather have her to himself. But as a one-night stand? Or more? She ignored the yearning ache inside her.

Dirk clapped a hand on Chase's shoulder. "Have you ever seen anything so pretty?" Chase grunted and shook the hand off, but the expression on his face told her he agreed.

Shannon glanced at the men and licked her lips. *Let's get this party going.* "I taste even better than I look. Want to find out?"

Chase's eyes flashed, the color changing to a brilliant yellow, and the intensity exuding from him doubled. "Shannon."

Shit, even the way he says my name makes me wet. I

wonder if my saying his name has the same effect on him. "Chase?"

"And I'm Dirk. Now that we've got everyone's names straight, how about we get down to business?" He took a step in front of Chase, but only a step.

Chase gripped the man's shoulder and pushed ahead of him, striding toward her like a man possessed. Shannon's breath hitched in her throat and for the first time she wondered what she'd gotten herself into. Could she handle this cowboy who sometimes acted more like a wild animal than a man?

He stopped a mere foot away from her, but didn't touch her. Her body responded, aching for that physical connection, but she held back from reaching out. *Come on, Chase, touch me.* He studied her for a moment, then motioned for Dirk to go around the table, placing him at Shannon's head. Dirk softly caressed her hair.

"Listen up." Chase's tone dipped lower and Shannon shivered at the sexual tension in his voice. "We're going to do this threesome, but it's going to go my way."

"Now wait a sec." Dirk's hand in her hair tightened. "I'm not taking any orders from the likes of you."

Chase growled—*growled?*—and lifted his lips in a snarl. "The only reason I'm sharing is because this is what she wants. It's a one-time thing."

He's getting protective really fast. But for the life of her, she couldn't find anything wrong with that. Not any longer. Something had opened up inside her at his possessive words and she'd almost heard the sound the crack made in her invisible wall. "Dirk?"

"Yeah?"

"We're doing it his way." She tipped back her head to see his face. *Holy shit. His eyes are amber, too. What the hell is with these two?* "Okay?" *Come on, Dirk, you know what I want. Help me out.*

Dirk blinked and she saw that he understood. "Fine. But only because you asked and only if I get satisfaction, too." He gritted his jaw and looked at Chase. "So? Do I need to fetch some catnip to get this thing going or what?"

Chase grasped one of her feet, pulled the spur off the heel and brought her legs over his shoulders as he sat in the chair. He scooted forward until he was inches from the cleft between her legs. "Shannon, suck him off. Dirk, play with her tits."

Dirk chuckled. "For once, I'm not going to argue with you." Quickly, he unbuckled his silver buckle and pulled his zipper down. Tugging the top of his jeans wide, he offered her his already-extending dick. Shannon started massaging it, running her fingers over the oozing tip. His cock jerked, growing with the attention.

"Good. Now draw him in."

She did as Chase commanded, slowly sliding Dirk's shaft into her mouth. The vein-covered skin glided into her mouth easily, until the tip struck the back of her throat. But she didn't choke. Instead, she concentrated on watching Dirk's face as a wave of desire wafted over him. He inhaled, then slowly exhaled. "Oh, man, that feels great."

"Play with her tits."

For a man who wanted her all to himself, he sure seems to be getting off on watching Dirk and me. But as long as he's happy...

"Don't mind if I do." Dirk palmed her, kneading, stroking her nipples between two fingers, whispering sweet words about her tits. He pushed her breasts together and rubbed the hardened nipples against each other. She moaned and continued to stroke his dick, matching the pace set by his hips moving back and forth.

Why isn't Chase doing anything? Please tell me he's not

content just to watch.

"Are you getting wet, Shannon? Can you imagine me lapping your juices while you suck him?"

She made a sound in her throat and hoped he'd understand. *Stop talking and do something.*

He spread her folds and she gasped, thankful that he'd finally touched her. She wiggled her ass to encourage him to do more. Dirk, his eyes closed and mouth parted, grunted each time she took his full length. His hands worked her, pinching her pebbled nubs, sending little stabs of pain into her chest. But she loved every bit of it.

I wish I could see Chase's face between my legs.

Cold metal struck her clit, the strange sensation making her jump. Quick jabs of pain flicked into her sensitive nub and ran in a straight line over her pussy, into her curls, around the outside of her snatch, then back up the slit.

Omigod. He's using my spur on me. She mewed, excited by Chase's inventiveness and again wishing she could watch him in action. She poised the tips of her teeth over Dirk's shaft and slowly moved his dick out of her mouth, razoring her teeth along the loose skin.

"Damn, oh, damn, but she's good. I don't know what she's like at your end, cat man, but she's got one talented mouth on her. Fondle my balls, sugar."

She looked up at Dirk, pleased at the rapt attention her breasts held for him and cupped his balls with one hand. He groaned in appreciation.

Chase dug the spur into her, shooting a little more pain through her, but she didn't care. Truth be known, she loved it. But she wanted more than metal against her skin. She took Dirk's cock out of her mouth and rubbed it against her cheek. "Chase, sweet man, please eat me. I need to feel your tongue on me."

Before she could take Dirk back inside, struck her clit, wiping away the ache and repla warmth of his hand. She jerked up, but he sticking to her like one of the broncs he'd bɪᴏᴋᴇɴ. ᴘᴜsʜɪɴɢ hard, he penetrated her pussy, shoving two fingers deep inside her. "Ah, Shannon, you're already dripping. So you like sucking on his dick? Or could it be you like getting finger-banged?" Slowly he dragged his fingers into her channel, then reversed direction. He moved his thumb over her clit, alternating the pressure he put on her growing nub. "Mmm, you smell sweet. Sexy, musky and sweet all at the same time."

Even what he says makes me hot. Shannon squirmed, urging him to push his fingers—or something bigger—back into her.

"Tweak her nipples harder, Dirk. I think she likes it."

Dirk nodded, keeping his eyes closed, and twisted her nipples harder. But not hard enough that she wanted him to stop. He groaned when she removed his cock from her mouth. "Damn it, Chase. Don't stop. Don't ever stop. Put your mouth where your fingers are."

"Take it easy, woman." He slammed three fingers into her. "You're going to love what I'm going to do to you. Just be careful not to chomp down on Dirk's little prick."

Little my ass.

"Little my ass." Dirk's eyes opened and narrowed at Chase as though he didn't trust him not to tell her to bite. "Don't anyone even think about doing any chomping."

How she could giggle with all the hot sensations rushing through her, she'd never know. Chase renewed his finger-fuck of her, slipping his fingers deeper, faster inside her. His thumb raked over her throbbing clit and she struggled to keep from screaming. *Not yet. If I yell too soon, he might stop. Or would he finally use his mouth on me instead?* She struggled with the cision, finally deciding to go with the flow. Besides, she couldn't keep her body from thrashing. The men, however, held her down, keeping her where she actually wanted to stay.

"Suck on him, Shannon. Pull it hard. Eat him up."

She obeyed, fervently hoping he'd take his own advice and eat her up. *He's definitely enjoying the show we're giving him.*

"Baby, tell me to eat you again. This time I might do it."

Chase's order was everything she'd wanted to hear. She let go of Dirk, against his growling protest. "Eat me, Chase. Eat me while I blow Dirk." Smoothly, she slid his cock back into her mouth.

"Oh, shit that feels so great, sugar." Dirk continued his pumping action, his breaths matching his movements. "Yeah, Chase. Eat her. Suck her. I want to see her squirm even more."

Chase clamped his mouth onto her pussy, making her gasp in surprise and relief, sending an electric bolt through her. She twitched, delighting in his attack, spasms flaring under his touch. His tongue joined his fingers, diving into her cave. He nipped at the pulsing nub, sucking on her, drawing her juices out of her. The sounds he made lapping at her wetness excited her, burning her skin with every lash of his tongue. "Oh, shit, Chase. Damn, that's good. Bite my clit. Please."

"I gotta be honest, man. Watching you eat her is turning me on big-time." Dirk leaned over and swiped his tongue over her nipple. Bumping the table, he continued nibbling at her tits. She brought his dick inside, then released.

Tremors rippled outward from her head and core, crashing together near her heart. She'd had several men at once before, but none of those times compared to these two.

Chase removed his fingers to dart his tongue inside and out. He licked her from her slit up to her clit, taking her pulsing nub between her teeth. Letting out a satisfied sigh, he slid back down to dive into her cave again. She clenched, wanting to keep him inside her as long as she could. Holding her folds wide with his thumbs, he caressed her with his fingers and lashed at her with his tongue. Panting, she rocked between the men, arching for one to take her tits and bucking for the other to drink her dry.

Chase slipped his tongue out of her and ran his hands down the outsides of her legs. She squeezed her legs together, trying to force him back down. He laughed and held her apart. "Look at me, Shannon."

She tried to raise her head and couldn't until Dirk gave her a boost. Her body shook, already exhausted by the encounter, but excitement still resonated within her. Chase smiled at her, raised his fingers coated in her sex and stuck them in his mouth. "You are the hottest, sweetest thing I've ever known."

"Shit, man. I want a taste." Dirk's voice was gravelly, filled with lust.

"I'm sure she has plenty left." Slowly, with the tips of his mouth eking upward, he slid his tongue along the inside of her leg from the valley behind her knee up to the cleft at the top of her leg. She inhaled, anticipating him to pounce on her pulsing nub yet, instead, he nipped her skin, marking a trail of increasingly stronger bites around her mons to the other side. Reversing direction, he ran his tongue down her other leg.

"You are driving me frickin' crazy. Fuck me, Chase. Do it now before I explode."

"I think it's time for a switch." Easing her legs off his shoulders, he placed the spur on the table, rose and motioned for Dirk to take his place. She watched, mesmerized by his smooth, cat-like walk. Had any man ever walked so fluidly? He moved with the grace of a dancer, yet with an underlying fierceness in every step. Unbuttoning his shirt, he tossed it to the side and quickly undid his jeans.

Instead of sitting as Chase had done, Dirk stood next to her leg and bent over, placing his face above her curly snatch. He crept his hand along the mound of her tummy, following her midsection up to take a breast. "First things first. I want to smell you." Burying his face in her curls, he inhaled, tickling the skin underneath. He gripped her boob, squeezing hard, and slipped his other hand between her legs to open her to his exploring tongue. Where Chase's tongue had been smooth and hot, Dirk's was rough and warm. She stared into Chase's face as he studied her reaction to Dirk's touch, then placed his mouth close to her ear.

"Shh, remember this. Dirk can't kiss you. Only I can kiss you."

His gaze sought hers again and she understood what he was asking of her. Kissing was somehow the most intimate thing they could do and he didn't want to share her kisses with Dirk. She nodded, silently pledging her kisses to him.

Chase growled, smothering her mouth with his. The sweet taste of her juices mixed with the musky manly taste that was all his. Covering her upper lip with his, he ran his tongue across her teeth. She swept her tongue into his mouth and he pursued it, holding it hostage for a moment. At last he turned her loose and raced her tongue back inside, flicking the tip of the soft flesh along the sides of her mouth.

Shannon whimpered, not knowing how she could stand more blissful torture, not knowing how she could ever stop. No one had ever kissed her like that, ever made her cream not from another man's mouth on her pussy, but simply from his tongue on her lips. He'd created a tornado in her. Her nipples ached not for Dirk's hand, but Chase's touch.

She took Chase's hand and placed it on her other breast. Biting her lower lip, she reached out again and peeled the flaps of his jeans. Breaking free of the kiss, she turned her head and took him inside her mouth. His abs contracted and he bent to replace his hand on her nipple with his mouth.

Chase growled against her tit, spilling warm air over her sensitive skin. She moaned and took his hard length, sucking hard on his shaft. He shuddered and gripped her breast harder. Dirk, licking like a thirsty dog at fresh water, suddenly covered her clit with his mouth. With Dirk's mouth on her pussy and Chase's dick in her mouth, an orgasm broke over her, spilling out of her pussy and sending shudders through her body.

Taking her by the hair, Chase urged her to return to his oozing cock. With his splendid appendage at her face, she took up where she'd left off just as Dirk resumed feasting on her. She worked her mouth up and down, from his curly-framed base back up to the oozing tip. The sucking sounds she made echoed those of Dirk and excited her even more, sending more juices to her soaked pussy. Reaching between Chase's legs, she cupped his balls, gently juggling them so they rolled over her fingers.

"Shit, Shannon, I love that. Here." He pulled his dick away and scooted closer to the table, moving his balls closer to her. "Put your sweet mouth on these, baby. Run your tongue over them." He chuckled and tracked his fingers through her hair. "But be careful."

She moaned, deep in her throat, and nuzzled her face into his sacs. His musky scent filled her nostrils, delighting her in the masculine aroma. Palming his balls, she tenderly stroked them with her tongue, taking turns to gently drag each into her mouth. Moaning again, she blew against the sensitive area and inwardly smiled when he shivered. She fondled him more, rubbing her forehead against the skin between his balls and his ass, coupling the balls first in her palm, then putting as much of them as she could into her mouth.

"Ooh, damn. Stop, Shannon." Chase stepped away and she grumbled, unhappy to lose her new toys so soon. "If you keep doing what you're doing, I'm going to shoot my wad all over your face."

She lifted an eyebrow at him that said "so what?" and grinned.

He growled a torturous sound. "Don't tempt me."

She arched, loving the sensation of each man's hand on her tits. "Don't be afraid to put a little muscle into it, boys. A little pain turns me on."

"Then let's use both of these." Dirk took her leg, lifting it until he could grasp the spur and yank it off the heel of her boot.

"Be careful with that Dirk Claxton," Shannon quipped lightheartedly. "Did your momma teach you how to safely hold sharp objects?"

"I'm pretty sure both of us were born with sharp objects, um, in our hands."

What an odd statement. But who cares? Not me. Not when they know how to handle a hot woman like me.

Chase reached out for the spur he'd left on the table. "Now let me think. Where, oh where, do I want to use this?" His eyes sparkled, growing more yellow. "I've got an idea."

Whirling the spur around, he laid it against her shoulder. She inhaled, holding her breath, excitedly waiting for what he had planned. Slowly, he pressed the rowels against her skin just hard enough to cause a slight sting, but not enough to draw blood. He held the heel band and carefully drove the spur along her shoulder and into the hollow at her neck. Following the spur's trail with his tongue, he moved on, skimming the spur over the rise of her chest and into the space between her breasts. He tenderly soothed the soreness the steel of the spur left behind.

Dirk sat between her legs and placed her boots on the edge of the chairs. Spreading her wider, he slid his spur in a circle, going into the curly patch of hair, down the crevice between her leg and her pussy, and back up the other side. But when he moved the spur on top of her throbbing clit, she knew she'd never again think of a spur in the same way.

Much as Dirk had done to her pussy, Chase circled her breast, kissing the trail he made with the spur. He topped the mound and skimmed a loop around her nipple, digging the steel a little harder into her flesh. Both men latched onto her—Dirk onto her clit and Chase onto her tit—jolting her. Cold steel met hot tongues and she closed her eyes to savor the intensity of the two sensations. She inhaled sharply, letting the multiple vibrations flow over her, and grabbed the back of Chase's head.

"Are we hurting you?"

"Chase. God, yes. I mean, no." She panted, trying to answer him without losing her hold on the delirious feelings running over her skin. "Ooh, wow. Spur me, cowboys."

"I'm thinking this filly needs a rider."

Chase left her tit bereft. "She does."

Dropping the spurs, Dirk and Chase left their respective sides, meeting at one end of the table, each ready to climb on top. Instead, she slid off the table, squeezing her body between them, and put one hand on each of their gloriously hard chests. The instant she touched them, she blew out a breath, letting her hands slide farther down until she had both of them exactly where she wanted them. Almost in sync, their shafts twitched, coming to attention. With a wicked laugh, she dropped to her knees and came face-to-face with her ultimate cream-filled dreams. Working her hands in and out, up and down, she bumped their wet cocks against her cheeks.

"I wonder which one I should take first."

"Oh, shit. Take me." Dirk's words came out in a whisper.

"No. Me." Chase's tone was all pleading.

Shannon rubbed their tips against the corners of her mouth and cast her gaze upward so she could watch both men's faces. Peeking just the tip of her tongue out, she flicked the end of one cock, then the other.

Dirk clutched her hair, holding on with both hands as he stared at her. Chase, with his own tongue snaking out to lick his lips, held his shaft for her, urging her to take more of his inside her mouth. Delighted, she fondled his balls, silently thanking him for his help.

"Ready?" If she hadn't had her mouth already busy again, she might've laughed at their urgent expressions and rapt attention. Both men nodded and she took a breath. "Good."

Opening her mouth wider, she slipped as much of each of their rods into her mouth as she could and sucked. The mixture of their individual tastes swept over her tongue, giving her a new and different taste. Where one was sweet, the other was salty. Where one was musky, the other tangy. She moaned as they did, wrapping her tongue to take both tips. With her hands cupped firmly around them, she pumped them, two shafts of desire in her mouth.

Dirk's hold tightened on her hair. "Holy shit. I'm going nuts."

Chase's answering moan echoed Dirk's awestruck tone.

The heat of their cocks scorched through her hands and into her body, sending a fresh wash of desire between her legs. Purple-lined veins throbbed against the skin of her palms while their juices tickled her tongue. Twisting around the tip of each man's shaft, she sucked, pulling every ounce of drink she could from them.

When she took a breath, she turned and brought Chase alone inside her mouth. Yet instead of complaining, Dirk simply groaned and covered her hand on his shaft with his, helping her massage him. Chase caressed her back and pushed his hips toward her, letting her draw another inch of him inside. She dragged him in, then released, repeating the motion over and over again. When she thought he'd reached the peak of his limit, she let him go and took Dirk's shaft in. Chase let out a satisfied "ah" but didn't complain.

"This, boys, is how to share."

With Dirk's hand cupping his balls and the other firmly entrenched in her locks, she worked him, twisting her hold around his engorged shaft, tugging him to her. Gripping Chase's cock, she echoed her head's movement with her hand.

She glanced up at Dirk's closed eyes and felt the rise coming to the forefront of his dick. *If I don't stop soon...* Checking with Chase, she realized that he, too, was nearing his release. She had to stop for fear of breaking the tenuous hold each man held on his restraint. Letting Dirk's shaft go with a satisfying pop, she stood, running her hands up the length of rock-hard abdomens and over their mountainous chests. Lifting her head, she looked at Chase and Dirk, and froze. *Amber eyes. Weird.*

Dirk cupped her ass, squeezed and made a rumbling noise in his throat as though he'd lost the ability to speak. Chase, his gaze locked on hers, took her tit in his hand and rubbed his thumb over the hardened nub. A wild, almost frightening glint in his eyes made her dart her gaze away.

She swallowed, determined to speak. "Now that we've learned to share—" Her gaze fell on the object hanging on the adjacent wall and she forgot the rest of what she'd meant to stay.

Chapter Six

When Shannon pushed them apart and sauntered away, all Chase could think of was getting his hot rod deep inside her. Whether he was first or second no longer mattered. Her sudden departure threw the werewolf, too, who growled his displeasure and pivoted to watch her. Shannon strode across the room, her naked ass wiggling enticingly.

"What's she up to?"

"How the hell should I know?" Yet even if Chase had known, he wouldn't have told him.

Shannon stopped in front of a crumbling fireplace, with bricks broken off the edges of the mantel and ashes piled over the grate. She glanced back at them, a wicked smirk on her face, and reached above the mantel to take a bullwhip off its hooks.

"Uh-oh. What'd'ya think she's going do with that, Mr. Kitty?"

A spark of excitement, mixed with a tinge of anxiety, flickered in Chase's gut. "I think a woman with a bullwhip can do just about whatever she wants."

Dirk dropped his voice to a whisper only a werecreature could hear. "Maybe she's planning on taming a wild animal? Did you tell her what we are?"

"No." Chase shook his head and concentrated on

Shannon's slow, seductive stroll toward them. Her breasts bounced, taut nipples pointing at him like heat-seeking missiles. The sway of her hips drew his attention away from her tits to the patch of slightly darker blonde hair below. His cock reacted, once more demanding he throw her to the floor and make her his.

Suddenly, he saw her again, taking Dirk inside even as she spread her legs, letting him slide into her bottom. He groaned, met the werewolf's eyes over her shoulder and sensed the unspoken message. *"Give her what she wants, cat-man. Rock her off her feet."*

Shannon stopped a few feet from them, fisted one hand on her hip, set her feet apart and shook the handle, making the popper dance above the floor. "Lookie what I found, boys." She moved her wrist in a circle, letting the whip snake next to her feet. "You two have your spurs and now I have my whip. It's time to stop messing around. Strip, you big studs."

Both men hurriedly shed their clothes and boots. Chase had enjoyed a session or two of bondage in his life, but this female with a whip was the first to ever make him sweat. Sweat in a good way, that is. If she wanted to whip him into submission, he'd let her. Then he'd give her the same treatment. Still, being vulnerable in front of an armed woman had its downsides, too. "Do you know how to use one of those things?"

"Nope." She swung her arm forward slightly, letting the whip flick out in front of her. "But how hard can it be?" She arched an eyebrow over the tantalizingly smiling mouth. "Your turn to follow my orders. Work 'em, big boys. Go on. You know what I want to see."

Chase glanced at Dirk who had already started stroking his cock. *You have to love a woman who knows what she wants.* He grinned and wrapped his hand around himself.

She nodded, slowly, smugly. "Good. You're doing real

good." Her grin grew. "But not good enough." Moving quickly, she swung her arm outward, raising it above her head.

"Shannon, stop before you hurt someone." Chase lowered his voice, but tinged it with a hard edge. "You obviously don't know how to use a whip."

Fortunately, she lowered her arm and let him take the whip from her. "Oh, so you're an expert on bullwhipping?" She frowned. "Or whatever it's called."

Winding the leather into a loop, Chase scanned her body. He lifted her chin with the end of the whip. "I'll show you how to use a bullwhip."

She caught his underlying meaning and swallowed. "Show me."

"A bullwhip has all kinds of good uses. To ward off attackers..." Chase gently placed the whip over her shoulder. "To punish a very bad girl." He jiggled the handle so the leather strip flicked gently against the delicate curves of her back. "I think someone ought to be taught a lesson. Don't you, Dirk?"

"Oh? But what, pray tell, did I do that was so bad?" She pretended confusion, but the twinkle in her eyes betrayed her excitement.

"Little girls shouldn't handle deadly weapons." Fire sparked in her eyes. "At least, not unless they know how to handle deadly weapons."

"And which deadly weapon are you talking about?" She bumped one eyebrow up and down in challenge and lowered her gaze. "The whip? Or something else?"

"The one you don't know how to handle," snickered Dirk.

Her mouth dropped in feigned "oh, my" surprise. "Good one, cowboy. So what's the punishment for my crime?"

His gaze met hers, silently asking if she trusted him. "Bend over and put your hands on your knees and you'll find out."

She hesitated, biting her lower lip in a way that made him want to bite it, too. Slowly, she turned around and placed her sweet apple-shaped butt toward him.

Her ass drives me crazy. She'll feel my whip on her ass and me inside her in a minute. Smoothly throwing his arm up, back and then outward, he sent the whip flying toward the milky white of her flesh. With a small *snap*, the tip of the whip struck her butt cheek.

"Oh!" Shannon bolted upward, slapping a hand over the small red spot where the whip had touched her. She twisted around, her face an unreadable mask.

For a moment, Chase was afraid he'd hit her too hard— until a slow smile spread across her face.

"That was fucking amazing."

She couldn't have said anything sexier. Unable to control his lust any longer, Chase strode over to her and pulled her ass against him. Using the whip as a rope, he loosely wrapped half the length around her waist, then around his, tying them together. The end of whip dangled temptingly down the side of her leg. Bending her over again, farther this time, he opened her buttocks to his inspection. "Wrong. *You're* fucking amazing." With a growl, he reached between her legs and found her dripping pussy. He speared two fingers into her wetness, pushing them in and out. Using his thumb, he skimmed the area around her bottom hole, making the sensitive muscles knot.

"Dirk, grab the lube and condom from my jeans pocket."

"Oh, Chase, please hurry. I want you to doggy-style me."

He cringed at the term "doggy-style" and Dirk's low chuckle, but shoved his irritation away when Dirk handed him the tube.

"Hey, what about me?"

Chase stared into the eyes of the werewolf. "You'll get

yours. In a bit."

Dirk's eyes flashed gold, but he didn't complain. After a tense moment, he nodded his agreement. Taking his hand away from her wet pussy, Chase sheathed himself, then parted her ass cheeks wider.

"Damn. She looks good front and back."

When the dog's right, the dog's right. Chase squirted the lube onto his fingers and rubbed them around her bottom hole, into her dark passage and back out. Her muscles flexed at his touch, making him ache with the need to put his cock where his hand was. "Easy, baby. Try and relax. It's going to be a tight fit." He shoved two fingers into her, felt her tense and then relax. Turning his hand in sideways motions, he worked her ass, loosening her up for his invasion.

She moaned and shimmied her butt at him. "Do it, Chase. Hard. I can take it."

His cock bobbed up and down, telling him to do as she ordered. But he didn't want to hurt her. At least not more than she wanted to be hurt. "Steady her, Dirk." *I want to watch her blow him, suck him as I fuck her.*

Dirk moved in front of her and took her by the hair. She grabbed his thighs, holding on for balance.

Chase lubed himself, running his hand over the length of his shaft, spreading the slick liquid from base to tip. *Damn, she's going to feel so hot around me.* Scissoring his fingers into her ass again, he pushed at the tightness, working her muscles, ordering them to give him greater access. *Come on, baby, take it easy.* Her tightness loosened up a bit but she needed more. Pointing the end of the lube slightly into her ass, he squeezed, sending the cool gel into her. She gasped, then shuddered. She bucked back at him to try and rush him, her panted breaths a sign of how much she wanted his cock inside her. He had to smile at her eagerness.

"Bend lower. Dirk will keep you steady."

She followed his directions, moving her hands farther down Dirk's legs. Dirk slid his palms down her back to grip her by the hips. The werewolf's eyes glowed brightly, arousal apparent not only in his hard dick, but in the rigid set of his body.

Chase positioned the crown of his cock against the puckered skin and pushed. She went still, held her breath, then slowly let out her breath. Her ass loosened up. He took his time even though he wanted to pump hard and fast, then pushed his shaft farther inside. *Clench, relax, push.* The mantra of their actions filled his head. *Clench, relax, push.* Her ring of muscles slowly released, letting him enter. He was halfway into her, but that remaining half throbbed to feel her hold around him.

"Use the whip, Dirk. Spank me while Chase bangs me."

Dirk took the end of the whip and slid it along her back. With a quick flick of his wrist, he feathered light *snaps* along her skin. Small pink marks traveled around the curve of her buttocks, then up the slope of her spine.

Her mews at the whiplashes swirled in Chase's gut and, for a moment, he wanted to change places with Dirk. Suddenly, the need to feel his cock fully inside her overwhelmed him, stripping him of any chance to stop, and he plunged his length into her. She cried out, nearly tumbling over at the force of his shove, but his impromptu rope binding them together and Dirk's sure catch held her upright.

"Shit, Shannon, are you all right?" He could barely speak, panting the words out. When she didn't answer, alarm at what he'd done skyrocketed. "Talk to me, baby." He leaned back, rubbing his hands over her gel-slicked ass. Blood whirred in his head, shaking all other thoughts out. *I need to stop. God, but I don't want to stop.* His concern for her, however, won out and he began to pull out.

"Don't you dare."

He paused, unsure that he'd really heard her speak. "Did you say—"

"Fuck me now!" She twisted her head around and glared at him. "Did you hear me that time?" She wiggled her buttocks at him and he took her at her word, plunging his cock inside her again. She screamed, louder this time, but he took it as a sign of her desire and kept going.

Chase growled, shifting to bring out his teeth and claws. He pulled out, only halfway, then rammed back into her, rocking her on her feet. The sweat from his brow and chest dropped onto the small of her back, and he wished he could lean over to lick the drops off her. Dirk reached under her and took her tit, his breathing labored, his eyes closed again.

His cock sliding in and out of her pink-flamed ass only made Chase hotter for her. He watched Dirk's arm muscles, imagining how the werewolf fondled and played with her tit. The harder, rougher he pushed, the more engorged he became, slapping his balls against her. Still her tight rings clamped around his shaft and wouldn't let go. *She's so tight, so hot. I'm not sure how much longer I can go on yet I don't want to stop now. Not yet.*

Her cry of release sent shockwaves shuddering through her, rippling along his cock and skimming to shiver against his balls. The sensation shook him, nearly sending him over the edge. With a groan, he forced himself to withdraw from her, pulling out quickly before he lost it. Fighting harder than any battle he'd ever fought, he kept his climax in check. Barely.

Retracting his claws and fangs, Chase threw away the condom, pushed Dirk's hands off her, then bent over so he could wrap his arms around her, over the whip. She was still shivering from the orgasm. "Are you okay?"

She giggled brokenly between ragged breaths. "I will be."

"Well, I won't be unless I get some ass." Dirk let her go and motioned for a change. "My turn."

Chase unwound the whip, lifted her into his arms and wrapped her legs around the upper part of his. As though specifically made for him, her snatch opened wide and he glided inside. Her moaned breath against his shoulder warmed his skin. "Can you handle both of us, baby?"

Shannon smiled that soft smile he loved and nodded. "I can't wait."

Taking her gently to the floor while keeping his shaft inside her, Chase leaned back on his calves and hands and waited as Dirk knelt behind her and cupped her ass cheeks. She lifted, placing a hand on the base of Chase's dick to keep it from slipping out of her. With a relieved groan, Dirk slid the tip of his shaft inside her ass.

"Oh, damn." She stiffened, somehow pushing at both of them, clinging to Chase.

His gaze locked onto Dirk's hands kneading her breasts as he gently worked his way into her from behind. The werewolf leaned over, trailing kisses along her smooth neck.

As long as he doesn't bite, I'm okay with it. Chase gritted his teeth, wishing he could balance her better and still put his hands on her. "Pinch her tits, Dirk." Dirk did as he asked and Chase licked his lips in appreciation. *She's so hot. Fucking both of us at once.*

She rocked slowly, going along with Dirk's careful movements. Dirk moaned, his eyes closed, as he pushed harder, slipping as far as he could inside her. A strange yet exhilarating feeling rippled along Chase's shaft. *Oh, shit. What the—*

He paused, his heart picking up speed, then shoved his shaft back inside her in the same moment Dirk drove into her from behind. *It's him. Almost like we're meeting in the middle.* Chase's breaths came faster. *Holy crap. No wonder men don't mind doubling up on one woman.* He wanted more, wanted to enjoy the new experience for all that it was worth. *Damn, this feels so good. Fuck her hard, Dirk. Make her shudder.*

"Shannon, play with your clit. Masturbate while he rams into your ass. Ram her hard, man." He stared into her face, watching the flashes of lust as she took both men at once.

Shannon fingered her pussy, keeping one hand steady on his cock. Dirk, his eyes closed, and with sweat running down his forehead, thrust into her harder, harder until she rocked with his pushes. Chase, the ache inside his gut roaring to be released, watched, mesmerized, enthralled and horny as hell.

"Good one, man. That's it. Make her pant." He puffed out air as he worked his hips, thrusting upward. He matched Dirk, push to shove, and was rewarded with the wonderful sensation again. Playing around with the new experience, he changed rhythm, the impression against his cock changing as the werewolf pulled out and he dove in. *Damn, this is great. Fucking her and feeling him fuck her, too. Hell, forget great. This is absolutely amazing.* Even the feel of Dirk's legs between his own, his tense muscles working to thrust his hips forward, excited him.

Shannon, throwing her head back, screamed in ecstasy and rode them both. Her arms pushed her tits together and she kept rubbing herself, stroking him as he drove into her. Flesh slapped against flesh, sweat dripped from one person to the next until he couldn't tell where one person's perspiration started and another's took over. Groans, moans and various sounds of desire filled the air until, suddenly, Dirk fell backward.

Feeling his own release nearing the brink yet again, Chase growled and lifted Shannon off his dick. Together they cried out as he did so, almost as though they'd somehow torn the other's soul out. Collapsing on top of him, Shannon's hard breaths pushed against his chest. "Damn, woman, that was amazing."

She giggled, then smoothed the hair away from her face to look at him. "Tell me we're not finished yet."

He laughed, twisted his head to check Dirk, his breathing only now leveling out, and shook his head. "I don't know about him, but I'm still in the game." Summoning his strength, he stood, taking her with him and carried her to the table. Gently, he laid her on top of it. He wiped the beads from her sweat-dampened brow, gazed into her eyes. *She's something special. Very special.* "I need to fuck you."

"You mean you need to fuck me again."

"Yeah. Again and to the finish this time."

"Hold up. Don't forget me." Dirk staggered over to the table, bent over and licked her tit.

"How about this?" She pushed her breasts together and smiled at Chase. "Dirk can fuck my tits while you get my pussy again."

"Sounds good to me."

Chase grinned at the man rubbing her tits. "Everything sounds good to you, man."

"Hop up here, Dirk, and I'll give you a ride."

Chase stepped to the side to let her scoot down the table until her legs hung over the edge and Dirk crawled on top of her upper torso. He licked the hollow between her breasts, lapping away like the dog he was. Finally, he straddled her, using his legs to push her breasts together. With a groan that burned a hole in Chase's gut, Dirk worked his cock between her breasts.

"Chase?"

He yanked his gaze away from her breasts. "Yeah?"

"How about eating me first?"

He swallowed. What man wouldn't? Placing a chair underneath him, he positioned her legs over his shoulders. Dirk pumped, his ass cheeks clenching and releasing as he thrust his dick back and forth between her tits. Chase closed his eyes, envisioning Shannon flicking her tongue at the tip of the werewolf's dick and expected to be disgusted. Instead, the fire burning within him increased and he pressed his face against her sopping pussy. She moaned, whether at Dirk's attentions or his, he didn't care. All that mattered was the sweet taste of her and the feel of his hand on his slick cock.

Her clit throbbed beneath his mouth, encouraging him to lick, stroke, nip at her. She bucked against him, her sensitive nub handling all his lashes, and he gripped her legs, keeping her down.

"Eat me, Chase. Please, I need you."

He opened his eyes to see the pretty patch of hair above her pouting pussy and growled, sending his hot breath onto her skin and getting a shiver of excitement in reward. Concentrating on the button pulsing for his full attention, he suckled strongly on it and listened to Shannon's moans grow louder. She came, arching, bending, nearly tossing Dirk off her.

"Oh, God, oh, God. Oh, oh, oh. Ohhhh!"

Her cries marked another orgasm and, with the sweet juices spread over his face, ratcheted up the burning heat inside his groin. Even watching Dirk's ass muscles constrict and release as he worked his shaft back and forth between her tits made Chase ache for her. When the werewolf rose up on his legs far enough for Chase to glimpse Shannon's enraptured face as she flicked her tongue over the tip of the other shifter's dick, he knew he wanted more. "Get off her. Now."

Dirk kept pumping, momentarily twisting around to glare at Chase. "You're fucking kidding me, right?"

"No, I'm not." Standing, Chase took Shannon by the legs and urged her to flip onto her stomach. "You want to come, don't you? And I want her to suck me off while you fuck her ass again."

Dirk's blank stare and obvious confusion lasted only a second. "Don't mind if I do." Dirk helped her to roll over and slide closer to the edge as Chase came toward her head. Guiding his shaft into her, Dirk groaned and gripped her ass. "Damn, but she's tight."

Chase, taking her hair to keep it out of her face, spread his feet and let her take his balls in her hands. With a quick whip of her tongue over his weeping tip, she deep-throated him. "Ahhh." For a moment, he closed his eyes, undone by the amazing sensation of her teeth, her tongue caressing him.

"Hey, cat man, didn't you want to watch?"

He opened his eyes, thankful of the reminder when his gaze fell on the slickened round hills of Shannon's buttocks. Her flesh quivered with each of Dirk's strokes and when the shifter slapped her on the cheek, Chase had to resist the urge to change places with him. He couldn't decide which way he wanted her the most. *This is better than anything I imagined.*

On her elbows with him, she still managed to lift her bottom higher for Dirk. Almost without noticing, Chase matched his rhythm to Dirk's. "That's it, baby. Pull, but not too hard. Ah, use your tongue. Good, that's good."

"I don't know how much longer I can last, man."

"Then don't."

With a loud groan, Dirk pulled out of Shannon, releasing onto her back. She squealed and tugged on Chase's dick a little harder. Dirk, spent but mobile, crawled off the table and grabbed a cloth off a nearby table. "Let me clean you up." Quickly, he wiped her down.

Unable to resist any longer, Chase pulled his cock out of Shannon's mouth and lifted her into his arms. Laying her gently on the floor, he entered her, shoving his dick into her wet and welcoming pussy. She grunted at the force of his move, then wrapped her arms around his neck and her legs around his waist. "Make me come again, Chase."

He gazed into her eyes, wanting to go deeper into those sweet depths, as deep as he now was inside her body. "More than that. I want to make—" She blinked and he knew she'd caught his near slip. *What the hell had I started to say? Surely not that word.* Yet, suddenly, he knew he'd almost said it all, telling her before he'd actually realized the truth. *I love her.* He sucked in air, stunned. *I want her to be my female, now and forever. She's my mate.* He studied her face, the myriad of expressions, and waited. *Does she already know? Can she sense my unspoken feelings? The unspoken word?*

"Make whoopie?" She tilted her head and gave him a look full of understanding. Her face softened and the corners of her mouth crooked up in an almost shy smile. They held that indefinable connection for a few moments more until, at last, she craned her head around to see a very satisfied Dirk standing at the end of the table, watching, listening. "Dirk."

Thrusting into her, Chase took her face between his hands and regained control of those wonderful eyes. "Later. We'll talk about this later."

Damp hair stuck to her forehead as she nodded. "Later." Then, squeezing her legs around him, driving back into him, she whispered, "I do, too."

His heart skipped a beat while hers pounded against his chest. With a roar, he lunged into her, spilling his seed into the woman he loved.

Chapter Seven

A hand fondled her breast, perking her tit into attention. Shannon stretched, arching her back to push her boob harder against the hand, and reached for Chase, who had been curled up next to her on the makeshift bed he'd thrown together. But abruptly the hand left her breast and the warm body next to her rolled away. The smile forming on her face morphed into a frown and she struggled to rid her mind of the sleep stubbornly clinging to it.

At last, she threw away the mental cobwebs and remembered. *Chase loves me. He didn't actually say the words, but I know he does. I felt it. Still, it'd be nice to hear him say it.* "Chase?"

Growls erupted near her, ridding her of the lingering sleep and making her stomach flip over in fear. Jumping to her feet, she snatched up her clothes, clutched them to her chest and whirled to find the two men punching, grabbing, yanking each other around the room. "Oh, my God, what the hell are you doing?"

Dirk landed against the wall, then slid down to land on his rump. Bottles from the shelf above him shattered on the floor around him. He scrambled to his feet, vibrations of rage flowing off his body, golden eyes glaring, flashing with anger. "No one throws me around like that." With a sound that was half shout and half roar, he lunged toward Chase.

Chase readied for the oncoming attack, his shoulders bulging, his face a frightening mask of fury.

Shannon shouted at Chase. "Why the hell did you do that?" *More like* how *the hell.* She didn't get far, however, before he grabbed her arm and pushed her behind him and away from Dirk. The enraged glint in his glowing amber eyes stunned her and she held her breath. *What is going on with this guy?*

"Yeah, catnip, what's up with you? Share and share alike. Just like before."

Chase, the muscles in his back rippling, ready to attack again, growled. "Not happening, dog breath. Things have changed."

Changed? He doesn't want to share now that he loves me. That's what's changed.

She smiled again, unable to keep the happy feeling from her face. "But, Chase, he doesn't know. He couldn't know what's happened. We have to talk. First you and me, and then—"

Before she could finish, however, Chase covered her mouth with his. He wrapped his arms around her, crushing her within their iron embrace. Dirk growled somewhere far away, but even that faded under the onslaught of emotions. At the mere touch of Chase's tongue to hers, lust—renewed and given added strength—raked through her. She drank him in, wanting to taste more of him, all of him. But what she really wanted, she'd already waited too long for. She opened her legs and wrapped them around his lean waist.

Chase, however, broke their kiss. Taking her face in his, he searched her for obedience. "I've had enough of this. I can't—" He struggled, his face showing the turmoil within, then determination set his features. "Tell him you want only me." His grip strengthened, yet she knew he was restraining himself. "Tell him."

The gleam in his eyes told her everything she wanted to know. *He really does love me.* A thrill lightened her heart. *He did a threesome with Dirk, but now he doesn't want to share me. He wants me all for himself. Now I, we, mean too much.* She continued to study him, searching his heart while searching her own. *I love him, too.* She took his wrists, not to break away, but to keep him close. *How the hell did this happen? When did I fall in love?* Grinning, she wiped the questions away. *Who the hell cares? All that matters is that we love each other.*

Without turning her eyes away from Chase, she tried to make Dirk understand—even though she barely understood herself. "Dirk, I'm sorry. Really. But the threesome part is over." She had to look at him. "Please understand."

Although still irritated, Dirk ran a hand through his hair, then gave her a curt nod. Finally, his familiar easy grin replaced the snarl on his lips. "That doesn't mean I can't watch, does it?"

"Good grief. You are such a dog."

"More than you know."

At Chase's remark she turned to him, hoping his answer would be the same as hers. She heard the grumble in his chest, but it was soon followed by a heavy sigh.

"I guess letting him watch is okay." Chase lowered his tone at Dirk. "But no more touching."

She laughed and swiped her tongue along his chin. "I think we've had plenty of foreplay, Chase. I need you to fuck me and fuck me hard. Right now. Right this—"

"Don't you ever shut the hell up?" Chase clutched her ass cheeks, holding her in place. He rammed his cock into her waiting pussy.

If he'd wanted her to forget how to speak, he couldn't have found a better way. Her head swam, dizzy with the feel of him forcing his way into her core. His kisses grew more intense, more possessive than before. And his cock, oh, God, his cock so deeply entrenched in her, called out to her with every shove, every push. She laid her head back, letting him bite her neck from her earlobe to her shoulder. Even when he bit her extra hard, digging teeth—*fangs?*—into her, she wanted more. *Am I bleeding? I don't care.*

Clutching his hair, she kept his mouth on her and arched, hoping he'd get the message to take her nipple into his mouth. She almost cried in relief when his teeth nipped at the swollen nub.

Another orgasm, bigger, longer than the earlier ones, swept over her, surprising her in its duration. She held onto him and rode it out. Yet before she could take a breath, another shuddered through her. She cried out and dug her nails into his back.

"Say you're mine." His rough panting tickled her nipples, but in an enticing way.

"I'm yours. And you're mine." She leaned away from him, pushing against his chest, and ground against his pelvis. Although she could feel his shaft at her inner wall, she wanted more of him.

She kissed him, his mouth, his neck, his ears and still couldn't give him enough. Suddenly, everything was clear to her. Jarrod's heartless abandonment, the months of clawing through the ensuing heartache, all the years of meaningless sex, all the men she'd used then forgotten, were in preparation for Chase. Everything she'd experienced, everything she'd lived, had given her the insight to recognize the truth of this moment. *I love this man.* He was hers and she was his.

He thrust into her again, going impossibly deeper, bouncing his balls off her wet slit below. Moaning, he dug his nails into her back and continued to ram into her. Yet this was no mere act of raw sex any longer. They were, as he'd wanted to say, making love.

The huge orgasm blindsided her, sweeping through her like a tsunami, rolling over her body, diving into her heart. She tensed, then started trembling and kept shaking with wave after wave racking her from head to toes.

Drenched in sweat, they clung to each other, one's tremors feeding into the other's. With a wild cry, Chase stormed his release, shooting into her. She smiled, happy to have his seed inside her. Contracting her muscles, she did her best to capture his come.

"Shannon."

"Yeah, I know. I'm yours."

His chuckle blew warm breath against her shoulder but, compared to the heat of their bodies, it felt cool. Slowly, he laid her down on their thrown-together bed. She held her breath, hoping he wouldn't walk away. With a sigh, he collapsed on top of her. She slid her hands along his sweaty back and hugged him.

"Whew. I sure hope that was as good for you as it was for me."

Shannon caught Chase's bemused look and, together, they turned to see a spent and very satisfied Dirk sitting on the floor, his still-erect cock in hand. "Believe me, Dirk. It was way better."

With a grin, Dirk curled up into a ball and quickly fell asleep.

"Just like a man." Shannon nodded at the snoring Dirk. "Fall asleep anywhere in no time flat."

"Just like a dog, you mean."

"Huh?"

He touched the end of her nose. "Never mind." Snuggling against her, he stroked her love-worn body.

She traced the line of his jaw, working her finger from his

kissable earlobe over to his even more kissable lips. He surprised her by snatching her finger into his mouth and holding it there while he lashed his tongue around it. She giggled, watching the motions of his tongue behind his cheeks. "You sure do like sucking on things, Mr. Reya."

He turned her loose, making an exaggerated popping sound. "What's with the 'Mr. Reya'?"

"Oh, I don't know. The name fits you. You know, all spicy and hot, yet cool and commanding."

"You get all that from the name Reya?" He snuggled his face into her neck, showering her with tickling kisses and making her giggle more.

"Yep." She wiggled her ass against his crotch. *I wonder how much longer I'll have to wait before he's ready for another go.* The growth beneath her bottom answered the question. "Uh, if you're thinking of growing any more, then I need to take a restroom break first."

He cupped her tit, licked across the swell of her breast. "Then you'd better head on out to the outhouse. Oh, and get dressed first."

She straightened up, pushing against his granite-hard pecs. "Are you serious?" She glanced around the small one-room cabin and realization hit her—in both the head and her bladder. "There's no bathroom in this place?" *Please tell me you're joking.*

Chase obviously enjoyed her dilemma. "You're just now noticing this?"

"Hey, I had my mind on other things."

He skimmed a hand along her thigh, over her leg and onto her curly snatch.

She squirmed against him, but this time it wasn't due to any desire to have sex. "So tell me where the real bathroom is."

"Out back. Just follow the dirt path and you'll run right into it." Chase stood, taking her with him.

Lying cradled in his arms, she splayed her hand across his steel-like chest, and wished she could answer the heat in her abdomen instead of the call of nature. She sighed and enjoyed how he carried her to the back door of the cabin and leaned over, flexing his muscles, to let her open it.

She peered into the dimming light and, although it was well down the path and obscured by bushes, finally spied the shed, which was not much bigger than a phone booth. "Holy shit."

"Haven't you ever heard of an outhouse?"

"Yeah, sure. Like in the movies. Doesn't everyone have indoor plumbing nowadays?"

"Not in these old cabins. Besides, it's not that bad. Just watch out for the spiders and snakes."

She dropped out of his arms and pushed him back a couple of steps. "Now that part better be a joke."

"Actually, no, it's not." He hugged her close. "Let me get a lantern and I'll go with you. I'll stand guard over you while you, uh, do your business. After all, I've seen everything you've got."

She glanced up quickly to see if he'd snickered at her and caught him rolling his lips under to smother a chuckle. *No way am I going Number One in front of this man. A girl has her limits, after all. Never mind him. I'm a big girl. I can do this.* "Get the lantern and don't let me hear you snickering."

Chase found the battery-operated lantern—*thank you for small mercies*—while she tugged on her clothes. "Here." Keeping a straight face, he handed it to her along with an old newspaper.

"Trust me. I'm not going to waste any time reading."

He coughed, quickly covering a laugh. "Uh, the paper's not to read. It's to wipe with."

She took the crumpled paper and stared at the dirty spots on it. "Don't we have any toilet paper?"

"I didn't see any. And I doubt anyone left some in the outhouse, either. Spiders tend to nest inside the roll."

She cringed, thinking of the tiny spider she'd killed back at the ranch. It had taken her thirty minutes to dredge up the courage to step on it. Her anxiety took over, imagining her baring her tush to tarantulas and cobras in the semi-dark of the crude structure. *Oh, shit. Was great sex worth this?* She studied Chase's handsome features and remembered his hands on her body. *Yeah, he's worth it.*

Gathering her courage, she stepped outside into the twilight and trudged through the brush and bushes, trying to follow the dirt path leading to the outhouse.

"You can do this, Shannon. You can do this." Repeating the encouraging words out loud didn't help much. But she half hoped they might scare a snake or two away. At last, after what seemed a very long time, she stood in front of the tiny building and reconsidered her decision not to let Chase accompany her. Steeling herself against whatever horrors lay behind the wooden door, she lifted the latch, flung the door wide and stumbled back a couple of feet, ready to be attacked by scores of spiders and snakes.

"Shannon? You okay?"

She jumped at the sound of Chase's shout, then gritted her teeth. "Yeah. I'm fine." *Does he really mean to check up on me? Or to frighten me a little more? The man definitely has a playful side. Too bad I'm not laughing.*

"Good. But I forgot to warn you to look out for skunks, too."

Skunks? Oh, come on! She spun around, checking the bushes around her, but saw nothing. She blew out a breath, settling her rattled nerves. *Playful, my ass. He's downright evil and when I get back to the cabin, he's going to pay for his little jokes.* She forced the knot forming in her throat back down into her stomach. *But what if he's not kidding?*

"I'll be in the cabin if you need me."

"Okay." She lifted the lantern and stuck her arm into the outhouse, illuminating the closet-like quarters. Spider webs hung from every corner but it was the hole serving as a toilet that nearly had her losing her lunch. *A frickin' hole? No actual toilet? So I'm supposed to pee into a hole in the ground?* She inched forward to peek closer. Thankfully, she couldn't see the bottom, but she had no doubt about it. This was the toilet. *Now I know where the term shithole comes from.*

Taking a deep breath—which she immediately regretted—she stepped into the outhouse and closed the door. She hooked the lantern on the nail on the back of the door and quickly lowered her jeans. *Please, oh, please, don't let anything bite me in the ass.*

Faster than she'd ever managed to do so, Shannon did her business, zipped up her jeans and pushed open the door. She stepped outside and inhaled, taking in the sweet mountain air.

A low rumbling sound froze her to the spot. *What the hell is that?* "Chase?" She swallowed and tried to produce more than a whisper. "Chase?"

The answering growl suddenly made her reevaluate the outhouse's appeal. Yet she doubted the rickety old shed would give her much protection. *If this is a wild animal, I have to make it back to the safety of the cabin and Chase.* She turned slowly, biting her lip to keep from whimpering. Every rustle of a leaf, every fleeting shadow left her shaking and trying to drag air into her suddenly constricted chest. *Is that something?* She squinted, trying to make out the shape in the bushes. *It's too big for a skunk. Way too big. So what the hell is it?*

The idea hit her and she nearly cried from relief. *I bet it's Chase. Funny how the man who'd seemed so stoic before today had morphed into a prankster.* "Chase, if you're trying to scare me, it's not working. And, by the way, that's one lame-ass growl. Shoot, I've heard poodles that sounded meaner." *And I've definitely heard him growl meaner than that.*

The growl was louder this time and definitely more menacing. *Okay, that really sounded mean. And dangerous. Oh, shit.*

"Chase?" Suddenly, her brilliant deduction of his playing a joke didn't fly. *That's a real animal.* The dark shape in the bushes moved closer, growing bigger and wider. She could hear the crunch of leaves with its every step. *Holy shit. That's a really big animal.*

Unable to break free from the dread striking her numb, she stood and waited for the animal to break through the bushes. Her breathing quickened and her heart raced in her chest. *Only a few more feet and I'll see it.*

A massive head covered in brown fur broke through the last bush between them and jaws opened wide, showing long sharp fangs dripping with saliva. The fear holding her in one spot exploded into absolute terror. She dropped the lantern and ran.

Chapter Eight

How long does a human female take to do her business? Chase paced the room and wished the cabin had a back window to go along with the back door.

I guess this is just one of many things I'll have to get used to now that I've found my mate. The smile slipping over his face surprised and delighted him. *My mate. I've found my mate.* She was human, but other werecats had taken human females for mates. Granted, he'd never expected this to happen, but now that it had, he wasn't about to let her go. He would explain everything to her, then bite her, changing her into a shifter.

His smile faded. *Will she want me once she knows what I am?* A knot formed in the middle of his chest. *What if she's afraid of me? Even if she can love me knowing what I am, will she want to become a werecat? What if she refuses to be my mate?* Growling at the fear clenching at his heart, he shoved the questions away. He'd find out soon enough.

What's taking her so long? He stared at the back door, willing her to come back. At last he forced himself to sit down. *If she isn't here in a few more minutes, I'll go get her.*

"Where's Shannon?"

Chase glanced up from his seat at the table—the table where he could still imagine Shannon's luscious nude body spread across its length—to scowl at the werewolf. Dirk stretched, pushed his body against the wall to stand, then scanned the room. "Out back."

The werewolf sauntered toward him, took a chair and flipped it around to straddle the seat. "She's one incredible female."

"She's *my* incredible female." Although Dirk had backed off earlier, Chase figured it couldn't hurt to verbally stake his claim one more time.

Dirk held up his hands, palms out. "Relax. You wouldn't want to cough up a hair ball. I get that you two have found something special. No problem. I mean, I would've liked to have had another go, but I'm willing to step aside for *true love*." He grinned, hinting at the truth behind his taunting words.

True love. As sappy as that sounded, those were the correct words to describe what Chase felt for Shannon. He just hoped the feeling was reciprocated. If what she'd said during sex—agreeing that she was his—was any indication, it was. Keeping his expression neutral, he let his thoughts wander to the day when he would take her into the mountains, showing her his world and her new home. His dick twitched at the thought of Shannon lying on her back amidst the forest, legs open, welcoming him.

Her scream ripped his fantasy apart, knotting his gut. Chase rushed through the back door, flinging it open so hard it nearly tore it off its hinges. Dirk hurried behind him, but alarm for Shannon kept him in the lead. He ran, his eyes quickly adjusting to the darkness. Another scream drove a wedge of panic through his heart and he picked up his pace by partially shifting. "Shannon, where are you?"

"There!"

He saw her in the same instant Dirk yelled. Stumbling through the brush, she fell, her eyes wild, cuts from the bushes streaking her cheeks. "Run! It's right behind—"

The bear was on her before she could finish her sentence.

To Chase's horror, the huge animal picked her up with one paw and tossed her several feet into the air. She landed behind the bushes with a sickening thud.

"No!" Roaring, Chase tore off his clothes, shifting all the way. Fur raced along his body, claws extended from the hands forming paws, eyes narrowed, morphing from the sight of a man into that of a cougar. His bones ground together, growing larger in some areas and smaller in others. Within seconds, he fell to the ground on all fours. He snarled, challenging the bear. Dirk stood beside him, a dark brown wolf, growling his own battle call.

The bear rose on its back legs, swiping the air around him with its gigantic paws and splitting the air with its terrifying roar. Dropping back to the dirt, it lumbered toward them, a furry freight train determined to pummel them under its feet.

Chase's muscles tensed and he crouched, ready to pounce. He flung his body at the bear, soaring over its snapping jaws to land on its massive back. The bear bellowed in anger and bucked, trying to hurl the werecat off him, but Chase dug his claws deep into the fur, into the creature's underlying skin. Snarling, he clamped his fangs into the thick neck. Blood gushed into his mouth, spurted from the sides of his jaws, splattering onto his chest and legs. Dirk darted in and out, keeping away from the animal's strikes, and landed his own blows to its underside.

Enraged by its inability to get rid of them, the bear spun in a circle, rubbing against the thick brush to try and knock them off. When that didn't work, the animal roared in frustration, buckling at the knees to begin a roll. Chase jumped, tearing away part of the beast's neck. He hurtled his body several feet from the rolling predator.

The severely injured bear struck out at them, but his now-feeble attempts to attack fell short. They continued to strike at him, Chase daring the gigantic jaws while Dirk slashed at its hind legs. Round and round they circled the animal, using their speed to stay clear of the bear's claws and fangs.

Lifting its head in a final roar, the bear hurriedly shuffled back from them, then twisted around and ran back down the path, leaving a bloody path behind him. Chase, his breath harsh and ragged, watched the bear disappear from sight, making sure it was no longer a threat, then turned to where Shannon had landed.

"Chase?" Shannon stood between two bushes, grasping limbs to keep herself upright. Dirt and blood covered her clothing and a gash made an ugly streak across her forehead. "Is that really you?"

Joy filled him and he shifted back to human form. She stared at him, mouthing something incomprehensible. A small cry escaped her as her knees buckled and she lurched toward him.

Chase caught her a second before she hit the ground. He knelt over her, lowering her gently to the ground, letting her face rest against the ever-growing pool of blood flowing out of her. "Shannon." He stroked her pale cheek, silently urging her to look at him. "Baby, please open your eyes."

A human Dirk stood over them. "She's losing a lot of blood, man. Too much blood."

Chase pulled off his shirt, pressed it against the gaping hole in her side and fought back the urge to take his fear out on Dirk. "Help me staunch the bleeding. We've got to get her back to the ranch."

Dirk removed his shirt, squatted on her other side and started ripping it apart for makeshift bandages. "I don't think we'd make it in time. She wouldn't survive the trip. Not the way she's bleeding right now."

Chase inhaled slowly and fully, then exhaled, trying to calm down enough to think. "We have to do something. I can't, I *won't* let her die."

"You have to do the only thing you can do." Dirk met his gaze and nodded, his face a grave mask. "You know what I mean. If she has any chance of surviving until we can get help, then you have to mark her and hope it's enough to keep her alive."

Bite her without her consent to become his mate? She'd said she was his, but she hadn't known that he was a shifter—or that she'd become one, too. What would she say later? What if she'd rather die than become a shifter, or his mate? Yet Dirk was right. What choice did he have? He had to change her to give her enough strength to make the journey back to the ranch.

Chase shifted again, just far enough to lengthen his teeth into fangs. He let her head fall backward to expose her lovely neck and her carotid artery, then paused, wondering if he'd seen her eyelids flutter as though she were trying to open her eyes. When she didn't, he opened his jaws and sunk his fangs into her. She gurgled a strange sound, jerked a few times, then grew still. Clutching her body against his, he held her, giving her the life force that he prayed would keep her alive.

The nightmare was always the same, with the same gigantic monster rising up in front of her, its glistening white claws flexed, ready to tear out her throat. Hard eyes locked onto her, freezing her very breath while shiny alabaster fangs dripped saliva in anticipation of sinking into her delectable skin. She struggled to get to her feet but, as it always happened in the dream, her legs refused to move.

Shannon opened her mouth to scream, yet no sound came. *Why can't I scream? Why can't I run? Where am I? Please, God, don't let me die.* Then in one last desperate attempt to scream, she mouthed the hardest question of all. *Chase, where are you?* With the ferocious bear towering over her, she prepared, as she always did in the torturous nightmare, to die.

When the beautiful mountain lion jumped in front of her, placing his body between her and the monster, she finally cried out, not in fear but in exultation. The cougar fought like a demon possessed, striking out at the monster, standing between her and certain death.

The cougar, aided by a swiftly moving wolf, attacked the enormous bear-monster, slashing at its throat, its underbelly; anywhere they could find a vulnerable spot. The bear was covered in big dark splotches of its own blood and soon Shannon could sense its desire to fight lessening. With an outraged roar, the bear whirled around, stumbling over its own feet, and rushed out of the clearing.

"Chase?" she whispered. "Is that really you?" *Why did I call the cougar by Chase's name?* Yet she knew without a doubt that the puma who had fought for her, perhaps sacrificing his life for her, was Chase. The blackness she'd grown accustomed to enveloped her again and she closed her eyes, unable to stop her legs from buckling beneath her. With an exhausted sigh, she welcomed the wet warmth against her cheek even when she realized that the warmth came from her own pool of blood.

"Shannon?"

She sighed again, not sure if she'd actually made a sound but not caring. The soft touch against her cheek washed through her, giving her comfort where no other could be found.

"Baby, please open your eyes."

She tried with every ounce of willpower in her to heed his plea but could only manage to peek between fluttering eyelids. In that second, she saw what couldn't be real. Yet deep inside, she knew with absolute certainty that it was. Chase, holding her gently in her arms, sprouted fangs, then sank them into her neck.

The pain racing through her neck burned through her skin, into her veins and down into her very soul. Jerking against the invasion of her body, she tried to cry out, tried to lift her hands up and push him away, but she was powerless. Giving up even the pretense of struggle, she welcomed the blackness surrounding her.

"You've been here the whole time. How about you let me take over and you get—"

"No. I'm not leaving her side." His words came out harsher than he meant, but the frustration and guilt he felt had to come out someway. *But not at her cousin's expense. Shannon wouldn't want that.* Chase glanced at Bob, hoping the distraught man would recognize his apology in his face. "I can't. I don't want her waking up without me here to help her."

It was the same discussion they'd had many times since he and Dirk had carried her back to the ranch two days earlier. The ranch's doctor—one who knew about the existence of shifters—had done all he could. With shifter blood running through her veins, taking her to a human hospital was out of the question. Now it was up Shannon to pull through and the only thing they could do was wait.

Why can't they understand that I'll stay by her side until it's over? No! Not over. Until she comes out of this...sleep...she escaped into. He cradled her hand in his, covering it with his other hand. *And she will come out of it. I know she will. She has to.*

"Chase, look, I know we're not best buds or anything, but you need to listen to Bob. What good will you do her if you collapse from exhaustion?"

He could sense Dirk standing behind him and shook his

115

head. The werewolf had remained nearby during the past days, surprising Chase with his unwavering support. "You know I can last a lot longer than that. Than any human ever could."

"Yeah." Dirk let out a heavy sigh. "I know. And I also know you did everything you could to save her."

Chase sprang out of the chair, whirling toward Dirk. Fangs shot out and claws sharpened into razors. Grabbing the werewolf by the collar, Chase shoved him against the wall. "Do not talk like she's dying." Barely controlling his rage, Chase spit out his words. "She is not going to die."

Dirk calmly unhooked Chase's clenched fists from his collar and moved him back a step. "I know, I know. I didn't mean it like that. I only meant that you need to stop blaming yourself."

Chase thrust the werewolf against the wall again, then hurried back to his place beside Shannon. "If I'd gone with her to the outhouse, none of this would've happened."

"You don't know that. In fact, if the bear had caught you off guard while you were playing kissy-face, then both of you might've ended up bits of meat right now, a tasty meal served up to the vultures. Instead, you heard her cry for help and you answered it. Hell, I hate like hell to admit it, but you saved her, man. So stop torturing yourself."

"She has to wake up."

"Yeah. And she will. Give her time. After all, she made it this far, she'll make it all the way."

Chase paced to stare out the window. "I don't know what I'll do if I lose her. Even when I finally realized I wanted her as my mate, I still didn't get how much I need her. How much I love her." He swallowed, trying to keep his voice from quivering. "She's everything to me."

"I envy you, man."

"What did you say?"

The slow easy grin that was Dirk's trademark smiled back at him. "Crazy, huh? A werewolf envying a werecat. But I do. Not because of what you are, but because of the way you feel." The grin faded as Dirk raised a finger in warning. "I'll deny up and down that I ever said this—" he dropped his finger and his features softened, "—but I'd give anything to love someone the way you love her."

Chase studied him, realizing how alike they really were. "I'm not so sure it's a good thing. What if she doesn't love me back? At least not enough to accept what I am. What I made her become." He moved to her side, wanting, needing, to stay close to her.

"Then you'll learn to live with it. As long as she's okay, you can live with the other, right?"

Yeah, I can. Chase smoothed a hair away from her forehead and willed her to respond. *Please, come back to me, Shannon.*

"Hey, Sleeping Beauty, it's about time you woke up."

Dirk.

Shannon groaned at the throbbing in her head and neck, the ache in her entire body. She swallowed, but her throat felt as though it had been sewn shut. "Water." She hoped he'd understand the word hidden in the croaking sound she'd made.

"Just a sec. I'll get her some."

Bob.

She peeked open one eye and, instantly regretting it, squeezed it shut again. *Oh, please let me die. Shit, shit, shit.* "Aw, shit. Someone close the fucking curtains before my head explodes."

Bob's relieved-sounding chuckle came from the other side of the room. "I bet the real Sleeping Beauty never talked like a cowhand."

117

"You do know Sleeping Beauty isn't a real person, right?"

Leave it to Dirk to point that out.

Someone sat down, dipping the bed, and a hand lifted her head to press a glass to her parched lips. Cool liquid slipped between her lips and she moaned in gratitude.

"Take it easy," he whispered, then cleared his throat. Stronger sounding now, he added, "You don't want to overdo it."

Chase. Thank God Chase is all right. She squinted, fearing the sunlight would split her head in two, but she had to see him. Had to know he was unhurt. Had to see that he was...a man. *Did I really see him change from a puma into a man?* She finally made her eyes obey and looked into his face. "Chase?"

"Yeah, I'm here."

The expression of tenderness, of caring—of love—in his eyes made her heart pound. Like before, the incredulous thought hit her. *He loves me.* She paused to enjoy the touch of his hand against her cheek.

"He never left your side."

She glanced at Bob, unsure of what to make of his statement, then back at Chase. "Are you okay?" His slight smile was all she needed to reassure her.

"I'm okay."

"Good." A wave of pain ripped through her and she hissed to keep from crying out. "What happened?" *Did you really turn into a cougar?*

"You played a little game of tag with a bear." Chase tried to sound playful, but his tone was deadly serious.

Dirk stepped to the side of the bed next to Chase and grinned. "And you lost."

Releasing a huge sigh, Chase echoed the other's grin and gave her another sip. "Don't you know better than to mess with a bear? Never mind. As far as I'm concerned, you won because you're alive."

"Are you sure?"

"Trust me, you're alive and getting stronger every day. But I'm glad you're finally awake. You've been in and out of it for four days."

"Thanks to Chase." Dirk winked at her, sharing a secret she wasn't sure she knew.

"Hey, take it easy. Let me help you sit up." With Chase doing most of the work, she rested against the headboard, wincing at the ache searing along her shoulder and neck.

"I remember running from the bear—oh, hell, I tripped and fell like some stupid bimbo in a slasher movie—and then suddenly I was flying through the air." *And landing really hard.* "I remember getting the air knocked out of me and my head feeling like someone had taken an ax to it."

"Brother Bear definitely laid into you. He gave you quite a gash in that hard head of yours."

Brother Bear? She sent Dirk a questioning look. It hurt like hell to move her forehead.

Bob took a position on the other side of her, capturing her hand between his two callused ones. "I don't know what you three were doing out there, but I'm damn glad Dirk and Chase were around to fight off the bear. I hate to think about what would've happened otherwise."

"Me, too." Had her head wound make her hallucinate? "Chase, did you—?" She glanced at the cowboys, unsure of whether to speak candidly or not. "I mean, could I talk to you in private?"

Bob nodded, told her he'd be nearby and kissed her hand before leaving. Dirk and Chase exchanged a telling look. Patting Chase on the shoulder, Dirk winked at her again and followed her cousin out of the room. *Now what's that about? When did those two become so chummy?*

"I love you, Shannon."

She promptly forgot the question she was about to ask and gaped at him instead. "Wow. Good thing I'm already in bed. Otherwise, that would've knocked me off my feet." *He loves me. Sure, I already figured as much, but hearing him say it makes it real. Very real.* "Did you just say you love me?"

He laughed. "Yep, I did." A frown fell into place. "And you love me, too. Or did I not understand what went on between us?" His features hardened. "Maybe I don't know how humans do this kind of thing, but I was sure—"

"Wait. What did you say? You don't know how *humans* do this?" Shannon used his arms for support and leaned forward to study him. "Humans? As in you're not human?" *Am I still dreaming? At least it's a new dream, but I'd rather wake up. Wake up now!*

He glanced over his shoulder, checking to make sure Dirk had closed the door, then faced her again. "Do you remember anything else about the attack? Like seeing something else?"

"Yeah, I do. I remember one helluva big cat. Bigger than any cougar I ever saw on television. In fact, I saw the cat change into...you. But...I had to be seeing things after getting hit in the head. That's the only explanation that works. Right?" Her heart pounded against her chest, at once terrifying and exciting her. She bit her lower lip and felt the pain that was more real than anything she'd experienced in her nightmare. Taking a deep breath, she got ready to hear the impossible answer. "What are you trying to tell me?"

He took her hands in his. "You didn't hallucinate. What you saw was real."

"Real." *Maybe if I repeat what he's telling me, I'll believe it. But do I really want to? The man who just declared his love for me is wacko. Or a supernatural creature.* "You're telling me you can change into an animal." *Please tell me you're joking.*

"Shannon, I realize this is difficult, especially after getting mauled and nearly dying, but you have to believe me."

No I don't. Yet she couldn't say the words. Whatever Chase told her, she wanted to believe.

"You've heard of werewolves, right?"

"Like in stories? Fairy tales? Uh-huh." An image flashed through her mind. She'd not only seen a huge cat but a very large wolf. Together, side by side, staring at her until she'd passed out. "Omigod, I remember now. There was a wolf, too."

"That's right. But it was a werewolf, not an ordinary wolf."

"And he was standing right next to the enormous cougar." *Omigod, he's serious. He thinks he's a man who can change into a cat. What do they call them in the movies? Shifters?* She had to look away from him to give her brain time to catch up with what her heart already knew. *I believe him.*

"I'm the cougar you saw."

Yet she needed one more stab at bringing her world back, the world where supernatural creatures did not exist. "You seriously thought I'd believe you?"

His earnestness deflated a little. "I did. But I guess you don't."

She smiled, hopeful that sanity was making a come-back. "Damn, Chase, next time give a girl some time to recover before you joke around like this."

"Shannon, I'm not joking."

A stab of alarm mixed with irritation brought out the dare before she could think twice about it. "Then prove it. Change into a cat, right here and right now." *Come on, Chase, give up the gag. Why is he playing this game when we need to discuss our future? Do we have a future?*

"Okay, I will. Brace yourself." Then, within seconds, Chase narrowed his eyes. They glowed with an amber, cat-like color, the color she'd seen before. He growled, that wonderful animal-like growl he'd done while having sex, then parted his lips. Long sharp teeth—non-human teeth—grew over his jaws. "And the wolf was Dirk."

She placed her palm on the bandage on her head and waited for her mind to stop reeling. "Holy shit. Omigod. You're telling me the truth. This is amazing." Stunned, she pulled her hands out of his and fell against the pillow and the headboard. "I, uh, I don't know what to think. How is this possible? How the hell—" *I've fallen in love with a supernatural being!*

"We're called shifters. Dirk's a werewolf and I'm a werecat."

"A werecat." She whispered the word, trying to make the word feel more natural, like any other word she'd say every day. "So you can change into a, a werecat whenever you want? Or does it have to be a full moon like for werewolves?"

"There's no moon out right now. The full-moon thing is pure fiction. Werewolves, like werecats, can shift anytime they want to." He started to reach out for her, but stopped as though he wasn't sure she'd let him touch her.

"And you and Dirk, in your animal forms, saved me from the bear." She giggled, unable to keep it contained. "Oh, shit, I finally get it. That's why you and Dirk are always arguing and calling each other animal names. Now it makes sense." *I had sex with two shifters! Are there others around me and I just don't know it? Are all the ranch hands shifters?* The life she'd grown to love on the ranch changed, making it more unusual, more thrilling.

"Shannon, baby, there's something else you need to know."

More? Is he going to tell me my cousin is a shifter, too? "What now?" Yet a part of her wanted to hear, was excited to learn about this other world and these strange wonderful people.

"You were badly hurt."

"Tell me about it. My head still feels like someone's standing on my shoulders and driving a sledgehammer into it."

"You would've died, bled to death, if I hadn't done what I did."

She inhaled sharply, afraid of what he'd say next. "What did you do, Chase?"

"Only a shifter could have survived your wounds. I didn't have a choice if I wanted to save you."

"You're scaring me, Chase." She swallowed, thinking about all the movies she'd seen where a werewolf bit someone and then they, too, became a shifter. Was it the same for cat shifters? "Just spit it out and tell me."

"Normally, I'd never have done it without your consent, without you saying you wanted me to."

"Chase, I swear if you don't tell me what you're trying to say, I'm going to... Well, I don't know what, but it'll be something painful to your crotch." She clenched the sheets, yet she was unsure if she did so to keep from running or from hitting him.

"I bit you and changed you."

She sat back, taking deep breaths. *Holy shit. Does he mean what I think he means? Did he change me into...* She paused, trying to decide how she felt. "You changed me? You mean, into a shifter? Like you?"

"Yes. Into a werecat." He hurried now, speaking quickly, urgently. "I love you, Shannon, and I want you to be my mate, my wife. I would've ended up changing you anyway if you'd said yes to mating with me. But when the attack happened and you were dying, I had to go ahead without your permission. So will you? Will you be my mate?"

His mate? A werecat mate? Will I change? Have I already changed? Grabbing the hand mirror lying on the nightstand, she held it up and studied her face. *Do I have fangs now? Do my eyes change color?*

He took the mirror from her. "You haven't actually shifted yet, but you will. But my bite, the bite that turned you, gave you the strength you needed to survive." He reached out, touching her chin with the back of his fingers. "I couldn't stand to lose you."

"But you did it without asking me first."

"I didn't have a choice. You weren't conscious."

Although part of her understood why he'd bitten her, another part of her rebelled against the act. "But you did it without asking me." She struggled against the turmoil, the confusion inside her.

"I know what I did. You don't have to keep saying it." Chase leaned away from her, annoyance closing up his features. "So you would have chosen to die instead? Or is it the fact that I made you my mate that bothers you the most?"

Her gaze met his and, instantly the confusion, the whirlwind of emotions within her evaporated. His anger flashed in those amber eyes, but so did his love for her. The love she'd wanted all her life. At last here was the man she could trust with her heart. *I would have said yes.*

"Shannon?" He frowned at her, unsure how to interpret her silence.

He changed me to save my life. Yes, without my permission. But hadn't he already changed me? I no longer wanted a life of endless sexual partners. Instead, all I wanted was Chase. And now I have him. "I'm glad you did what you did."

The relief he felt swept over his face, erasing the stiffness in his body. "Does that mean you'll be my mate? You'll come with me to my mountains?"

She searched his eyes, saw the love she'd hunted for all her life and gave him the only answer she could. "Well, after all, I already was a cougar. You just made me more of one. So when do we leave, Mr. Cat?"

"Oh, hell, not you, too." Chase's laugh echoed around the room.

Epilogue

"Shilah's a full-blown bitch."

Chase covered his laugh, hefted the backpack onto his shoulder and followed the path leading them higher into the mountains. "You know why, Shannon. Haken changed her without her consent, against her will, and brought her to his home. She's not adjusting to our life very well."

She fell into step beside him, doubling her steps to keep up. "Oh, boohoo. You didn't ask me first, but you don't hear me whining." *Well, maybe I did when he first told me. But not for long.*

"Yeah, but I bet that old cat Haken is hell to live with. Besides, you got the better man, er, shifter."

"Not a bit conceited, are you?" Her chuckle softened the jab. "Still, I don't see why we have to visit them. Aren't werecats supposed to be solitary creatures?"

"We get together when we choose. And I owe Haken. If he hadn't sent me to your cousin's ranch, I never would have met you." He grabbed her arm, spinning her around to face him. "Where would I be without you?"

She leaned into him and swiped her tongue over the hollow of his neck. "Absolutely nowhere." Purring, she slipped the backpack off her shoulders, letting it fall to the forest ground. "How about we take a break?"

He skimmed a hand over her breast and pushed his pack off. "Hmm, I do like the way you think, my mate."

"And I like it when you call me your mate." Shannon stepped away, already working on the buttons of her shirt. Her jeans and boots followed with Chase working to rid himself of his clothes.

Within minutes, Shannon, naked and shuddering with delight, reached out to run her hands over his bare chest. His rough hands gripped her breasts, lifting them to his mouth. He nipped, then flicked his tongue over her taut nipples, sending sparks of lust spiraling into her abdomen. Moisture flooded the crevice between her legs and she tugged him to the ground beside her. She arched her back, giving her breasts to him.

"Shannon."

The simple yet sexy way he said her name made her quiver with excitement. She wanted to answer but couldn't. He lavished her nipples, tossing all her coherent thoughts away. Already ready for him, she felt his shaft pressing against her thigh, his dick growing stronger, thicker. Soon she tugged him on top of her and slipped his cock between the crevices of her folds, teasing herself, teasing him.

Chase trapped his face between her breasts. "I love you," he mumbled between licks around her globes. Pausing, he looked up, the adoration apparent in his eyes.

Shannon shuddered in pleasure at the heat in his look. "I love you, too. More than I can say."

"No. I love you more."

She laughed at their familiar argument. "Then prove it." Pushing his shoulders, she guided him between her legs. "Gobble me up, big cat."

He obeyed her, sliding lower, then bringing her legs over his shoulders. His tongue moved slowly over her inner thigh, tingling her and making her jerk with every swipe. Growling his warm breath onto her skin, he latched onto her clit. His tongue whipped around her throbbing nub, sending her shooting toward the sunlit trees above.

"Oh, yes. Yes!"

He pulled her closer and drank deeper.

"Oh, shit, Chase. Don't stop." Bucking under his hold, she tensed, then released time after orgasmic time. She shuddered, panting, trying to level out her breathing.

Wiping his mouth, he crawled over her, placing wet kisses along the way, to position his face over hers. He nibbled at the corner of her mouth, softly, reverently until she could stand it no longer.

"Chase, I'm ready. Hell, I'm more than ready. Take me now."

"Impatient, huh? No problem." Spreading her legs, he plunged into her. The force of his thrust reverberated through his chest, rippling the muscles in his pecs. With his hands planted on either side of her, he pumped faster, harder, burying himself deep within her.

Gasping from the force pounding into her, she watched him, wanting to see his release. Amber eyes slanted and fastened onto hers. "I'm coming. Make me scream."

He doubled his movement, moving faster, his hips thrusting. She ran her fingers along his back, delighting in the feel of his muscles working for her, and clamped her hands onto his ass, holding on to him as he tightened and relaxed his buttocks.

"I don't know how much longer I can hold on. You're so hot, so tight." Chase stiffened, readied for his release and turned his head to the side. His cry echoed through the forest, sending birds flying from their perches.

Hugging him, she held him close, loving the way each wave rushed through his strong body. She closed her eyes, wanting to feel his seed gushing into her. She luxuriated in the heat of his skin against hers, the warmth of his breath against her neck.

"Shannon?"

"Hmm?"

"Are you really happy I turned you? I mean, if I hadn't needed to do it to save your life, would you have wanted me to bite you?"

How can he doubt my love for him? "Very happy. Of course, if I'd had a choice—" He tensed at her abrupt stop and she bit her lip to keep from giggling. "If I'd had a choice, I would've skipped the getting-torn-apart-by-a-bear part."

Chase chuckled, relaxing to fall beside her. "Yeah, I could've done without that, too."

They lay together for several minutes, listening to the sounds of the forest, enjoying the slant of the light as the sun moved higher in the sky. Shannon, her head on Chase's chest, sighed and turned to look at him. "Do you know the only thing that could make this moment better?"

His eyebrows dipped between his eyes. "How could we possibly improve upon perfection?"

She bopped him gently on the nose. "Near perfection."

"Okay, I'll take the bait. What would make this time, this place, and us even better?"

Shannon paused, resting her chin on her hand to stare into his face. "If I were pregnant. That would make it better."

Chase grew serious and hugged her closer. "Yeah, that would definitely make it perfection." Suddenly, he rose onto his elbows and studied her. "Are you saying what I think you're saying?"

"No, not yet."

Disappointment flitted across his features. "Not yet?"

"Nope. But that means, of course, that we'll just have to keep trying." She licked her lips and arched an eyebrow. "So, my big strong pussycat, are you ready?"

"You're really into the animal pet names, aren't you?"

"Yep. I like 'em a lot."

He grinned and nuzzled against her neck. "Whatever makes you happy."

"You make me happy, Chase. So, are you ready to make a little kitty?"

"Baby, I am ready, willing and able."

Before she could anticipate his move, he leaned back and shouted his joy. Shannon wrapped her arms around his neck and laughed.

Wild Cat

Dedication

I usually thank my supportive and loving husband who gave me the first nudge into the writing world. However, I think it's time to thank the other two big supporters in my life: my parents. They suffered through my early creative years, *oohing* and *ahhing* over one awful poem after another, then into my tumultuous teen years and, finally, into adulthood where I found not only my singing voice, but my literary voice as well. Thanks, Mom and Dad!

Chapter One

"Shit, shit, shit." Alex skirted the bloodied area and knelt beside the mutilated carcass. "That's the third one today."

Batting the flies away, she held her breath against the putrefying stench and was glad she'd had the forethought to tie her hair into a ponytail. She wished she'd brought a handkerchief to cover her nose.

Once again, Alex reconsidered her decision to track the rogue werecat responsible for the cattle attacks. But it wasn't like she really had a choice. She could either accept the growing suspicion that her brother was the killer, or she could volunteer to find the real culprit. Either way, the situation sucked, but she'd made her choice, coming down on the side of proving her brother's innocence.

Understanding why her people assumed that Bryer was the killer wasn't difficult. After his mate had been fatally shot by hunters, he'd changed, growing bitter and angry. Then, when the council had refused his demand for retribution, he'd spurned the pride, vowing to make them pay along with the hunters. Bryer's words of hate and pain the night he'd stood before the council, condemning them, ripped through her, taking her away from the gruesome mutilation.

"Alex? Did you hear me?"

She jerked, bringing herself back to the present. "Uh, no. I'm sorry. What did you say?"

Conner, Alex's best friend and childhood companion, squatted beside her. "I said that, from the way she's torn apart, the cat must be a massive one. Definitely bigger than any regular mountain lion and much bigger than any werecat I've ever seen…"

She could almost hear the unspoken "with the exception of your brother" hanging in the air. Glaring at her friend, she gritted her teeth and counted to ten, letting the rush of irritation pass. She couldn't fault Conner. After all, he'd chosen to come along with her when no one else would. He'd come with her not only to support her brother, but in hopes of scoring points with her. Once again, she wondered if she could have a life with Conner as her mate. After all, if anyone had proven his love for her, it was Conner. But the extra spark, the underlying connection she yearned for, just wasn't strong enough.

Alex studied the handsome shifter. He was tall and lean with enough muscles to make her feel safe in his arms. His long black hair fell across his forehead, serving to highlight the sparkle in his obsidian eyes. In short, Conner was exactly the way she liked her males. Not for the first time, she sighed, easily imagining sex with him, her limbs wrapped around him, holding him to her. But was sex the extent of any relationship they could share? In fact, knowing he wanted her for his mate kept her from accepting his sexual advances. Even after she'd started using sex to drive away the loneliness, the hole in her life her brother had left, she'd kept her friend at arm's length. Still, if she relented and took him to bed, would that help clarify her feelings for him? As she'd done so many times before, she pushed the questions away and focused on the present.

She nodded, then moved away from the rotting animal. "Yeah, that's a werecat's work, all right. Just like the others."

"Like I said, one helluva big cat, too." He paused and released a heavy sigh. "One as big as Bryer."

She whirled on him, flashing fangs and sprouting claws.

"Bryer didn't do this. He couldn't be this cruel, this wasteful. And he wouldn't put the pride in danger by stirring up the ranchers. I don't care what he said that night at the council. You know my brother, Conner, so how can you think that?"

She fisted her hands, not to keep from hitting him, but to rid herself of the uncertainty clawing its way into her gut. Memories of her brother sobbing on her shoulder, then swearing to tear human hunters apart flashed through her mind, but she forced them away. She looked away from Conner. Bryer had no one left, no one else to stand by him. She couldn't, wouldn't, give up on him.

"He's changed in the past year, Alex. After Lara died—"

"Leave his mate out of this." If only Lara had lived, then maybe Bryer wouldn't have changed, wouldn't have grown cold and hard. But multiple wounds had proven too much for the young werecat and the baby she'd carried. Alex swallowed the lump forming in her throat, defiantly lifted her head and confronted Conner.

Although she could see the argument in his eyes, Conner raised his hands and nodded in agreement. "Okay, okay. Take it easy, Stretch."

The childhood nickname, given to her because she'd towered over other female werecats, didn't lessen the anguish twisting her heart. Again she pushed away the horrible images trying to invade her thoughts and drew her body straighter. Instead, she pictured her brother chasing her around the hillside, tumbling over her in good-natured roughhousing. He'd grown from a pesky little brother into a wonderful, caring man. A man who'd had everything, a bright and happy future. Until the day Lara died. From that day on, he was no longer the playful free spirit she loved. Oh, how she missed his spontaneity and joking nature. It was as if the world had gone dark. She glanced at the carcass and shook her head. She had to believe in the brother she'd once known.

"Do you two like tearing dumb animals apart? Or is it because you like your meat rotten?"

Alex's snarl matched Conner's and together they spun toward the voice. She squinted into the sun, trying to see more than the outline of the figure standing on the nearby rocks. Resisting the urge to change into her werecat form, she slowly raised her hand to shield her eyes from the glare. Shadowed from the light, she could see the man clearer, his long form spreading wide at the muscled shoulders. His chest pushed against the denim material, highlighting the rock-hard abs beneath. A lock of dark hair flopped over his forehead, but it was his bright blue eyes that caught her attention. The laughter in them unsettled her and she dragged her gaze past the sensuous lips to the strong jaw. The tug inside her abdomen hit her, throwing her emotional equilibrium further off-base. Her vaginal walls tightened, cueing her libido's quickening. If ever she'd wanted to eat a man alive, this was the one. Then he grinned and she almost moaned with desire. His sexy, devil-may-care grin shot a hot lust-filled rush through her that had her swaying on her feet.

She cleared her throat, making sure her words wouldn't come out in a bedroom breath. "Who wants to know?"

"Oooh, she's a feisty little kitty." His grin grew wider. A grin reminiscent of the kind her brother used to brighten her day. She fought the smile tugging at the corners of her mouth.

She tilted her head and took a harder look at him. Not too many humans could recognize a shifter so quickly. "Trust me. My claws are a whole lot sharper than a kitty's. You'd better hope you don't find that out."

Conner stepped to her side, his body coiled and ready for action. "Listen to the lady and leave, cowboy, while you still have the chance."

The sexy stranger glanced at her friend, then turned back to her, dismissing him. "And let you bring down another one?

Uh, nope. Not happening."

"We didn't do this. Or the others." Intrigued, she narrowed her eyes at him and wondered why he wasn't worried about facing off, unarmed and alone, against two werecats. Alex crossed over to the other side of the small clearing, putting the sun to the side of her. "Besides, how do we know you're not the responsible one?" Yet she instinctively knew he wasn't. After all, this wasn't the work of a human. *If* he was human. She sniffed, wanting to catch his scent, but he'd done a good job of keeping upwind of them.

"Ah, so you know there's been more than one sacrifice."

"Sacrifice?" She eased closer, her predator instincts kicking in, her body tensing for a fight. In the past—before Lara's death—she wouldn't have been so cautious. She used to greet others openly, curious to meet new people. But Bryer wasn't the only one who'd changed that horrible day.

He studied her movements, the tips of his mouth quirking upward again. "From the amount of meat left on the carcasses, the animals weren't used for food. Besides, even a full-grown cougar wouldn't bring down three cows in one day. Nope. These killings are for show. Ugly presents to stir up the ranchers." His gaze met hers, relaying knowledge of her game. "But I'm pretty sure you already knew that."

She almost smiled in return, but caught herself again. Better to not let him know how charming he was. However, she couldn't stop the quickening of her pulse. How long had it been since she'd enjoyed the company of a fun, sexy man? Conner was smart and handsome, but he lacked the clever wit, the quick laugh she'd always found attractive. Catching a questioning glance from Conner, she vowed to keep her head on the business at hand and ignore the other parts of her body trying to monopolize her attention.

"Alex, why are we bothering with him? We have work to do." The tension radiating off Conner prickled her skin and her arousal won out over the truth of his words.

The man with the sparkling eyes hopped off the rock outcrop and landed a few feet from her. "Relax, furball. I believe your lady friend when she says you two didn't do this. Of course, that doesn't mean you don't know who did. In fact, I think you do know. What with you being werecats like the killer."

"What business is it of yours? Did he kill any of your cattle?" She cringed at her use of the telltale "he".

His eyebrows jumped up, noting her slip, but he didn't say anything. Irritated with herself, she scanned his lean body, searching for a weapon, and found none. If he was a rancher, he'd have a weapon, even if only a pistol.

His chuckle was so full of life she could barely resist the urge to laugh along with him. "Nope. But some friends of mine did. They've asked me to stop the varmint causing all the problems. So, pretty little pussy, what's your story?"

She ruffled at the term "pussy" but decided it wasn't worth commenting on. Besides, she didn't think he'd meant it in an offensive way. His manner was more easygoing, exuding a live-and-let-live kind of attitude. The way Bryer had been. "Suffice it to say we take care of our own."

She didn't need Conner's low rumble to urge her to stop talking, but this man was so interesting, stopping was difficult. And not at all what she wanted to do. If she could get information from him, then what was the harm? Enjoying the bulge in his jeans was simply an added benefit. She struggled to lift her gaze from his crotch.

With another chuckle, he started circling them in an easy graceful way until he'd put the slight breeze behind him. "Go on. Take another whiff. Enjoy the sweet aroma."

She inhaled, expecting to find a mix of human pheromones and sweat. Instead, the unexpected scent assaulted her nose.

Werewolf. Alex stuck out her hand, keeping Conner, who'd also taken a sniff, from lunging at the shifter. Frowning, she inhaled again. *Oh, shit. I'm attracted to a werewolf.* "Aroma? I think stink is a better word."

He pressed a hand over his heart and feigned a hurt expression. "Oh, my lady, you injure me so. You might as well stab me in the heart."

Alex laughed, finally unable to deny his charm, then suddenly wished he wasn't a werewolf. For the first time in a long while, she was attracted not only physically, but intellectually, to a man and he turned out to be a werewolf. She sighed and cursed her luck. She'd had sex with werecats and her share of humans, but never a werewolf. Hell, she'd never even considered it. But maybe...

"With pleasure." Conner hissed and lengthened his fangs.

The werewolf merely cocked an eyebrow and tipped his hat. "Calm down, kitty litter king. No reason to go all adversarial. How about we take a step back and start over? My name's Dirk. Dirk Claxton of the Cannon Pack."

"The Cannon Pack, huh?" She'd heard of the werewolves based near Colorado Springs and knew they were considered to be a decent bunch of shifters. Rarely bothering her kind, they stuck to their own business and kept out of everyone else's. At least until now. "Why are the Cannons helping human ranchers?" She shot a look at Conner, then signaled him to back down. He did so, albeit with a couple of grudging mutters.

"We're on good terms with the ranchers around here and owe them a favor. I said I'd look into this and get rid of the problem."

She eyed him as he walked over to examine the body. He knelt down, a gesture signaling that he no longer thought they'd attack him. "You needn't have bothered. We take care of our own." Damn, but she liked that cocked eyebrow. She wanted to lick that eyebrow and every other inch of him. Slowly, she ran her tongue along her upper lip. Catching Conner's frown out of the corner of her eye, she cleared her throat and adopted a stern expression.

"Yep, and it looks like you're doing a bang-up job of it, too."

"Alex, let's leave this flea-ridden mutt here to clean up the mess. We've got better things to do than to waste time flapping our yaps at him." Conner took a step away, then paused, surprised when she didn't follow him.

"Alex, huh? So daddy cat wanted a boy?"

His quick perception of her chauvinistic father surprised her, but she kept her face neutral. "My father liked the name Alexandra."

"Got a last name, Miss Alexandra?"

His gaze glided down her, then headed slowly back up, halting briefly to linger over her chest. Not that she didn't appreciate a man who found her body appealing. She waited until his eyes met hers before answering. "I'm Alex Grayson and this is my friend, Conner Walkman. We're part of the Grayson Pride. Ever hear of us?"

"Oh, sure. I know you guys." His mouth twitched, fighting back another grin. "Didn't I read something about you in *All About Cats* magazine? Oh, yeah. You guys invented a new brand of catnip, right?"

Conner's growl forewarned her, giving her the seconds she needed to block him. She struggled to keep from giggling. "Cute. Very cute. But Conner's right. We don't have time to waste playing audience to your standup routine." She moved away, pausing to let Conner catch up—and to take one last look at the werewolf. Then, setting the pace, she jogged to the edge of the forest surrounding the clearing. She'd gone only a few yards when her hearing picked up the sound of footsteps behind her. The footsteps of *two* pairs of feet.

Quickly she twirled around, with Conner doing the same a moment later. Dirk slammed to a stop a few yards away. "Where the hell do you think you're going?"

Enjoying a conversation with a witty werewolf was one thing, but having him follow her?

"With you, of course." The werewolf strode forward, closing the distance between them.

A skirmish between irritation and a strange delight played out. "No you're not." She fingered the small moon-shaped stone she kept in her pocket as she always did when uncertain. Conner had given her the stone years earlier with his name etched on one side and hers on the other.

"Yes, I am. Because I get the definite impression you know something more than I do about these dead cows. And I aim to find out what that is."

She could easily outrun him, but should she? Maybe he could prove beneficial to her mission. Making her decision, Alex sprinted, eager to see if the persistent shifter could keep up with her.

Dirk was still on their heels two hours later. Werewolves weren't as fast as werecats in short distances and he'd struggled to keep Alex and Conner in sight for the first mile. Or was it his imagination and she'd taken it easy, allowing him to stay close? If she had shifted, she would've left him choking in her dust. For whatever reason, once her initial burst of energy had passed, the staying power of his inner wolf had allowed him to catch up.

He ran through the intriguing idea of working with the werecats and watched the way her firm ass moved with each stride. The appealing bottom, however, was only part of her attraction. When she'd first turned toward him, ready to fight, he'd fallen straight into her fiery jade eyes and hadn't been able to think straight since. How could he when her body was all toned desire, rounded, womanly and perfect for a man's hands? The bobbing of her long reddish-hued hair, tugged back into a ponytail, kept rhythm with the sound of his boots striking the ground. He considered surging past her to see her full, perfect-for-his-hands-sized boobs but rejected the idea, opting to play it safe—for now.

He'd never had sex with a werecat but according to a couple of his pack mates the experience was one he'd never forget. Not only were the females eager for sex, they were wonderfully uninhibited in bed. Hell, in bed, in a car, in a cave—wherever sex could be had. Her butt cheeks jiggled, making him wish he could sink his teeth into her soft flesh. Maybe it was time he tried getting some real pussy. Swallowing, he concentrated on keeping one foot in front of the other.

Following the two werecats hadn't been part of his strategy. But once he'd seen Alex, then gotten the definite impression that she knew more than she was saying, he'd changed his mind. The fact that she made his johnson rise to attention in under ten seconds was a bonus. Besides, he'd seen something in her eyes, a deeply rooted pain and vulnerability, that had tugged at him, enticing him to take care of her, keep her safe and protected. He puffed out a breath, ridding himself of the unusual thoughts, and paced himself, keeping a few yards behind the pair.

Attempting to get his mind back on business, he switched his attention to Conner. The male shifter stayed neck and neck with Alex, glancing over at her, a questioning expression on his face. Again, Dirk gave careful consideration to the possibility of her wanting him to stay close. He smiled, enjoying the idea. Could he help it if females, shifters as well as humans, found him irresistible and wanted to keep him around?

Then his smile faded. He wouldn't kid himself. Alex

Grayson was no ordinary female. If she wanted him around, it was because she wanted something from him. Something more than sex. Again, the idea of keeping her safe, locked in his arms, swept over him.

Maybe he could goad her into telling. "I bet the sex would be phenomenal."

Alex slammed to a stop and confronted Dirk, shifting enough to bring out her fangs. Before he could react, her snarling lips were an inch from his face. Conner was by her side in an instant, imitating her partial transformation. "Dog, don't get on my nerves."

Her beauty intensified with her anger, making her green eyes flash. His balls ached just looking at her. Thinking on his feet, Dirk adopted an impromptu expression that was as fake as a three-dollar bill. "Who, me?" Once he saw her stern expression, however, he quickly gave up the pretense. "Look, we're after the same thing here. We both want to stop the asshole who's making trouble. Whoever this is has all the ranchers riled up and taking to the hills, shooting at any cougar or wolf they see. Hell, anything that's big enough to have done the deed. I figure if we work together, we have a better chance of stopping him before any other innocents get harmed. Then both of our packs, er, *peoples* are safe."

Something about the way she considered him told him she'd given the idea some serious consideration during the run. "I hate to admit it, but you may have a point."

"Are you crazy? Do you want a damn werewolf slowing us down? Flapping his jaws and getting in our way?" Conner paced a few feet away, running his hand through his hair. "Come on, Alex, get real. What would the council say?"

"Who the hell cares what the council thinks? Do you see any of them lending a hand?" Alex's tone left no room for argument.

Beverly Rae

"So I was right. You can use the help." Dirk smothered the fuck-you expression he so wanted to shoot Conner. "And for the record, I was right on your heels. Maybe it's you who'll hold us back."

As he expected, the shifter's hackles rose. Conner pushed against Dirk, chest against chest. "Keep it up, you reject from the pound, and you'll find your nose buried in the dirt hunting for your own leg bone."

Instead of accepting Conner's challenge, Dirk narrowed his eyes and glanced between them. "Hmm, that's unexpected. I thought werecats rarely start a ruckus unless they have a dog in the fight, if you'll forgive the expression." He let a shit-on-you grin explode. "Oh, I get it. So you and Alex are a couple, is that it?"

He held his breath and hoped she'd deny it.

"No we're not." Alex winced at the intensity in her tone, then shot a "forgive me" look at Conner.

Conner backed away from Dirk to scowl at Alex. Relief and joy sprang to life in Dirk, but he kept his composure.

"Not yet." But Conner's tone didn't sound confident.

If Dirk hadn't wanted to take Alex to bed himself, he would've found the tension rippling between the two werecats amusing. As it was, however, he knew he'd have to tread carefully if he wanted to get her on her back. "Sorry, man, but it looks like she's not interested."

"Conner and I are really good friends. Close friends."

Dirk grimaced. "Oooh, ouch, dude. You're in the friend zone. Or are you friends with benefits?"

If anyone could be friends with benefits with Alex, he wanted to be that friend. A friend who could lie between her legs and lap up her fetching feline juices.

Conner took Alex's hand, pulling her attention away from

144

Dirk. "Alex, what the hell are we doing? Let's keep searching and talk later." He shot Dirk a glare. "Alone."

"You mean before or after she gets with me?"

Dirk ducked, letting Conner's swing stir the air above his head. Yet before he could execute a punch of his own, a shot rang out.

Chapter Two

"You two wanna get your hands off my butt?"

Crouched between Conner on her right and Dirk on her left, Alex stared straight ahead through the leaves of the bushes where they'd taken shelter. How they'd ended up with her in the middle and each man fondling her ass, she wasn't sure. Not that it was an unpleasant feeling. It felt good. Really good.

Conner immediately took his hand off her. Dirk, on the other hand, squeezed her cheek. Hard.

"Watch it, Dirk." She halfheartedly meant the menace in her warning. In fact, if she had her way she'd like his hand on another part of her body. She reached for Dirk's hand, but didn't get it in time.

Conner grabbed the shifter's hand, knocking it away from her. Dirk stared at his hand, then chuckled. "Now how did that get there?"

She'd always been a sucker for a sense of humor. "Yeah. I wonder." Alex snorted and scanned the trees surrounding them. "The shot wasn't far off. But at least it was downhill of us."

"I'll bet it's one of the humans out to bag a cat trophy for the wall above his fireplace."

Conner tensed along with her. The werewolf was probably right. "No doubt."

"It sounded like it came from the nearest ranch." Worry

gripped her, ridding her of the heated thoughts about Dirk. What if a hunter had shot her brother? They could easily mistake him for the killer in their zeal to shoot any unlucky cougar. She rose, her heart lodged in her throat, her jaw clenched. Holding on to her belief in Bryer's innocence, she prayed he'd gone into the mountains and away from the turmoil surrounding the killings. Still, she couldn't shake the fear clinging to her spine.

"Let's check it out." Dirk took a few steps, then realized they weren't following. "Uh, troops, that's your cue to fall in line."

Alex and Conner glanced at each other and she sent him a silent plea. "I suppose we should. Check it out, I mean. You know, if only to ease our minds."

"Ease your minds? I don't understand. I thought we were tracking this menace."

Conner turned away from Dirk's scrutiny, apparently giving Alex the choice of telling him about her brother. But she wasn't ready. Sure, Dirk was friendly and she was beginning to trust him, but she wasn't ready to tell him such personal information. Not yet, if ever. "Never mind. Lead the way."

"Finally. But since it's getting dark, I suggest we shift and investigate in our animal forms. That way we'll have our night vision. Plus, we'll get in and out faster."

She had to admit the werewolf had good ideas. Too bad her own brain wasn't functioning on high speed. "Agreed."

"Good. Then let's get going. We can leave our clothes under these bushes."

She'd undressed many times in front of Conner and other werecats, shifting whenever they'd wanted to run in the woods. But, strangely, the idea of changing in front of Dirk left her embarrassed. What if he didn't like her body? Either her naked human body or her cougar form? The cat inside her reared its independent head, ratcheting up her stubborn streak. What was she worried about? About how a werewolf would see her? Besides, she'd had plenty of men tell her she had a great body. But still she had to wonder. What was it about this man that made her so self-conscious and yet ready to rumble in a sexual romp? Annoyed, she nonetheless placed her back to Dirk. Undressing as quickly as she could, she started the transformation before all her clothes were off. By the time she was nude and ready to run, all four paws were on the ground.

Conner, in his dark brown cougar body, snarled at the still fully clothed Dirk. She added a snarl and swished her tail at him. Why hadn't he changed?

"Oh, sorry. I was so mesmerized watching you get naked that I flat forgot to take off my clothes. But can ya blame a guy? You, sugar, are smokin'."

She couldn't help it. She preened. Flattery, especially from a handsome stranger, was always a welcomed treat. The next snarl came from Conner.

Sporting that sexy grin, Dirk unabashedly shucked his shirt, boots and jeans in quick succession. Still in human form, he hid his clothes next to theirs under a pile of leaves, then stood up and stretched, giving her the full picture.

If she was smokin', this man was on fire. She raked her gaze along his body, taking in the scars lining his back and highlighting his firm torso, the slight curve of his waist and the touch-me roundedness of his buttocks. The sudden urge to run her tongue down the crack of his ass overwhelmed her and she padded forward. If Conner hadn't put his body in her path, she would've flattened her tongue against that tanned human flesh. Dirk turned, giving her a front-row seat to the steel-like mounds of his chest, and her legs suddenly went wobbly. A spattering of dark hair highlighted the rippling muscles and played tour guide to the flat abdomen. Her gaze fell on his prize and her mouth dried up. His cock, so big, so thick, so amazing, curved all the way to the perfect end. She tilted her head, inhaled slow and long. If he was that big without an erection... She couldn't help it. She licked her lips.

Surprised at the intensity of her lust, she heeded Conner's warning and, as difficult as it was, averted her eyes from Dirk's manhood.

Dirk, however, caught her gaze and shot her a knowing look that said, "It's okay to look. But wouldn't you rather touch?" With a short chuckle, he let his inner animal take over. Muscles lengthened, bones creaked and snapped as the change swept over him. Dropping to the ground, he gritted his teeth together until fangs replaced them. Smooth human skin quickly disappeared under brown fur and a bushy tail sprouted. In less than a minute, Dirk the human had shifted to Dirk the powerful werewolf.

She wanted to rub against his silky fur, nuzzle his ear. Anything to touch the huge wolf staring at her. Recognizing the sexy lift at the corners of the werewolf's mouth, she smiled.

Dirk yipped at them, flicked his tail and started down the trail leading into the valley and to the ranch. They let him take the lead and followed, keeping first to the trees, then the brush. At last, the open field spread out before them and they ran toward the ranch house and barn. Ducking under the fence marking the outlying boundary of the ranch, the three shifters slid toward the pasture where cattle lazily fed.

Dirk led the way, keeping to the shadows of the falling light. Hearing angry human voices ahead of them, he veered to the left along with the two werecats and took shelter behind a broken-down lean-to. He crouched next to Alex and lowered his tail.

Four ranch hands stood around a dead bull. One man

hunkered next to it, examining the body.

"It's definitely the work of a big cat. Nothing else could've taken Thunder down. Not this easily. But what I don't get is the why of it. Why is this thing killing but not feeding?" The older man stood and wiped his hands on his jeans.

The burly cowboy next to him shifted his rifle to the crook of his arm. "We must've interrupted its meal when we ran it off, Ben. But Luke here got a good shot at it."

Dirk sensed Alex cringe, but didn't turn quickly enough to catch her full reaction. A flash of anger darkened her features and then, suddenly, her face was a neutral mask. The only remaining evidence of her rage was the hard look in her eyes. He studied her, trying to understand her. Wanting to understand her.

"Jim's right. But I missed, goddamn it." Luke spat a wad of tobacco.

"Seems like the thing's slaughtering cattle for the fun of it. Like it's personal or something."

"Yeah, right, Ben. The cougar's mad at you for not taking it to the dance."

Unlike the others, Ben didn't find the joke amusing. "Damn it all. This is the fourth one I've lost this week. We've got to do something."

"We need to send out a hunting party like the other ranchers did, that's what. Sooner or later, someone's gonna bag the beast."

Now it was Dirk's turn to cringe. He hated to think of how many innocent werecreatures, not to mention forest animals, were going to end up dead before this was over.

"And wind up killing some stupid camper, Jim?" Ben shook his head. "No thanks. I've already heard about a couple of accidents and I don't intend to have my head blown off trudging around those hills."

"Then maybe we should put out some traps? They're not as effective as a bullet to the brain, but at least we'd get the damn thing." Jim toed his boot into the side of the dead bull. "And if we get really lucky, it'll die a slow agonizing death."

Dirk couldn't help letting a small whine escape him. And immediately heard Conner scoff. He silently answered, lifting the edges of his mouth to show his fangs.

"Maybe." Ben muttered a few expletives. "We've had predators before, but this one's got me stumped. It's almost as though it can think like a human and stay two steps ahead of us."

"Maybe it's one of those creatures people say live in the mountains."

"Yeah, right. You've heard too many spook stories, Jim."

"I'm just saying, is all. So what do you want to do with Thunder, boss?"

"Leave him. I'm not paying someone to come out this far and haul him off. Let's head back to the main house and put our heads together."

Staying low to the ground, Dirk started backing up. Alex matched his movements, creeping alongside him. Conner, however, whipped around, flashing his tail from behind their barrier.

"Look! There it is!"

"Shoot it!"

A shot shattered the night. Without thinking, Dirk threw his body in front of Alex, blocking her from the hunters. Conner yowled and jumped into the air, twisting like a sidewinder snake, then landed on his side several feet away.

Alex snarled, turning toward her friend, but Dirk blocked her from going to Conner. Letting out an urgent bark, Dirk pushed her ahead of him, forcing her toward the safety of the trees and growled his words. "I'll get him. Now go!"

Once she was off and running, he rushed over to Conner, putting his body in between the injured werecat and the hunters.

"Move, cat-man, move!"

Conner scrambled to his feet, snarling his pain, then dashed after Alex. Another bullet whizzed past Dirk's ear, too close for comfort. He hunched down, digging into the dirt for traction, and raced after the werecats.

They kept running until, at last, they arrived at the same location where they'd hidden their clothes. Dropping to the ground, Dirk panted, exhausted but relieved to see that Alex was unharmed. She fell to the ground beside him and changed.

Dirk shifted, all the while keeping his gaze on the beautiful woman. Her long body, taller than any woman he'd ever known, glistened with sweat. Stretching to rid herself of the after-shift aches, she lifted her arms to the moonlit sky, reminding him of a forest goddess he'd once seen in a movie. Her full breasts perked higher, tempting him with brown areoles and taut nipples. He swallowed and followed a bead of perspiration as it trailed between her breasts, over the flat stomach and down to the curly patch of hair below. His mouth dried up and he desperately wanted nothing more than to quench his thirst by drinking her sweet juice.

"Why did you do that?"

He lifted his head to peer at her. "Do what?"

She stared back at him. "You know what I'm talking about. You threw yourself in front of me. You shielded me, kept me from getting shot."

"Well, isn't it obvious? I didn't want that pretty hide of yours riddled with gunshot holes."

"But why? Why put yourself in harm's way to save me?" Her scrutiny made him nervous, like she was diving down into his soul, ready to drag out the truth. "And then you did the same thing for Conner."

The answer came quickly enough, but he wasn't ready to reveal the truth, let alone admit it to her. "Let's chalk it up to chivalry, okay? And as far as saving the cat-man's ass..." He shrugged. "I figured it'd be easier than trying to recover his dead body and explaining what the hell he was. Don't make such a fuss. It wasn't a big deal."

"Yes, it was. You risked your hide to help us. No matter what you say, it's a very big deal to me." Alex gave him an indecipherable look, a look highlighted by a soft glow in her eyes. She started to reach out, then withdrew her hand at Conner's grumbled protest. "Thank you, Dirk."

Her gratitude flowed over him like a soft breeze. "No problem, sugar." For a moment, their gazes held and he took a step closer. She started to move toward him, then blinked at Conner's groan, breaking their invisible link. Tucking her head, she turned toward her friend.

"Conner, how badly are you hurt?"

Wrenching away from the tantalizing sight of her to the wounded man beside him took a lot of effort. Conner, returned to human form, dug his clothes out from under the brush and struggled to pull on his clothing. "It's only a flesh wound, Alex. Nothing to worry about." He brushed off Alex's attempt to look at the gash on the back of his leg. "And for the record, I didn't need his help."

"Yes you did and you were lucky he was there." Alex shook her head at him. "Why didn't you stay like you were so you'd heal faster?" She grabbed a piece of clothing and began wiping away the already drying blood.

"Hey, that's my shirt." Dirk snatched the shirt from her, but at her glower, grudgingly tore off a section from the shirttail she'd already used. "Fine. Here. But next time, use his shirt, okay?"

Alex dabbed at the area where the injury had been although only an angry red slash remained. "Let's be thankful it wasn't worse. Worse, as in mortally wounded. Thanks to Dirk."

Conner palmed her cheek and tilted his head so he could make her look at him. "Getting shot was worth it if it means knowing you care."

"Don't be silly. You know I care." She placed her hand on top of his. "Please be careful. I couldn't stand the thought of losing you, too."

Dirk started to ask what she meant, but decided he wouldn't interrupt. Still he had to wonder. Who had she lost?

"No, Alex. I mean really care." The two werecats stared at each other, a silent message zipping between them.

Dirk knitted his brow, confused by the jealous twist in his stomach. Their affection for each other, their connection, was obvious. He didn't like the unfamiliar sensation tightening his chest, yet he couldn't shake it.

"Conner, you know how I feel." Alex caught Dirk watching and abruptly averted her gaze. "But let's not get into it here. Not now."

"Hey, don't mind me. Far be it from me to interrupt mates. If you two lovebirds want to get it on, I'll be happy to stick to the sidelines." Falling back on his usual cavalier manner, he added with a wicked grin, "Or not."

"We are *not* mates."

Her forceful denial delighted him and Conner's scowl added to his pleasure. "Even more reason for us to get busy in the bushes."

"Back off, Fido. She's a feline. She doesn't lie down with mangy mutts."

If the male cat wanted to get under his skin, he was doing a great job of it. Yet instead of taking the bait, Dirk kept his attention on Alex. Her lips thinned at Conner's outburst.

"I suggest we get some rest. It's late and I want to get an early start tomorrow."

"Are you seriously suggesting we sleep with him, Alex?"

"Yes, Conner, I am. I'm exhausted and we need each other's body heat during the night. Plus, I think Dirk's got the right idea. If we work together—I mean, really work together—maybe we'll have better luck. God knows we need to try something different." Pushing leaves and twigs together to form a bed under the overgrowth, she lay down and curled into a ball. "Are you two joining me? Or would you rather huddle together, just the two of you? Do whatever you like."

"The lady doesn't have to ask me twice." Dirk slid close to her, spooned her, and tried to wrap his arm over her only to have it slapped off. "Hey, you said we could do whatever we liked."

"Try that or anything remotely similar and I'll do more than slap at you." Her tone, however, contradicted the threat in her words.

"Oooh. You are such a spunky one."

A mumbling Conner took her other side, lying so he could face them, and pressed close to her body. "We're going to discuss this so-called cooperation with a werewolf again in the morning."

"Whatever, cat-man." Dirk made a show of snuggling closer to Alex, barely managing to suppress the smile tugging at his lips.

The light grew dimmer around them, the night blanketing the world, and the sounds of nocturnal animals added their bedtime music. Alex kept her eyes closed but couldn't sleep. Memories of Bryer and Lara, happy and contented together, churned inside her. Too many *what ifs* whipped her mind into a whirlpool of thoughts and emotions, keeping sleep away. Although she'd tried talking about the tragedy to Conner and others, they could never quite understand, never feel the pain the way she did. Feeling alone as she had for so many nights, she sought comfort from the closeness of the males.

She sighed, enjoying the warmth surrounding her. How could she not think of sex with two very masculine, very well-endowed men sandwiching her? Conner's wide chest rubbed against the tips of her nipples which, of course, reacted in a perfectly natural way. With Dirk's hard pecs pushing against her back, she developed a whole new meaning to the phrase, "caught between a rock and a hard place". Not that she was about to complain.

Trying to keep from touching anything too personal, she tucked one arm under her head and rested the other along her leg. Soon, however, her legs grew stiff and she needed to move. Trusting Conner more than the wily werewolf edging ever closer to her, she lifted her leg and gently laid it on top of Conner's. He tensed at her touch, then relaxed, his breathing evening out.

If only she could sort out her feelings for Conner. She loved him, adored the friend she'd grown up and knew he'd make a caring and supportive mate. Logically, he was a great choice. Yet, although she was sexually attracted to him, would take him to bed if he wouldn't make more out of it than merely a sexual romp, she couldn't, wouldn't take a mate until she found the extra sizzle simmering right below the surface that meant a lifetime of passion. She sighed and wished Conner thrilled her that way.

Something hard bumped into her buttocks, coming to rest in the cleft between her cheeks. She inhaled, knowing exactly what that something was. Her first instinct was to slap it away as she'd done his arm, but she held back, enjoying the way the long rod grew even longer and thicker against her sensitive backside. Dirk's shaft was impressive. Impressive and very insistent. Hoping he'd think she was moving in her sleep, she arched her back, pushing her breasts harder against Conner's chest and wedging Dirk's cock deeper into her butt crack. He groaned, making her freeze. Was that a good groan? Or a frustrated one?

She took a peek at Conner. His eyes were closed, but his lips were parted, almost as though— She gasped as Conner's tongue snaked out to lightly touch her mouth, then slowly glided toward the corner. Squeezing her eyes closed, she wondered if Dirk could see what Conner was up to.

Suddenly, the rough texture of a different tongue tracked along the curve of her neck. Alex shuddered, pleased, excited and a little guilty. What would Conner do if he knew? She didn't think the werewolf would mind sharing, but her friend would. She'd heard about werecats having sex with werewolves, but she'd never considered it—until Dirk. But what about sex with both a werecat and a werewolf? Her heart pounded at the idea.

Dirk's hand found her left buttock, then fingered its way under her T-shirt and along the curve of her waist. Moving her arm barely enough for him to slip under it, she remained motionless and waited to see where he'd stop. He paused, then let his hand fall, coming to rest over her belly button. Conner scrunched closer and placed his hand on the side of her breast.

Fearing that Dirk would move his hand higher and run into Conner's, she feigned a stretch over her head and, keeping her eyes closed and her breathing even, rolled onto her back. Both men stirred and she waited to see if everything was good to go. When neither man complained about the other, she let out a small sigh.

Almost in sync, each man took hold of a breast. Dirk scooted closer, his dick pushing hard against her leg and his face close to her cheek. She could smell his breath on her, and slowly drew in his scent, relishing the musky aroma. Conner removed his hand from her breast to pull her leg over his, catching it in between his two, and spreading her apart. Gently, he placed his hand over her crotch.

Alex wondered how much longer this enticing interplay would go on, then prayed that it would.

Dirk's thumb caressed her already peaked nipple and she fought to keep from squirming. At first, he pressed lightly, then increased the pressure until, at last, his thumb rubbed slow forceful circles over her bud. She bit the inside of her mouth to keep from moaning.

Conner undid her jeans, tugged them wide and snaked his hand between her legs. His fingers found her sensitive spot, one rubbing her nub while the other fingers massaged the sensitive skin beside it. She couldn't stop her moans any longer. Wetness flooded her, oozing over his rapidly moving fingers.

She glanced at Conner's face, the dim light of the moon aiding her heightened senses. Checking Dirk's face, she found his eyes closed, but a soft smile curving the ends of his mouth. Did they know? How could they not?

She bit her bottom lip, resisting the burning compulsion to lick the corners of Dirk's mouth. But if she did, he'd know she was awake. Silently, she sent a prayer skyward, praying for them to keep their eyes closed. She shut her eyes again, eager to find out where they would take her.

Dirk's tongue flicked across her nipple and she couldn't squelch a tremor. To cover, she stretched again, pushing her breast into his face. She silently urged him to suck her aching bud, harder, stronger. As though he'd heard her unspoken command, he brought her nipple into his mouth and suckled. She moaned again, unable to suppress her pleasure any longer.

Conner rubbed harder, more insistent, and she spread her

legs wider. Giving up the pretense of sleep, she lifted her butt, signaling Conner to slide her jeans down her legs. With a hard kick, she freed her legs.

"So you were awake all this time, Alex?"

She felt more than heard Dirk's quiet chuckle at Conner's question. "Well, duh. Who can sleep with you two touching me?"

"Wait. Both of us?"

The irritation in Conner's voice flowed over her. "Yes, both of you. Now get back to business, boys." At once, guilt washed over her. "Conner, if you don't want to, I'll understand."

Yet she yearned to touch him, to give him a part of her. She hoped he'd go along with the threesome, especially since her desire to have Dirk was on full steam ahead.

"Yeah, Conner, don't do it if you don't want to. But in the meantime..." Dirk chuckled again, then latched onto her nipple. He pulled, tugging at her, cupping her breast and molding it to his face. Conner lifted onto his elbow and took her chin in his hand.

"Conner, don't stop. Please."

"You're right. I don't want to do this. Not with a damn—"

She put every ounce of frustration she could muster into her shout. "Conner!"

Chapter Three

Her cry stopped him. She held her breath to keep the harsh words inside and glared at him, half-pleading, half-demanding.

"I've waited so long to have you, Alex. But not like this."

She held his gaze, not giving into the impulse to look away. Yet when she failed to voice a response, he gritted his teeth, then groaned and scooted down, running his hand along her leg until he could move into position. Lifting her legs over his shoulders, he dove in, pressing his face against her warm pussy. He fingered her folds apart and raked his tongue over her, ramming it hard against her swollen nub. Sucking, nipping, licking, he continued to plunder her while Dirk suckled one breast and fondled the other.

Mewing, she no longer tried to hold back and released loud sounds of enjoyment. Dirk and Conner became vocal, each moaning, murmuring sounds of lust, as they worked her body, at once treating her tenderly, then roughly. She reached down to help Conner by holding herself open to him, then ran her hand down Dirk's back, keeping him close.

"Oh, oh, oooohhh, Conner!"

Listening to the noises Conner made lapping up her juices made her wetter, wilder, hornier. Lust coursed through her, churning her insides, flaming her body. She squirmed, wanting more, yet fighting for a few seconds to recover from the delicious torture. He plunged his tongue inside her, using his fingers to massage her throbbing nub. Heat, unexpected in its quick arousal, burned into her, sending her flying. She climaxed and waves of delight shuddered through her. "Oh, please. Don't stop."

Dirk got on his knees, brought her breasts together and forced his face between them. The vibrations of his pleasured groans reverberated against her chest. He stroked her nipples with his thumbs, then pinched them between his fingers. "Suck on my nipples, Dirk. Make them ache. It's okay. I like it rough." He answered with his mouth and teeth, pulling, nipping at her.

Conner answered, too, breathing air onto her sensitive clit. The warmth hit her, shooting her into another orgasm and she clutched at Dirk's back, digging her nails into his flesh. Gripping her bottom like he'd never let go, Conner kept her to him, unrelenting in his pursuit. He ducked a little lower, piercing her with his tongue. She bucked, not wanting to get away, but unable to stand the delicious sensations any longer. "Oh, shit. Oh. My. God. If I'd known what you could do..."

Conner stopped to question her with a look, but unwilling to explain, she pushed his head down again. "Don't you dare stop now."

Dirk, however, wasn't one to stand by and watch. He ran his tongue between her breasts, moistening her skin. "How about I get on top and fuck your tits?"

"No!" Conner shoved her hands away. "Don't let his cock near you."

She started to tell him he couldn't make demands, then thought better of it. How could she deny his request when he was pleasing her in spite of his dislike of Dirk? For now, she would acquiesce. "Not now, Dirk. But I wouldn't mind watching you take care of yourself while Conner eats me."

Conner growled, but she ignored him and quirked her eyebrows at Dirk. "Well?"

"Don't mind if I do." Dirk quickly unzipped his jeans, pulled out his all-too-ready dick, spat on his palms and started massaging himself.

She gasped and wished for a brighter moon to see his massive shaft.

Conner darted his tongue in and out, fucking her as she watched Dirk work his cock. She wiggled to a better position, trying to keep her hands on the werecat's head and her gaze on the werewolf. Dirk pumped his shaft, sliding his hand back and forth from the curly dark hair at the base to the curve that led up to the mushroomed cap. "Faster, Dirk. Go as fast as you can. As fast as Conner's tongue and fingers."

Both men took the challenge and increased their speeds. Dirk's heavy pants grew faster, his rapt attention centered on her every move. Lifting her breasts toward her mouth, she swiped her tongue over one taut bud then the other and was rewarded with an agonized sound from Dirk. "Ooh, Dirk, I love it when you growl."

Not to be outdone, Conner added his thumb to the agonizingly wonderful attack, wrenching her focus away from the werewolf. She stared at her friend, amazed at how he controlled her even as she bucked against him. He stayed with her, using her jerks to coincide with his licks, his head remaining buried between her legs. The familiar whirlwind of impending release whipped through her and she thrashed about, her moan heralding her pleasure. At last she could take no more and she cried out, her body jerking with orgasmic spasms, her breasts jiggling. Gasping for air, she watched Dirk tense, readying for his release. His eyes changed, the brilliant blue morphing into glowing amber in the darkness as his explosion overtook him.

The tension inside grew, forming stronger waves of lust, and she knew her ultimate orgasm was near. The turmoil of desire built up inside her abdomen, speeding up and down in rolls of heat. Suddenly, she exploded, soaking the tender flesh between her legs. A deeper blackness than the night swept over her and she struggled to stay conscious.

Climax after climax rocked through her until, at last, she could stand it no longer. She heeled herself away from Conner, breaking his hold. Going to his knees, he undid his jeans, took his shaft in his hand and masturbated. Her gaze glued to his, her breaths still racking her body. He stiffened, groaned, then released.

"Alex."

Alex wondered at the lust, the excitement and, more, the love in Conner's tone. Shuddering, he fell to her side, keeping one hand possessively on her thigh. Had she made a mistake? Should she have let him tongue her? She bit her lip and hoped the sexual romp wouldn't make him even more determined to mate with her. But, oh, God, how wonderful he'd been! She couldn't deny it. She'd loved every second with both shifters.

Turning away from Conner, she caught the expression on Dirk's face and gasped. The compassion and, more, the absolute understanding filling his features left her breathless. Suddenly, he reached out and covered her hand and, for the first time in a long while, she was content.

"Shit! Get away from me, you mangy mutt!"

Conner's angry words ripped apart her dream—a wonderful dream of delicious sex with Dirk—startling her awake. She leapt into a fighting stance, ready for an attack by a faceless killer. Instead she found Conner backing away from Dirk, his hands fisted, his neck red with fury.

"What the hell is going on?"

Dirk, sporting his mischievous grin, shook his head and continued to brush the dirt and leaves off his body. "Nothing.

163

He's getting all excited—oops, poor choice of words—over nothing."

"Nothing? You call waking up with your arms wrapped around me nothing?" Conner spat onto the ground and stalked a few feet away.

She couldn't help but laugh. "Well, seriously, Conner, what's the big deal? I mean it's not as if you haven't already seen his he-haw."

"He-haw?" Dirk's expression was priceless. "If you're referring to my manly package, I'll thank you to use a more fitting term."

"You—" Conner pointed at Dirk. "You are a freak. Stay away from me, got it?"

"Aw, Connie, you're hurting my feelings. I thought we shared something special last night."

Alex choked back her giggle although she wanted nothing more than to let it loose. It had been a long time since she'd laughed like this. A long time since the one person who could always make her laugh had changed. "Okay, okay. Fun's over. Conner, calm down. I'm sure it happened after I got up to, uh, use nature's facilities, then lay back down on the other side of you. He probably rolled next to you thinking you were me."

"You do have a very feminine side to you, cat-man."

Conner darted toward Dirk, hands open to throttle him, but Alex jumped between them, blocking his way. "Don't we have more urgent matters to attend to?" The two men grumbled but stepped back from her. "How about we agree that last night never happened?"

Not that she ever wanted to forget and she hoped they felt the same way. When she was sure Conner wouldn't lunge at Dirk again, she moved away, already concentrating on the real problem. "I was thinking. We shouldn't have shifted into our animal forms to check out the ranch. After all, there's less chance of getting shot, at least intentionally, as humans. Granted, we won't cover as much territory, but at least we won't wind up dead."

"Agreed." Dirk bit his lip, humor showing in the lines around his eyes. "Is that okay with you, cat-man?"

Alex frowned and shot him an imploring stare. Granted, he was funny, but Conner obviously didn't agree, so why keep baiting him?

Dirk caught her meaning, coughed and did a one-eighty. "Uh, seriously, man. What do you think? Should we stay in our human forms?" After she rewarded him with a soft smile, he added another attempt to get on her good side. "And how are you doing today, anyway? Wound all healed?"

"Alex, so help me, I'm going to chew him up and spit him out." Conner's face flushed a purplish-red.

"Actually, Conner, I think he's sincere." She couldn't help but wonder, but decided to give the werewolf the benefit of the doubt.

Conner didn't appear to agree, yet grumbled a curse at Dirk and nodded. "I'm fine." He put his back to Dirk who made a "hey, I tried" shrug. "I think we should tackle the next ridge near the two smaller ranches."

"I agree with ca—with Conner. From the locations where the bodies were found, it looks like the killer's moving in that direction." Dirk's grin was gone, seriousness replacing any sign of mirth.

She had to admit she liked his serious side almost as much as his jovial one. Her thoughts drifted back to last night's activities and landed squarely on his excellent package. Of course, his physical attributes put both those other sides to shame.

"Alex? Did you hear what I said?"

She blinked, wiping away the sexy image. "Yeah. I heard

165

you, Dirk." Avoiding their silent perusal, she forced her mind back to her mission. "So what are we waiting for? Get your tails in gear, men."

She marched off, leaving the men to follow her.

A skimpy breakfast of berries-on-the-run and twenty minutes later everything was forgotten except picking up the trail of the killer and trying to stay out of gunshot range of the armed humans scouring the hills. Using hand signals to relay his intent, Dirk ordered the other two shifters to spread out, moving out of eyesight of each other but close enough for their sensitive ears to hear a shout.

A noise to his right had Dirk ducking, narrowly avoiding being spotted by two hunters. Hiding behind some bushes, he let them stroll past him as they argued about which baseball team would win the championship. How they expected to hunt while flapping their gums he'd never know. In fact, if they'd all stay home, he could make better time. He resisted the urge to stand up and tell them so. Now that he had Alex to worry about, he couldn't take unnecessary risks.

The implication of his thoughts struck him, making him stay behind the bushes a little longer than necessary. Why should he worry about Alex? Not only was she competent enough to take care of herself, she had Conner. Yet he couldn't shake the need to protect her. Hell, he wanted to protect her. Wanted to keep her safe from not only the hunters, but from anything else that might hurt her.

Once the hunters were out of sight, he rushed off in a different direction, his footsteps barely making a sound. He then circled around, making sure he stayed close to Alex's position.

Conner's exclamation alerted him and he took off in a run.

A few minutes later, he dashed into a clearing to find Alex and Conner standing over a dead cow. "Damn it! Not another one already."

"Looks like it." Alex's scowl, a scowl that couldn't mar her beauty, matched his inner turmoil.

Conner knelt next to the carcass. "Yep. It's definitely the work of the same cat. Same earmarks. Same everything. And it happened recently, too. The body's not even cold yet."

"But how does he do it?" Dirk scanned the surrounding tree line for any signs of the killer, but found none.

"What do you mean?" Alex kicked her toe against the cow's still-limp leg. "He attacks and rips out its throat. Exactly like he did to the rest."

"That's not what I meant. I'm asking how does he strike so fast? And with all these hunters around? I spent most of my time hiding from them instead of tracking him."

"Why would you hide?" Alex held her hand up to shield the light coming through the trees. "I thought you liked humans."

"I like them well enough, I guess. But if you called out and they heard you, then they ran into a beautiful woman—" he covered the length of her with his gaze, then landed back on her face, "—they might question what the hell you're doing out in the wilds."

"Which is why I stayed hidden, too." She blinked and he could almost read her thoughts.

Taking compliments wasn't easy for her, but it was more than that. He reached out to her, hoping to dive behind the pain he'd seen all too often since meeting her. She saw his gesture, started to smile, then caught him studying her and forced a passive expression. Instead of pulling her into his arms, he dropped his hand uselessly to his side.

Conner cleared his throat, loudly, rudely. "If you two are through discussing the obvious, maybe we can get going?" He pointed to an area of grass where drops of blood were scattered. "Wait a sec. This is different."

"How so, cat-man?"

"It appears Bry—uh, the killer decided to take some of the meat along with him this time."

Tension between the two werecats rippled in the air. Alex bristled at Conner, then abruptly turned in a different direction, placing her back to Dirk. Dirk took them both in, tried to understand the conflict, then decided to bide his time and ask questions later. Adding more tension wouldn't gain him any answers. Until then, he'd have to wonder what Conner had started to say.

"Well, at least we know he has to eat. But why this time and not before? He's always torn the cow apart, then left all the meat at the site of the kill." Dirk searched the ground around the cow but didn't see any signs that he'd fed beside his prey.

"Probably because of the hunters."

Dirk shook his head at Conner's explanation and pointed toward the sky. "I don't think so. He's never worried about them before so why start now? I think maybe it's because of that storm coming in. If he's smart—and obviously he is—he's heading for shelter."

Alex's and Conner's gazes followed his direction. Black clouds formed nearby, darkening the sky to the west of them. "Crap. The rain will wash away his tracks."

"That and catch a lot of unprepared people in the mountains. Including us if we don't find someplace to hunker down and wait it out." Dirk pivoted on his heel and started toward the nearest ranch.

"Hey, hold up, Dirk. Where're you headed?"

"Um, to find cover, of course. You know. Like at a ranch. Personally, I don't like flash floods, and I kind of thought cats didn't like getting wet, either."

"Very funny. Look, I don't like getting wet, but I don't like the idea of trying to explain who we are and why we're hunting the killer cat, either. Didn't you say they'd wonder about a woman being out here?" She glanced at Conner and lifted her eyebrows in question. "I know a safe place the pride uses."

"Alex. No." Conner obviously didn't like the idea of showing a werewolf one of the pride's secret hideaways.

"Conner, we don't have a lot of options."

"Why do I get the impression that you two are speaking in some kind of feline code?"

She chuckled, ignoring Conner's sour face. "Follow us, werewolf. We'll keep you safe and dry." Alex turned toward the mountains and the rock outcrop situated on higher ground. The men followed behind staying silent and matching her pace for pace. Together they left the valley, traveling through the forest and onto the rocky ledges until Alex stopped in front of a large growth of bushes. With a glance at Dirk, she pulled at the branches and the false barrier fell away, revealing a large cave. The mouth of the cave reached above their heads and was wide enough for all three to stand side by side.

"Holy shit. I've spent a lot of time in these woods, but I never knew this was here."

The clap of thunder following Dirk's remark sent them scurrying into the cave.

Alex stared at the flashes of light slashing through the falling darkness. "Am I imagining it or was that lightning too damn close?"

"Freaky damn close." Conner scowled at Dirk. "The storm must be our ancestors telling us how displeased they are by our hanging around with a werewolf."

"Conner, my friend, you do have an interesting way of viewing the world." Dirk puffed out an exasperated breath and dragged in a leveling one. "Not a good view, but an interesting one."

Why did Conner have to be such a prick? Especially since Dirk had tried so hard to be nice to the cat-man to make Alex happy. But a man could only put up with shit for so long before it stuck in his craw. He gritted his teeth and returned Conner's snarl. "For Alex's sake, I'm trying to control the part of me that wants to flatten you and stomp your furry butt into the cave's rocky floor. Hell, *through* the floor." Yet when his gaze fell on Alex standing at the mouth of the cave, he immediately forgot about Conner.

Lightning lit up the world outside, bursting splashes of brightness across her upturned angular face. Soft shadows played with her features, accentuating the high cheekbones, the way she jutted her chin out in a defiant manner. The fire of lights outside made the copper in her hair sparkle with its own flame. She stared into the night that had arrived with the storm, her eyes darting from one point to another, searching. She pursed her full lips together, plumping them as though waiting for a kiss.

He'd love to kiss her. To ravish her lips, her eyelids, her pussy. And, surprising even himself, her mind. Captured by her beauty, Dirk let his eyes devour her. She was taller than most women, even most shifter females. The way she stood, her shoulders thrown back, gave her a regal posture and, if he believed in such things, he would swear she was a Greek goddess returned to Earth. From the rounded curve of her shapely buttocks to the long, lean length of her legs, he took her in, his mouth watering at the idea of her lying beneath him, writhing in lust-filled ecstasy.

A clap of thunder jolted her and she jumped. Her gaze locked onto his, her green eyes glowing, sprinkled with brilliant golden flecks. Shifter flecks. The night's storm called her inner beast just as he could feel his own animal heeding the call. His animal roared to life inside, aching to answer her unspoken summons to take her. His gut twisted in the familiar stirring of lust, but stronger than he'd ever felt it, different than he'd ever felt it. He let his fangs grow and returned her stark perusal. *"Alex, I need your legs wrapped around me, holding me."*

She swallowed and narrowed her eyes at him, almost as though she'd heard his thoughts. Then her pink tongue flicked across her kissable lips and his knees nearly buckled in the rush of desire. He swore at that moment that he heard her answer in his mind. *"Then come to me, Dirk. Take me. I'm yours."*

A soft rumble rolled in his chest and he took a step forward—until an arm pushed against his chest.

Chapter Four

Dirk's growl rumbled out of him and he glared at Conner. "Get your stinking paws off me, you oversized mouse-chaser."

Conner dropped his arm, then took a step in front of him. "Alex, get away from the entrance of the cave."

Alex, still uneasy on her feet after the unnerving connection with Dirk, could merely nod. Normally she would've balked at such a brusque order, but she was in no position to argue. At least not until she'd figured out what had happened.

When she'd stared into Dirk's eyes, she'd experienced a bond unlike any she'd ever had with any of her werecat lovers. Somehow she and the werewolf had come together, emotionally, sexually, without physically touching. If Conner hadn't broken their connection, she would've gone to Dirk and begged him to take her. At that moment, she'd wanted him to push her down and ride her from behind. She'd wanted him to tell her what to do and how to do it. She still wanted him to.

Another flash of light and the resulting clap of thunder shook her from her fantasy. Dirk frowned, a crease marring his forehead, but he never stopped staring at her.

"Conner, could you gather some firewood and start a fire?"

Conner glanced at Alex, then at Dirk and frowned. He opened his mouth to speak, but clammed up at Alex's hard look. With a curt nod, he eased into the darkness outside the cave. She swallowed and paused, half expecting Conner to return, then tossed her hair over her shoulder. Glancing at Dirk, Alex hastened into the interior of the cave. Voicelessly, she begged him to follow her.

The plea was in and out of her mind before she realized what she was thinking. Was she going crazy? Or was it her imagination playing out with the storm's eeriness? She quickened her pace and kept moving toward the rear, into the blacker recesses of the cave that ran approximately fifty feet deep. What would Conner think? Moreover, what would he do if she hooked up with Dirk? The other night had been unplanned and spontaneous. But this time she knew what she wanted, had even instigated it. Suddenly, her strength left her and she leaned her shoulder against the cool wall. Did she dare continue this sexual escapade? She chuckled, speaking her answer before logic could talk her out of it. "Hell yes."

"Hell yes what?"

She whirled, placing her back against the wall to find Dirk standing close to her. Too close. "What did you say?"

The intensity in his eyes echoed the frown on his face. "That's what I'm asking you." She instinctively knew that he understood what she wanted before he spoke. "Or do I already know what you're saying yes to?"

"You're a strange man, Dirk Claxton." She needed time to think. Not caring if he responded, she looked down and immediately regretted it. Her gaze fell to the bump in his jeans, his cock pressing against the material. Her breathing shortened and she struggled to look elsewhere, at anything else.

"Strange but sexy, I hope."

She forced her words to come out stronger than she felt. "A bit conceited, are we?"

He touched a lock of her hair, spreading the strands between his callused fingers. "Hey, when you've got it, why deny it? You're not exactly a dog, you know. Although some of the female dogs I've known have been real knockouts."

She laughed at his joke, letting out some of her anxiety along with it. "Gee, thanks. Your flattery is underwhelming."

"Okay, then let me say it straight out. You're the most captivating woman I've ever known. And I'm not talking just about the way you look, either. I think you know that. You can sense this thing between us like I can."

Dirk lifted her chin to make her meet his eyes—his gorgeous ocean-colored eyes filled with amber speckles—and she blinked at the passion in them. Suddenly he pressed against her, his muscled chest flattening her breasts. His mouth crushed hers and he thrust his tongue between her lips, past her teeth to seek out hers. She inhaled, as much from delight as surprise, and met his forceful kiss with her own. Pulling the bottom of his shirt from his jeans, she slipped her hand along his muscled back, running her fingers over his scars. "How?"

His chuckle spread warmth into her mouth. "How? I figured you already knew how. But if you don't, then not to worry. I'm a great teacher."

She gasped as he nibbled at her ear, sending delicious spirals of desire along her neck to the tips of her breasts. "I'm talking about your scars, wolf-man. How did you get the scars on your back?"

He paused, then took her face between his hands, forcing her to look at him, his gaze delving deep inside her. "Seriously? You want to talk about my scars?" But when she didn't answer, he continued, "They're souvenirs of a bad time in my life when I fought with everyone and everything I could find. Including a man with a whip." He tilted his head. "Why? Do they bother you?"

She slid a hand over a large scar and shook her head. "No.

In fact, I think they're kind of sexy."

His wicked grin melted her from the inside out. "Sugar, you're the sexy one."

His mouth crushed against hers, ridding her of the need to answer his flattery. Instead, she pulled him close, trying to mold his body to hers, *into* to hers. He lowered his head, trailing his tongue down her neck to the rise of her breasts, then back up to capture her mouth again.

At first, she wasn't sure if the rumbling sound came from her or from him. The vibration that traveled with the low hum, trembled through her breasts to spread inside her, touching her heart not with a mere physical awareness, but with something more, something stronger. His tongue lashed at hers, sliding over hers to suck her taste into his mouth. Musky raw flavor filled her and she wanted to drink in every bit. Dirk growled again and angled his head to nip at the corners of her mouth. She moaned and ignored the chilly rock pushing into her back.

Suddenly, he changed places with her, then pulled her to him. Grabbing her buttocks, claiming her like the animal he was, he lifted her and she gladly wrapped her legs around him. With a sigh of desire that filled his mouth, she thrust her hips forward, grinding into his hard bulge.

Supporting her with one hand, he moved his palm under her shirt to her braless breast, taking it, making it seem small in his large hand. Another growl rumbled from him to her and she warmed at the now-familiar feeling. *Please take me. Fuck me and fuck me hard.* Silently, she hoped he'd hear her thoughts again.

With a half-growl, half-groan, he pushed her away even as she clung to him. "Here? Now?" he whispered.

Unable to speak, she nodded.

"What about—"

She snarled her warning, breaking off his irritating

175

questions, and started unbuttoning his shirt. He growled again, relief mixing into the urgency this time, then reached for her jeans and started unzipping them. Unlacing her legs briefly, she chucked off her boots and let the jeans slide to the floor.

"I'm so glad you're a commando lover like me."

At last, she found her voice. "Makes for a faster shift." She grinned, knowing her grin was as mischievous as his. "Or a faster lay." In a hurry, she threw his shirt to the floor and started on his jeans while he worked on his boots. "Come on. I want you bare-assed."

"Damn straight. Whatever you want, sugar, you'll get."

"And speaking of damn straight..."

He shoved down his jeans, his cock thrusting outward to prod against her mons. "Is this straight enough? Although I've always heard that the ladies like the curve at the end."

She mewed at the engorged shaft and slipped her hand down to fondle him. He moaned and lifted her again, his fingers digging into her ass cheeks. Dark brown hair framed his dick, already oozing with his pre-come. She licked her lips, ready to taste him. She smiled at the idea. Dirk had her licking her lips a lot. "Damn but you're hard. Hard and wet."

"The better to take you with, my dear."

His playful words, combined with the sensual growl of his tone, made her pussy flood with cream and her nipples pebble. A pulsating need raced through her. "Take me, Dirk. Now."

"Take it easy. That storm's not going to let up anytime soon. We've got all night." He skated his hand between her legs and dipped his fingers between her folds. "You're wet, too. So slick and slippery."

She groaned her frustration into his ear, followed with a lick down the side of his neck. "Then slide on in."

Catching her throbbing nub between his fingers, he

pinched her, making her yelp. "Ow!"

"I like it rough, lady. Can you handle it?"

"I can handle anything you throw at me, wolfie."

He moved his fingers, rubbing, stroking, pinching her nub. She wiggled against him, loving the sting that came along with the pleasure. Her come flowed out of her, raking her release through her and outward in ragged pants.

"Already?" He nuzzled his mouth against her collarbone, warm breath tickling her skin.

"Don't worry. I have more where that one came from."

"Argh." Gently, he lowered her along with himself, placing her on her back against the chilly cave floor. "I've got to have you."

He pushed her T-shirt over her head and threw it away. Sucking on her nipple, he tugged and pulled at her breast. Fingers of lust spread into her breasts and splintered outward to thread through her body.

"Condom."

"Shit." He reached over to rummage through his jeans pocket.

"Do you always bring a condom along while hunting a cattle killer?"

"Hey, ya never know. I was a wolf cub with the Boy Scouts so I'm always prepared."

She laughed out loud. Dirk reminded her of Bryer, the way he made her laugh, his lighthearted attitude toward life. Sadness at the thought of her brother trickled into her, but she roughly pushed it away and concentrated on the sex. On Dirk. "Figures you'd be a Boy Scout."

Dirk quickly put on the condom. "What's your pleasure, little lady?"

"My pleasure would be for you to stop talking and start

working." Alex spread her legs wider, leaned her head back and gasped at the delicious rush of pleasure Dirk's hands and mouth gave her, then let her head fall to the side. She gasped, her nails digging into his shoulders.

Conner sat on the other side of the cave, watching them. His eyes, glowing with amber, narrowed at her, intent on taking everything in. But it was his expression that had her breath hitching in her throat. A mixture of hurt and arousal played across his features.

Why hadn't he said something? She searched his face, waiting for him to see her question, but he didn't act as though he'd noticed. "Dirk, look," she whispered.

She couldn't understand Dirk's mumbles from between her breasts. Taking Dirk's hair, she tugged his head up.

"Ow! I like it rough, but hair pulling isn't very cool."

Taking his chin, she twisted his face away from hers. "Conner's here."

Dirk stopped moving to glower at the werecat. His body tensed and not in a good way. "So you like to watch, huh, cat-man?" His easy tone contradicted the rigidness of his body.

The strange expression on Conner's face dissipated, replaced with an irritated one. "No." His gaze matched Dirk's and held, then moved to her and softened. "I lit a fire at the entrance like you asked and then wondered where you two had gone. When I saw—"

"When you saw us, you decided to sit a spell and take in the show." Dirk checked Alex. "Not that I mind. As far as I'm concerned, he can watch all he wants. Still, the lady may not like it."

She pushed a hair out of Dirk's eyes and hooked it behind one ear, keeping her gaze—and her hands—where they were. "Conner, are you all right?" *I wonder if...* She paused, gave the new idea another thought and decided to forge ahead. "Would you like to join in?" She ran a hand down Dirk's back, enjoying the texture of his scars against his smooth skin. "You don't mind, do you, Dirk?"

The slight crease of his forehead belied his words. "Naw. I don't mind. Personally, I prefer my threesomes with two females, but whatever catches your fancy, sugar."

"Conner?" Had she gone too far? As much as she wanted Dirk, she'd hate to hurt her friendship with Conner. She sent him a smile, one filled with both hope and a plea for understanding. "I want you, too, Conner."

"Come on, man. It's a good way to pass the night."

Alex shot Dirk a warning look, caught the twinkle in his eye, then tried a different approach. "Please, Conner. I've always wondered what it would be like. Haven't you?" She knew he had. But would he let her give this to him? Would he give this to her? She tilted her head and tried on a sexy expression. "And after last night, I really want to."

He blinked, his eyes suddenly darkening, then added a quick nod. "Of course I have. But just with the two of us." His eyes darkened into a deeper yellow. "Not with him."

"Be reasonable, man. What the lady wants, the—"

Alex flattened her hand against Dirk's mouth. Once she was sure he'd finally gotten the message to shut up, she tried again. "Conner, this is what I want. Please. I can almost taste you." She ran her tongue over her upper lip as an extra enticement and was rewarded with a flicker of desire across his face. Reaching out, she beckoned for him. "Come here. Let me have this. Let me have *you*."

The added emphasis did the trick. Slowly, Conner rose from his seated position, kicked off his boots and crossed over to them. "Only for you, Alex. I'd do anything for you."

Alex tried to ignore the commitment behind Conner's words and, pushing against him, encouraged Dirk to back off. She got on her knees and offered her hand to Conner. Yet instead of taking his hand, she reached for his jeans and undid them. "Then do this. I promise you'll enjoy it."

Slipping his jeans to his ankles, she wrapped her hand around his hard cock, then slid her mouth down the length. He tasted wild, musky, wonderful. He inhaled sharply and pulled off his shirt. She sucked harder, drawing him deeper than before. He wavered on his feet a second and tracked his hands through her hair to keep his balance. Moaning, he fixed his gaze on her, watching her move his penis in and out.

"Hey, don't forget about me." Dirk positioned himself behind her, taking her butt cheeks in his grip and spreading them wider. His shaft slid into her crack, rubbing his shaft against her.

Keeping her focus on Conner, she cupped his balls and gently massaged him. He moaned louder and planted his feet apart.

"Oh, shit." Conner pulled her impossibly closer, holding her to him. "That's so good. Ahhh. Yeah, Alex."

She increased her rhythmic motions with Conner, tugging, pulling, sucking him. Wrapping her tongue around him, she ran one hand up his firm abdomen and thrilled at the tiny ripples of pleasure coursing through his skin.

Dirk groaned, leaned into her and nipped her on the shoulder. "Damn, but I love your ass. I've been watching it all day, wanting to stick my dick into you."

"Then do it." Alex trailed her tongue along the bottom of Conner's shaft, breathing in the scent that was all male werecat.

Dirk grazed his teeth across one cheek, down the dip in the middle and over the other cheek. "Bend over a little more and open wide."

The wetness between her legs erupted into a flood. She

moaned and bent forward as Conner fell to his knees, leaning back to give her a good angle to take him into her mouth again. Dirk pushed her cheeks apart and used his fingers to rub something cold and wet around her anus and inside.

Dirk was prepared for anything. Instead of saying so, however, she continued to eat the prize in front of her. Conner's cock was hard, highlighting the purple veins laced from tip to bottom.

Dirk slowly pushed his fingers into her, carefully, gently. "Breathe, Alex. Breathe and relax."

She closed her eyes, fondling Conner's balls and concentrating on the wonderful heat in her hands and body. Taking long slow breaths, she opened for Dirk.

Dirk quickly replaced his fingers with his shaft and slid the huge cock slowly, inch by delicious inch into her butt. She tensed, then relaxed, easing him inside her. Dirk rocked back and forth, grunting as he did so, his hands on her hips to keep her in place. "Awww. God, you're so tight. So sweet." Suddenly, he rammed into her, pushing her forward. She would've fallen if Conner hadn't held her shoulders. Every time Dirk thrust into her bottom, she used the motion to take Conner's shaft deeper into her mouth.

"Ooooh!" Saying the word with Conner still in her mouth, Alex felt the warm air flow over her hands and down his shaft. Another climax broke free, shooting out from her pussy in waves of ecstasy. Smaller pleasure waves rippled along her legs, threatening to weaken her knees. Dirk, however, sensed her weakness and held her tighter, keeping her with him.

At last she could stand no more and let go of Conner's shaft. "Oh, hell, yes. Someone better do me right now. I can't stand it any longer. I need a man's cock inside my pussy."

For a moment, she wasn't sure if either man had heard her. They went still, neither one moving. Glancing up, she could see the dare in Conner's face as he glared at Dirk.

"I'll have her first."

"Well, technically, cat-man, I already did."

"Dirk, shut the hell up and get Conner a condom." Alex pulled away from him even as he tried to hold on, then twisted to face him. If she hadn't wanted sex so much at that second, she would've found his surprised expression amusing. Lying on her back, she opened wide and motioned to Conner. "Now, Conner. Dirk, take the condom off and let me suck you dry."

Again the men paused before moving into position. Conner leaned over her and took one of her breasts. Lifting her legs, she wrapped them over his shoulders, lifting her pussy toward his prize. With a half-moan, half-growl, he slammed into her, scooting her head into Dirk.

Dirk shifted to the side, giving her better access and held his dick in his hand. "You're so damn wet. I can see your come on him."

"Give it to me." Alex took his shaft and guided it into her mouth. She closed her eyes, savoring the new taste of werewolf. The taste was slightly different from Conner's. Thicker somehow. Earthier. She dragged on him, keeping her gaze on his lust-filled face.

"Suck me, Alex. Use your tongue, sugar."

Rocking back and forth from Conner's rhythmic pounding, Alex drew Dirk in and out, holding then releasing over and over, sweeping her tongue around the thick rod. His impressive shaft curved at the end to tap at the top of her mouth. So big. So long. So right. Tasting Dirk while Conner fucked her pussy was beyond her wildest fantasy. She'd had threesomes before, but never with two men who were so very different. And never with a werewolf.

Conner groaned, leaned over and flicked his tongue over her taut nipple. Taking his cue, Dirk reached out to pinch her other sensitive nub.

She slurped Dirk's shaft inside, released him, then did it again. He groaned and spread his legs wider. Cupping his balls with one hand, she slid the other around his thigh to grip his tight butt cheek. Feeling powerful and in control of the two men, she tightened her legs around Conner and tracked her tongue down Dirk's length, kissing it along the way, only to plunge him back inside her mouth.

"Oh, shit, I'm going to blow." Dirk groaned and pulled out of her mouth, turning away with a shout.

Conner, soaked with sweat, increased his speed, pumping her harder and faster. She reached down, fingering her nub, driving her pulsating pussy to climax. The moment she tensed, then let the climax roll through her, Conner stiffened, threw back his head and roared his release.

Chapter Five

"Damn it. Another day gone and we're not a step closer to finding him. So much for three heads being better than two. Especially when one of the heads is a werewolf's." Conner wiped the sweat from his brow and scowled at Dirk.

"Last night's storm didn't help matters, Conner. The tracks we were following have washed out." Dirk could've said more. In fact, he wanted to tell Conner to shove off, but he resisted the urge to take Conner's bait. The werecat was as worn out as he was and taking it out on him. Besides, he didn't really dislike Alex's friend and, in fact, could understand why Conner resented him. The werecat had to have noticed the chemistry between Alex and him. A chemistry that simply didn't exist between Alex and Conner.

Dirk studied Alex as she arched her back, thrusting out her breasts, trying to work out the soreness from several hours of running. She bent her head, rubbing her neck, and he bit back the sudden desire to massage it for her. Instead he watched her, fearful of disturbing her, like scaring away a timid doe in the forest. Impossibly, she was more beautiful now than when he'd first seen her—like a female werewolf but with an exotic edge. Getting to know her had added to her charm, making him want to know her even better.

Alex sighed a mournful sound, then turned toward him, her gaze meeting his before moving on. Yet he knew she hadn't really seen him. Instead she was far away, lost in her thoughts, her memories. Dirk inhaled, stunned at the loneliness and grief in her eyes. For several moments, he studied her, wondering what tragedy could fill her beautiful eyes with such extraordinary sadness. Her face, as captivating as ever, seemed older, as though filled with lines he couldn't see. Her lips parted and he expected her to speak but knew if she did, her words would not be meant for him but for someone only she could see. He inclined his head to her, hoping the movement would catch her eyes, but still she looked past him into an unseen world.

Unable to bear the ache in her eyes any longer, he dropped his perusal from her face to her breasts. Her firm and pebbled breasts dried his mouth and he wrenched his attention farther down, eager to devour her other treasures. He followed her long legs, watched the way she held her body tall and straight, denying the inner turmoil he'd seen hidden in her gaze. She was a strong woman and he loved how that strength revealed itself in sex. A spark of excitement tickled his cock. Last night was great, but he wanted more time with her. Alone time with her. He glanced at Conner and barely kept the snarl from his lips.

"Alex?" Dirk whispered, fearful of startling her. She blinked but didn't show any other sign that she'd heard him. He took a step toward her, raising his hand to her. Conner hissed at Dirk, stepped to block him, then reached out to touch Alex's arm. Without warning, Dirk's gut clenched, twisting with an unfamiliar emotion.

"Stretch?"

Alex jolted out of her trance, pulling away from Conner's touch. She glanced between the two men, confusion etched on her face. "What?"

"You okay?" Conner's lowered tone was gentle, his demeanor suggesting he'd seen her this way before.

"Oh." Alex shook her head, then tugged at the ends of her hair, her gaze wandering anywhere except on the two men. "Of

185

course I am."

"Are you sure?" Dirk studied her, ready to do whatever she needed. "Is there something I can get you?"

"I said I'm fine, Dirk."

"Good. For a minute there, I thought—"

She ground out her answer, her glare telling more than her words. "Like I said. It's nothing. I was just thinking about...the weather." She looked skyward toward the darkening horizon. "We need to find shelter again, boys."

"You're right, Alex." Her gaze, firm yet tender, locked on to his and his stomach took another hit. This time, however, he recognized the feeling as good old lust. "There's a ranch not far from here. I know the rancher and I'm sure he'll put us up for the night. Besides, I could use a hot shower."

Alex lit up at the mention of a shower, her attitude returning to a friendlier mood. "Oooh, hot water. I can almost feel it running over me. Are you game, Conner?"

"The idea of Dirk getting his stench washed off sounds good, but not much else. Staying with humans? I don't know."

"You don't smell like a bed of roses either, furball."

Alex laughed, directing her attention to her werecat friend and wrenching Dirk's heart in the process. A nagging idea tugged at his awareness, but he couldn't bring it to the forefront of his mind. Why was he so hung up on this female? Sure, she was hot, but he'd had his fair share of sexy females. No, it was something more, an intuition that they were alike, sharing not only an internal unhappiness, but a hope to see the joy in life. In short, Alex was special.

"I'd prefer a cave to a human's home."

Dirk opened his mouth to argue but, fortunately, Alex chimed in with her decision.

"Not me. I'll take four walls and, hopefully, a bed over a

cold rock any day." Her eyes sparkled, radiating the excitement in her body. "Dirk, lead the way."

He nodded and started off at a slow trot. The two werecats followed, mucking through the mud left from the previous night's storm until, at last, they saw the ranch nestled in the clearing below. Dirk picked up their pace toward the main house.

An older male stepped through the front door and watched their approach. When they were close enough for him to see them clearly, he held up a hand in greeting.

Dirk stopped them, motioning for them to stay where they were. "Let me do the talking." He strode to the house and up the porch steps to extend his hand to Bob Tally, the ranch's owner. "Hey, Bob, how's it hanging?"

Bob gripped his hand, firm and hard. "You tell me. Are you having any luck?"

"Not yet. But I've enlisted a couple of friends to help out." He nodded toward Alex and Conner. "I'm hoping you'll let us stay the night to rest up before we head out again."

Bob's knowing gaze skimmed over Alex and Conner. "They don't look like Cannon Pack."

"They're not." Although Dirk sensed that Bob wanted more information, he assumed the seasoned cowboy would figure it out on his own. "I'll vouch for them."

Bob studied Alex and Conner as though rethinking his decision. "Well, since they're friends of yours..." He tipped his hand to Alex. "We can't have a female staying in the bunkhouse so you'd better stay here in the main house. I just finished supper, but you're welcome to make yourself at home in the kitchen."

"I'd appreciate that, Bob. I could use a good meal."

Bob glanced at Dirk, then at Alex and raised one eyebrow. "There's plenty of spare rooms upstairs, but I expect you won't be needing three rooms."

"I'm hoping you're right." Dirk kept his back to Alex and Conner, not letting them see the wink he gave Bob.

Bob chuckled, then waved Alex and Conner forward. After brief introductions, he led the trio into the house, then excused himself and went upstairs.

Alex turned to Dirk, resting her hand on his chest. "Are you sure this is okay?"

"Trust me. Bob wouldn't have said yes if he didn't mean it."

"But are we safe here? What will the other humans say?" Conner squinted through the window and into the settling darkness at the bunkhouse directly across from the main house.

"We can leave at first light so they won't know we were here." Taking Alex's arm, Dirk led her upstairs toward the guestrooms. "Let's check out the accommodations first, then head back down for a meal."

Dirk strode to the first bedroom door and swung it open. "You can bunk in here, Conner." The werecat peeked into the room and slowly entered. "Don't be shy about taking a shower. We'll all thank you for it." He caught Conner's scowl a second before he closed the door.

"Why do you love irritating him so much?"

Dirk feigned a "who me?" expression, but soon gave in. "It's my nature, I guess. Besides, he's just so damned easy to prod." Pushing the next door wide, he motioned for her to enter. "M'lady, your home for the evening."

Alex smiled her thanks, touching his arm as she passed to enter the dimly lit room. Awareness of her ripped through his arm at her touch and quickly found its way to his shaft.

Following her inside, Dirk searched the cozy interior and located the small lamp on the bedside table. The lamp cast a golden glow, filling the room with warmth.

Alex turned toward him and he inhaled sharply, startled by the sight of her. The more he looked at her, the more beautiful she became. The golden light softened her face and added dancing highlights to her copper hair. Wrapped in the almost ethereal light, she was transformed from a worldly beauty to a mesmerizing spirit from another land and time. "You're amazing."

Appreciation lit her eyes and her lush full lips parted. "Oh." Shyness overtook her, making her look away. "I, uh, don't know what to say. Shoot, I'm never at a loss for words." At last she lifted her gaze to his. "Thank you."

"You're welcome." *If I can look at her for the rest of my life, I'll die a happy man.* At first he was stunned at his thought, yet he knew with absolute certainty that he meant it. "Uh, the bathroom's right here." He motioned to the closed door to his right, feeling more like a bellhop than a hopeful lover.

"So I guess you've stayed here before?"

"Yeah, Bob and the pack go way back. I normally bunk with the ranch hands, but I've also been allowed inside the big house." He grimaced. He'd made it sound like he was some housebroken mutt begging for scraps at the dinner table. A heat he hoped she didn't notice traveled up his neck and into his face. "Um, I'll be in the adjoining room getting cleaned up. You know. If you need anything."

She stepped forward and pressed her palm to his cheek. "You don't have to play host, Dirk." The tip of her tongue peeked out to tempt him. "Besides, I like the way you smell right now."

Sliding his arm around her, he closed the gap between them. "I'm not playing host. It's just that I want you to feel comfortable. Relaxed and—"

"Safe?" She ran her thumb along the stubble on his chin,

sending flashes of pleasure down his spine. "I do, Dirk. I feel very safe with you."

"I'm glad. I want you to know you can trust me. That you can tell me anything."

She sighed and leaned into him to rest her head on his chest. "I'd like to. It's been a long time since I had someone to talk to. Someone who hasn't already judged my—"

A loud bang jolted them, breaking them apart. Together, they pivoted to find Conner standing at the door. He struggled to remain calm, fisting then flexing his hands. "How about we eat something, then get some sleep? I'm starved."

Dirk saw the same regret in her eyes that he felt. She'd wanted to open up to him. "You interrupted us, Conner. Why don't you back on out and give us a few minutes?" But, instead, Alex stepped away, leaving his heart and his body bereft.

"Conner's right. We do need to eat."

She'd let the moment go and Dirk had to let it go, too. "Okay, sure. But let's let the lady choose." Not exactly words of wisdom, but that's all he could manage. While one head was raring to go, the other was fresh out of ideas. "What do you want to do, Alex? Eat first? Or finish our conversation?"

She wavered, opened her mouth to speak, closed her eyes, then opened them with a new glint lighting them. Her entire demeanor changed, going from serious to playful. "Actually, I want more of what I had last night. How about it, Conner? Are you up for another threesome?"

Although he hadn't expected that answer, in fact was surprised at her fast change, Dirk was pleased. He'd have another time for her to tell him what he wanted to know when she was ready. *Until then, I'll wait for as long as it takes.* The thought physically rocked Dirk on his feet. Alex made him think in strange and unexpected ways. In wonderful ways. But it was Conner's reaction that really threw him.

"Yeah, sure. Why not?" Conner's frown, however, belied the lighthearted nature of his tone. "If that's what you want, Stretch."

She licked her lips and took a step toward the old-fashioned iron bed. "I hope this thing can hold all of us."

"Well, there's only one way to find out." Dirk slid his hand down her spine, delighting in the way she shivered at his touch. His heart rate sped into high gear and he swallowed the sudden flood of saliva. "Let's make this interesting, okay?"

She faced him, excitement lighting her features. "Okay. How?"

"Yeah. How?" Conner moved to the other side of the bed, his face a mask of suspicion. His posture, however, said he was ready for anything they could throw his way.

"Easy, man. All I'm suggesting is playing a little blindfold game." Conner might not want to admit it, but he definitely liked the idea. "Alex?"

"Sure, why not?" She tugged her T-shirt over her head, toeing off her boots at the same time. Her jeans soon fell to the floor, leaving her naked.

Shucking his clothes in easy moves, he took in the wonder of the woman ready to do as he asked. Dirk caught a glimpse of Conner, still clothed. If only he didn't have to share her...

"Conner, are you going to get undressed or what?"

The werecat male jolted as though coming out of a deep trance, took one look at Alex then Dirk, and started disrobing.

Alex ran her hands over her breasts, stopping a second to tease her taut tips. "Let's do this."

"That's my girl." The words were spoken before he knew it. For a moment, the three shifters stared at each other, each deciding how to interpret his statement. "You know what I mean. It's merely a phrase."

Taking a blue handkerchief from his back pocket, Dirk made a circling motion with his finger, telling Alex to put her back to him. He folded the handkerchief, then laid it gently over her eyes, letting her guide it into place. Once it was tied, he took her by the shoulders and positioned her legs against the edge of the bed. "Crawl on the bed, sugar."

She did as he commanded, the ancient bed frame creaking as she moved to the headboard, then flipped over onto her back. Conner watched silently, his body tense in anticipation.

"Now spread those luscious legs wide." She complied and he thrilled at the way she obeyed him. "That's good, sugar." Her pussy, already glistening with drops of desire, nearly drove him insane. "God, I want to eat you up."

"Then do it, wolf-man."

Alex could barely wait for one of the men to make the first move. She'd wanted to tell Dirk about Bryer, had started to tell him before Conner had arrived. But her courage had fled her. As she'd done so many times in the past year, she pushed away the agonizing emotions that thoughts of Bryer always brought and focused on something simple, easy and mindless: sex.

The bed creaked, the mattress lowering under the weight of someone sitting on the edge. A hand touched her leg and she jumped, then silently cursed herself for being so skittish.

A hot mouth closed over her left breast and lashed a tongue over the tip. She gasped, loving the feel of the tongue running back and forth over her chilled skin. Goosebumps that had risen because of the cold air warmed. Rough fingertips, callused from hard work, dragged up and down her side, tormenting her as she inwardly begged for them to move closer to her center. The fingertips continued, slipping into the crevice between her legs and her torso, yet staying too far away from her aching pussy. She groaned. "I didn't know you planned on torturing me." She spread her legs wider, hoping to entice one of them to drink her juices.

A warm chuckle slid over her breast. "You ain't seen nothing yet. Suck on her, cat-man. Make her moan. That's it, sugar, arch your back. Shove it at him." Dirk ran his tongue over her bud and pressed against it, then nipped at it to give her a thrill of pain.

A different hand, Conner's, took her other breast and squeezed it, pushing more of her nipple inside his hot mouth. His chest leaned against her side and she slipped her hand around his neck, keeping him to her.

Dirk moved his hand across her pelvis, up the soft curve of her belly to return to her side again. Dragging his fingers, he skimmed his hand past her thighs then along the inside of her leg to her quaking knees and back up the inside. He paused and she held her breath, hoping he'd take her mons in his palm. She almost cried out when he didn't, instead moving down her leg.

"Tell me you want me to finger-fuck you, Alex."

She groaned and reached out for him. "I want you to do more than that." More? She'd spoken the truth, but wasn't certain what she'd meant by it. More sexually? Or *more*?

"Then tell us what you want, sugar."

Conner echoed her groan, then palmed both her breasts, bringing them together so he could suck on them at once. He nipped at the tender tips, zapping little bits of pain through her. But he soothed the sting soon with flicks of his tongue.

"Oh, Conner, I love it when you suck on my breasts. Suck harder. Lick me, too."

Dirk ran his hand along her leg, over to her folds to spread them just wide enough for him to thumb her wet clit. She mewed, ready for more yet not wanting to rush him.

"Do you love that, too? Your pussy is so hot, so wet. Come on my fingers, Alex. I want to lick your sweet juice off my fingers."

An orgasm rushed to do his bidding and she lifted her ass toward him, pushing against the thumb driving her crazy. "Oooh. Please. Do it harder."

"If I rub you any harder, sugar, I'll rub the skin right off."

"I don't care." Conner squeezed her breasts together again, then drove his face against her, licking the hollow between them. She gasped at the roughness of his tongue. "You two are making me so horny. Dirk? Conner? Someone eat me. Now."

"My pleasure." Dirk clamped his hands around her ankles, pulling her sideways to the edge of the bed. "Sorry to take away your treat, Conner, but I've got to have a taste right now."

A cool wet tongue licked her pussy, pushing against her throbbing peak, driving her over the edge again. She exploded and heard Dirk let out a satisfied moan. She lifted her hips, squirming in ecstasy. Her legs shook, threatening to buckle until, at last, he shouldered her legs and held her firm. "Stay right here. I've just started to lap you up."

Dirk stabbed his tongue inside her dripping pussy, licking the inside of her cave then sucking her juices out of her. His breath blew against her as he took her nub in, then abruptly let it go. First flicking his tongue of sweet agony over her distended fleshy bead, he then dragged his tongue flattened and hard against her. He held her, restraining her thrashing and keeping his mouth and tongue on her. She moaned in pleasurable anguish, but he didn't stop, instead using his teeth on her tender bead. She cried out, unable to imagine how much more delightful ecstasy she could stand but not ready to have it end. "Ahhhh, please. Keep doing what you're doing."

Dirk's chuckle warmed her skin, taking his teasing tongue away. "But, sugar, there's so much more I want to do to you."

"I want a taste." Conner let go of her breasts and more creaking sounds came as he placed his body sixty-nine style over hers. "Suck on me, Alex, while I suck on you." His thick shaft nudged at her mouth, tempting her to take him inside.

Wrapping her hand around his shaft, she pulled him into her mouth. His taste, so wild, so tangy filled her mouth. Slowly, she dragged her teeth along the smooth skin, stopping every once in a while to suck or lash her tongue around him. His moan, filled with sexual tension, encouraged her and she pulled him in, released him, then deep-throated him.

Soft kisses feathered her mound and a tongue flicked over her skin to tease the vee that led to her pussy. While Conner kissed her, edging closer and closer, Dirk ran his fingers along her legs and moved, dipping the bed. He lowered his body to place her heels on his shoulders, opening her wider still. Turning his head, Dirk jabbed his tongue inside her, matching Conner's quick kisses along the top of her mons. Together the men pleasured her, Conner keeping to the area above her pussy while Dirk stabbed his tongue in and out, over and over, sucking on her wetness.

"My turn." Conner's voice was low and gravelly.

Dirk paused and she held her breath, hoping the two shifters wouldn't start fighting.

"Fair enough. But I'm still going to use my fingers."

Two fingers pushed inside her, moving swiftly to caress the tender skin of her vaginal walls. Conner lowered himself closer to her body, then latched on to her aching nub. She inhaled sharply, throwing her head back, side to side. Pure lust-filled bliss filled her.

"She's so tight. Hurry up, cat-man, and get your fill. I've got to have her and I mean soon."

An irritated rumble from Conner tickled her skin, but was swiftly followed by breathtaking sucking that turned the ripples of desire into waves of hot hunger. Her blood pulsed in her nub, echoed in her ears, pushing another, bigger orgasm close to the surface. Soft kisses replaced the sucking, leaving for a moment to circle the sensitive skin around her nub. Dirk sped up, plunging his fingers deep inside her, thrusting in and out of her, doubling the intense build-up.

She wondered how close Dirk's fingers were to Conner's mouth, then promptly pushed the worrisome thought away. Like her own desire, their craving was too strong for them to complain. Instead, she cupped Conner's balls in one hand and gently squeezed as she deep-throated him.

Alex tried not to writhe too much, not wanting them to lose contact. Instead, she lifted her hips, grinding her sex against them. Conner answered her by pressing his mouth fully against her, enclosing her tender clit and pussy lips. He pulled them into his mouth and the only thing she could do was to scream. The orgasm rocked through her, first in a giant tidal wave and followed by smaller waves of release. She clung to Conner's legs and waited for the delicious bliss to subside.

"Conner, move out of the way. I have to have her." Dirk waited for Conner, a silent message she couldn't understand passing between them. "You know what I mean."

Alex thrilled, wanting Dirk more than she'd ever wanted a man. She heard the intensity in Dirk's tone but kept her mouth firmly around Conner's throbbing shaft. Pumping him, she sucked his cock in again and again, feeling his release coming closer and closer. Suddenly, he shouted, heralding his release, and she pushed on Conner's hips, moving his body away from her.

"Alex."

She heard the love in his voice and bit back the tears welling in her eyes. Could she make him understand? She'd finally figured out how she felt, once and for all. But if she told him, would he remain her friend? After taking a steadying breath, she took off the blindfold. Conner covered her mouth and she tasted the musky tang of her own juices. The kiss lingered, bringing with it all the emotions they shared. He finally broke free and studied her. Realization, then hurt filled his face but quickly vanished. Slowly, he settled by her side.

"I can't wait any longer." Dirk climbed between her legs and tore open a condom package. Taking a firm hold under her butt, he pushed her legs toward her chest. He slid into her, his eyes closed, his face tensing with control. She gasped at the size of him, lifted her head to watch his hips move back and forth, diving in then retreating from her cave.

Conner cupped her under her chin and made her look at him. He dove into her eyes, making her feel more exposed and vulnerable than any nudity ever had.

"Conner, I don't—" Words failed her as she stared into her beloved friend's eyes.

"It's okay." He glanced at Dirk. "I can see what we don't have." His sweet smile lifted at the corners, reminding her of Dirk's wicked one. "Mind if I watch?" He skimmed his hands over her breasts, fondling them and tweaking at the firm tips.

She tried to return his smile but failed. Instead, she gripped his hand and squeezed. "I'll always love you... Always need you..." She opened her mouth to say more, but words failed her.

"Come for me, Alex." Conner glanced at Dirk, then tweaked her nipple.

The smile she'd wanted to give him finally came.

Dirk thrust into her, rocking her toward the headboard. Conner rested on his elbows to place light kisses along her shoulder, down the curve of her breast and over her nipple. Dirk slammed into her wet pussy, working harder and faster. Pushing against her knees, he opened her wider and rammed into her, driving all the way inside her. Alex arched, clutched the sheet, and gripped Conner's neck. "Yes. Oh, hell, yes!"

Her pussy clenched, tightening around Dirk's cock, trying to hold him in place. Dirk stroked her hard wet nub and she exploded, screaming louder than before, uncaring who heard her. He came a second later, roaring his release. Tremor after tremor shook through her into him, then came back to her. Blood rushed to her ears, dulling the sound of Dirk's grunts. The final burst of her sex almost pushed her into the darkness. She closed her eyes and held on until the ride was over.

"Alex?"

"Stretch?"

Conner using her nickname told her that they would remain friends. "Yeah, boys?"

"Damn, after what we just did, I'd hardly call us boys. What do you think, Conner?"

"I think you've got that right."

Alex opened her eyes to find them lying on either side of her. She lowered her gaze, first at one, then other, finding their shafts nestled against her legs. "Agreed. You two are most definitely men."

Alex stretched her arms above her head, warmed by the sun's light bursting through the window to spill onto the bed. Although the idea of waking up with Conner and Dirk beside her had been a tempting one, she was glad that she'd sent them back to their respective rooms after raiding the kitchen for a late-night supper. Sometimes waking up all alone in a big comfortable bed was even better than sex. Okay. Not better than sex with Alex and Conner, but damn close.

Conner. The image of her friend played in her mind, but for once, she wasn't conflicted. Although Conner was everything a woman could want, he would never be more than a friend to her.

She slipped out from under the sheet, padded into the bathroom and checked the clothes she'd washed by hand the night before. Finding them dry, she pulled them off the shower curtain rod and laid them on the counter. "Time for another hot shower."

Testing the temperature of the spray, she stepped into the shower and let the water cascade down her body. A sigh escaped her and she closed her eyes to savor the wonderfully soothing sensation.

"Want someone to scrub your back?"

An excited tremor rushed through her to find Dirk standing in the doorway. "Good morning, Dirk. Have you had your shower yet?" She couldn't resist. She had to tempt him, knowing he'd take the lure and run with it. "Or are you still dirty?"

His smile widened into the mischievous grin she adored. "Hell, yes, I'm dirty. Even though I already had a shower." His lustful gaze scoured her body, leaving her breathless.

"Then I guess you should take another one." She opened the shower door and gestured for him to come inside. He moved quickly, shucking his boots and jeans. She tugged at his hair, roughly bringing him toward her. His mouth found her nipple, seizing it, pulling it. She struggled to unbutton his shirt, pushing it away from his shoulders to fall to the bathroom floor behind him. As their lips connected, nipping, pulling, licking, she brought him into the shower.

They crushed together, unable to let their bodies separate for even a second. Leaning against the shower wall, they let the warm water flow over them, mixing the hard taste of well water with the musky juices of their kisses.

Dirk took each breast in a hand, shoved his face between

them and licked each one, circling around their fullness several times until his spiral led him to her hardened nipples. As his thumb caressed one nipple, he nipped the other, the pain becoming the pleasure she wanted.

But she needed more. She wanted him to take her as any male should take a female. As she'd always dreamt of her mate taking her, controlling her, making her his. She needed him to possess her, to take her sex and claim her heart.

His hands played with her bottom, slipping his fingers between her butt cheeks. Reaching above her, she angled the spray nozzle and showered his back with the warm water, loving the way his muscles channeled the stream down the contours of his back, over the rise of his butt and into the cleft of his ass.

He took the nozzle from her, the sparkling eyes she adored twinkling at her. "My turn." Reaching between the cleft between her legs, he lifted one leg and placed it on the built-in shower seat. Running his hand over the small mound of her abdomen, he bent to his knees, taking the nozzle with him. "Hang onto my shoulders. I wouldn't want you to fall when your knees give out."

"Modest much, are you?" She sank her fingers into his shoulders and gasped as the warm spray struck her, coursing the water around her, inside her. Spreading her folds, he aimed the water at her center and she gasped again as the spray throbbed against her aching nub.

"Oh, hell. Oooh! Dirk. Oooo, yeah, but that's— Oh, yes!"

"Go ahead, sugar. Mix your juices with the spray and let me drink." His tongue joined the water to lick her clit, drinking in her juices along with the rivulets coursing along her skin. She cried out, barely holding on to him as rush after glorious rush ripped through her body.

"Dirk. Oh, wow, Dirk." Wanting more, wanting all he could

give, all she could physically stand, she spread her legs wider. Her release exploded and was followed by two stronger ones. She cried out in delight, hanging on to him to stay upright.

Moving the nozzle an inch to the side, he drove his tongue between her folds and sucked. She threw her head back, closing her eyes to concentrate on the delicious rush of emotions flowing through her. She craved him, needed him. More than she'd ever imagined she could. But once they'd found the killer, he'd leave her and she would miss him. When had this man, this werewolf, come to mean so much to her? She gasped from the realization and gripped his shoulders, holding on to him, physically keeping him with her.

He took his mouth and the water from her, making her shout in protest. She begged him with her eyes and her words. "No. Please. Don't stop." She bit back the words she wanted to say. The words begging him to never leave.

Yet when he lifted his head to her, his eyes darkened in desire, she knew he wouldn't desert her.

Without a word, he brought the pulsating water back to her. This time she couldn't keep her knees from buckling as the force of the water struck her nub and she climaxed again, the glorious waves of pleasure rolling through her.

Dirk gently guided her to sit on the seat, letting the shower nozzle fall to the side. "I'm still thirsty and something tells me you've got more orgasms to give me. Spread 'em, sugar."

She obeyed, murmuring a soft mewing sound, and slid her bottom toward the end of the seat. Leaning her shoulders against the wet tile wall, she caught her breath, ready when his mouth fell on her mons. First he teased her, licking away the water streaming over her skin. His tongue slid over her, easing across her, making her ache for him. At last, he moaned and slid his hands under her legs to lift them over his shoulders. Using his fingers, he opened her to him.

Dirk knew how much pressure to put on her, when to lick, when to suck, when to bite. She'd reached the precipice time and time again, but he'd changed position and left her hanging over the edge of her orgasmic cliff.

"Dirk, please. Don't make me suffer." She wanted to say so much more but didn't have the strength.

Again his answer came in the physical way, using his fingers to explore her vagina. Crushing his mouth against her, he renewed his attack. She moaned, her voice growing louder with each rub of his fingers. Clutching his wet hair, she kept him to her, moving her pelvis up and down in rhythm. Like an avalanche moving faster and faster as it rushed down the mountain, her muscles tightened everywhere, tensing in preparation for the next eruption. Shudders of orgasms, each one bigger than the last, rushed through her.

He stopped, giving her time to rest and catch her breath. Her pulse slowly returned to a seminormal pace, and she tugged on his hair to pull his face closer to hers. Before the cascading water could wash it away, she ran her tongue over his lips and tasted her juices on them. "Hmm, good stuff."

"You don't need to tell me." He fondled her breasts and growled his excitement low and deep in his throat.

"Your turn."

"I thought that was my turn, sugar."

She pushed against him, making him stand while she stayed seated. He did so, the corners of his mouth tweaking upward as he flattened his hands against the wall behind her. She ran her hands over his hard abdomen and licked her lips, tilting her head to the side to appreciate how the rivulets of water coursed over his six-pack abs, through his bush of curly hair and dripped off the tip of his purple-veined penis. She flicked her tongue over the end of his cock and watched it jerk in response. Glancing at him, she opened her mouth just enough to run her tongue over her lips and watched the water drip off his nose as he locked his attention on her. Smiling, she took his shaft in her hand and drew him into her mouth.

He inhaled sharply and spread his feet wider. She cupped his ass, keeping him close to slip him in and out of her mouth.

"Damn, Alex, I don't know how much longer I can hold on."

"You have to because I'm not finished yet." Alex sucked harder, pulling on every inch of his shaft in a slow drag. She wrapped her hands around his dick, working him. His pleasure moans grew louder, signaling his imminent release.

"Damn it. I can't—"

Abruptly, she let go and stood. Putting her back to the wall, she lifted a leg to the seat, opening for him. "Take me, Dirk. Now."

He rammed into her, knocking her head against the wall. She cried out, but he kept on, taking her bottom in his hands to slip his fingers into her crack. He fondled her buttocks, pulling her close, rocking her backward with his thrusts. She cupped one breast and brought her nipple to his mouth. "Harder, Dirk."

Obeying her, he grunted with the strain and pounded into her. Her muscles clamped around him, keeping him a willing captive inside her. She tightened and released, giving him as much pleasure as she could. He quickened his strokes, increasing the friction inside her, rubbing against the sensitive spot.

"Go deeper. Give me everything you've got."

Groaning, he lifted her off the floor then crushed her with his body. She cried out and slipped her hands to his butt, feeling his cheeks clench to drive into her farther, deeper. She bent her neck, enjoying the quick bites he trailed from her ear to her shoulder. In and out he worked, pushing his dick farther inside with each stroke. She ran her hands over his back, taking time to caress his scars.

She climaxed again and again, too many times and too fast for her dazed mind to count. Bringing his mouth to hers to smother her cries, he tensed for a minute, then roared his release into her mouth. His body shook, his climax thundering against her, and she matched his climax with the biggest orgasm of all. All too soon, his body rested against hers, quivering.

"You, sugar, are amazing." His breathing settled into a normal pattern and he let her legs slide to the floor. Placing his hands on either side of her head, he leaned in and gave her a soft, tender kiss. "I want you."

"Wow. Again? So soon?"

His eyes deepened, still amber like before, but holding a different intensity to them. "Alex, you don't understand. I mean I want you now, tomorrow—"

"No, don't say it." She laced her fingers over his lips, her breathing quickening. Did she want to hear what he would say? Fear mixed with joy, tearing her apart, confusing her. Was she ready for whatever he wanted to tell her? Would he tell her he wanted to stay? Or would he tell her he could stay, but only for a short time? And what about when he finally left her? Could she endure another heartbreak?

"Alex."

Startled, she and Dirk turned toward Conner. Strangely embarrassed, she kept her body blocked by Dirk's.

"Damn, Conner, don't you ever knock?"

Conner's fangs flashed at Dirk, then he hid them behind an emotionless face. "I came to say goodbye."

Chapter Six

"What do you mean? We haven't found—" Alex clamped her mouth shut, cutting off Bryer's name. Instead, she stared at Conner, willing him to say that he was joking.

Conner avoided her glare, giving her time to recover from her near mistake. He lifted his head again, this time fixing his attention on Dirk. "Take care of her or you'll answer to me."

Instead of his usual banter, Dirk agreed in a solemn tone. "You can count on it."

Alex grabbed the towels hanging on the rod, tossed one to Dirk, then wrapped the other around herself and hurried over to her best friend. "I don't understand. Why are you leaving?" She struggled to find the answer. "If it's about last night— Or maybe this morning, I—"

Conner pressed his fingers against her lips, stilling her. "Don't, Alex. We both know why. And it's okay. *I'm* okay."

Her heart cracked open, spreading until the pain tore her soul apart. "Oh, Conner, I'm so sorry. Please stay. Let's talk about this." She pressed her palm to his chest, then clutched his shirt. "Please don't do this. I can't lose you, too."

She had to make him understand, had to make him stay. After losing Lara, then losing Bryer in an even worse way, she couldn't imagine losing her friend, too.

"You're not losing me. Not in the way you think." He shook

his head and rubbed her arms, but his attempt to comfort her didn't work. "But I can't stay. Don't ask me to, Alex. I thought maybe we could be together, that we could be mates. I gave you the time you needed to decide." His gaze flew to Dirk, then back to her. "I want you to be happy."

"Then don't leave." A small cry escaped her and he drew her into his arms. She leaned into him, taking in his familiar scent. Wrapping her arms around him, she held on to him, physically keeping him there but knowing he'd already left.

"Shh. It's not like we'll never see each other again." He offered her a small smile, then moved her back to look at her. "I'll always be there for you, Stretch. No matter where you go or who you go with."

Alex swallowed the lump in her throat that threatened to cut off her breath and forced herself to talk. She unclenched then clenched her fists, unable to let go. "But you promised to help me find...the killer. Our job isn't finished yet." She couldn't let him leave. How could she keep going without him?

Dirk saw her unspoken plea. "Look, man, don't go on my account. Alex needs you more than she does me. Maybe I'm the one who should leave." He paused, waited for her to respond. "I'll do whatever Alex wants. All she has to do is say the word."

"No, Dirk, it's not that." Keeping one hand on Conner, she reached out for Dirk, then drew her hand back. How could she make them understand that she wanted them both?

"I've given this a lot of thought and I think you and Dirk will have a better chance of finding the killer without any distractions. Instead, I'll report back to the council and let them know how the search is going. Maybe I can get them to reconsider sending help."

"But we need you. *I* need you."

"No, you don't. You and Dirk will be fine. He'll take care of you." He took her face in his hands. "Come on, Alex. Don't make this harder than it already is. You know this is what's best."

Ignoring the truth of what he said, she tried to protest again, but he wouldn't let her. He took her wrist, breaking her hold on him, and moved her arm to her side. She studied the all-too-familiar stubborn expression. His mind was made up and once his mind was made up... "Won't you please reconsider?"

"No. My decision is made. Trust me, Alex. I need to leave."

She searched his face, trying to think how to make him stay, but she knew he was right. They'd sidestepped the unspoken problem between them long enough. Even if Dirk hadn't come along, they would've had to confront it. But she didn't want to think about that. She'd let it go for now, saving it for a later time, a time alone when she could cry. Slowly, she picked up her jeans lying on the counter, reached into the pocket and pulled out the moon-shaped stone. "I want you to take this back."

"But it's yours. Why would you give it back? We're still friends, right?"

"I want you to have it so you'll remember how much you mean to me. How much you'll always mean to me. No matter what happens between us or whoever comes into my life. Keep it safe for me."

"Okay. But you ask for it anytime you want. It'll be something we'll always share."

"Agreed. We'll keep it special, just between us." Her attempt to smile failed under the weight of her heart. Conner moved away and her stomach rolled, anguish forming a knot in her abdomen.

Conner's expression matched the werewolf's. The two men gripped each other's right forearm and studied each other. With a nod at Dirk, Conner broke their handshake to give her another hug. She held her breath, somehow keeping her arms at her sides, and closed her eyes, once again taking in his essence. He stepped away, slicing an agonizing rip into her heart, turned briefly to give her a soft smile, then closed the door behind him.

Letting out a moan, Alex fell against Dirk and clung to him. How much more of her life did she have to give up? Why did she keep losing the people she loved?

Dirk enveloped her, leading her to the bed to lower her on the edge. Sitting next to her, he hugged her, cooing soft words of comfort. She reached for his hand and held on, using it as her anchor in a world suddenly turned upside down.

"Why did he have to go? I thought we were doing okay, the three of us." She tightened her grip on Dirk.

"We were and we weren't."

It wasn't fair of her, but she didn't care. She shoved him away, frustration whirling with anger. "That's the dumbest thing I've ever heard."

"Alex, you're hurting, I know. But once you calm down and have some time to think about it, you'll know it was for the best."

"For the best? How the hell is running off my best friend for the best?" She glared at him, wanting to hurt him, to make him feel her pain. Even if she was wrong in doing so.

"You didn't run him off, you know. He's still your friend, will always be your friend. In fact, I envy him that. He's lucky that he's known you all these years. The only difference between then and now is that he realizes that's all he'll ever be."

She stood, pacing across the floor to the window. Scanning the yard below, she searched for Conner, but he was already gone. She leaned her forehead against the pane and closed her eyes. "I can't believe I hurt him this way. If we'd never gotten together, hadn't had sex..." Yet she couldn't regret giving that

208

part of her to him, if only for a short time.

"Do you mean you and Conner? Or me and you?" He waved the questions away. "Never mind. He would've had to come to grips with it some other way."

She turned away from the yard, unable to stand the emptiness. "I know. But why couldn't he have stayed with us, helped us search? I should have made him stay."

"You really would have hurt him then." He waited for her, hands clasped in his lap. "You're doing what's right for him by letting him leave now."

She hated the fact that he was right. Hated the fact that she knew he was. A tear, the first one she'd shed in the year since Lara's death, slid down her cheek to wet the corner of her mouth. She licked it away and tucked her chin, averting her eyes.

"Alex, what is it that's hurting you? Not just Conner, but the thing that's deep inside you?"

She gasped, then raised her gaze to meet his. "I don't know what you mean."

Seeing the refusal to accept her lie reflected in his face, she turned away.

"I can tell you've lost someone. Maybe more than one?" He was by her side before she could force a response. "Please, Alex, tell me. I see the sadness in you and I want to help. Trust me to shoulder some of your pain." He tipped her chin up. "I may make a lot of jokes, but I know what it's like to suffer a loss."

"I don't like to talk about it." Would he understand? Could he? She tried to shrug him off, but he wouldn't let her.

"I get it, Alex. You've gotten really good at pushing the bad thoughts aside, haven't you?"

She took a calming breath and released it, the air shuddering out of her. Biting her lip, she searched him, wanting to believe. "How do you know? How could you tell?"

His smile, so full of empathy, lifted her spirits. "Oh, sugar, you know what they say. It takes one to know one." A cloud darkened him, in his body, in his tone. "A hunter killed my father when I was a teenager. But it was the same as if he'd killed both my parents. My mother was never the same after that. She withdrew, lost interest in everything, including her children. At first, I vowed revenge, hated everyone and everything around me. I let my anger out the only way I knew how, by killing cattle for no other reason than the need to inflict my pain on someone or something."

Like her brother had? She opened her mouth to ask, then closed it, unable to voice her greatest fear.

"The rancher who owned the cows punished me by putting these scars on my back."

"Oh, Dirk, I'm so sorry."

"It's okay. I wouldn't have admitted it at the time, but I deserved it. He could've done much worse. After that, I withdrew from everyone. Hell, I barely said a word for two years."

She touched his arm, skimming her hand down his shoulder to take his hand in hers. He linked his fingers with hers. "Still, it's a horrible story and I'm sorry you went through that." Knowing he would understand, she managed a smirk. "But you not speaking? I don't believe it."

He chuckled, patted her arms in much the same way Conner had. "Yeah, but I swear it's true. After that, I found another way to cope. I changed into the smart-talking lovable hound you know so well." His smile faded. "But it's only a defense thing. Something to keep the grief from rearing its ugly head." He narrowed his eyes. "So, now that you see I understand where you're coming from, tell me. What's eating you up inside? Stop hiding, Alex, and let me in."

She licked her lips, trying to moisten the dryness, trying to decide what to do. Yet when he touched her face, ran his thumb over her cheek to wipe away a tear she hadn't realized she'd shed, the words began flowing. "My brother Bryer was my best friend. Even closer than Conner. He made me laugh, made me believe that anything was possible. Life was good then. Unburdened."

He led her back to the bed, retook their seats. "And then something happened to Bryer?"

"In a way." For a moment, she could see Lara and Bryer, happy and alive, announcing their union to the council. "Bryer fell in love with a beautiful werecat, a lovely woman named Lara. They were the perfect couple." She sighed. "I prayed I could find joy the way they had."

"But something happened, didn't it? Go on, Alex. Don't stop now."

She put her head on his shoulder, committed to continuing, relieved to finally tell him her secret. "They were married less than a year when it happened. Lara—she was always so adventurous—went too far away from our home." He cradled her hand in his and she stared at their hands, amazed at the way hers fit perfectly in his.

He stroked her hair and she closed her eyes, drawing strength from him. "You loved her."

"More. I loved and respected her. Lara was fearless in everything she did."

"But that fearlessness cost her her life?"

She nodded and choked out the words. "Her father found her the next day. She'd fallen off a cliff and we thought it was an accident. But then Bryer saw the wounds in her head, the bullet holes..."

"I'm sorry, Alex. For you and for Bryer."

She leaned back so she could see his face. "But it was

211

worse than that. Bryer died that day, too. Not physically, but emotionally. He changed from the second he saw her lying at the bottom of the cliff. My funny, lovable brother changed into a cold, cruel person I no longer knew."

"Then it's like you lost both of them. One was dead, but the other wasn't really alive either. I know how that is."

He understood. She touched him, making sure he truly existed, wasn't merely a dream. She'd never found anyone in the past year who'd understood how she felt. Conner had understood, but not in the same way. He couldn't have. Only someone who'd suffered the same way she had could understand completely. Did she dare tell him the rest?

"Alex, you can trust me. Go on."

All she needed was to hear him ask. She released the hurt in a rush of words. "My people, even Conner, think my brother Bryer is the rogue werecat. They think he's trying to stir up trouble between the ranchers and the pride. He blames all human hunters for Lara's death and the pride for not agreeing to his need for revenge. He feels like the pride is betraying him and they think he's trying to start a war where both shifters and humans will get hurt. A war of revenge for Lara's murder." She dragged in air, then let it out in one quick breath.

"And what about you? Do you think it's Bryer?"

She shook her head, then stopped. "I don't know. Part of me can't imagine my brother doing this, instigating all this trouble." Placing her trembling hands in her lap, she closed her eyes and forced herself to go on. "But another part of me can't deny that it makes sense. In a very real sense, my brother died a year ago, and this person walking around in his body is a stranger."

"You've had a hard time of it, haven't you?" His tone was lower, gentler.

Alex inhaled, held her breath, then let it out in a slow sigh.

The anger, the agony, hell, the guilt for wanting to live her life without the heartache crashed together inside her, forming a whirling ball of grief she could no longer force down. Clutching Dirk, she nodded, then sobbed, finally giving voice to the blackness that was her sorrow.

"Pick it up, Dirk." Alex quickened her step, taking the lead and leaving Dirk struggling to match her pace.

"Will you quit running me to death? I know you miss Conner, but you don't have to take it out on me."

She slowed her pace until he was by her side. "I'm sorry. I didn't mean to— I miss him so much."

His silence said more than his words ever could have. After comforting her, he'd stayed with her, holding her close, her tears wetting his chest.

She listened to the padding of their feet on the forest floor. Dirk's stride and hers matched, mixing together in an easy way that was both new and familiar. "Thank you for this morning."

"I'm glad you confided in me."

"Me, too." They jumped in tandem over a fallen tree. "I feel better about Conner now that I know he'll still be my friend." Did she dare say the rest? Dirk and she had grown closer, letting her believe in him. She shot him a smile filled with thanks. "I'm glad to have a friend who understands what I went through. What I'm still going through."

"I'll always be here for you, Alex." She sent him a questioning look that he caught and tried to dismiss. "Isn't that what friends do for each other?"

A warm glowed filled her, taking some of the loneliness of Conner's absence away.

"In fact, it's good that Conner realizes where he stands.

Now he can move on." Dirk's hand touched hers, his sensuality rippling off his body and into her like waves onto a beach. "He'll move on and then you'll do the same. When the right person comes along."

The right person? She watched Dirk, his hard body glistening in the sun, and her stomach did a strange flip-flop. Shyness hit her and she tried to keep her face neutral, not wanting her thoughts to show on her face. "I guess you're right." She suddenly brightened. "Oh, wow. I just had the best idea. I know the perfect lady for Conner. She's always had a crush on him."

"See? Things have a way of working out for the best." His sly smile crept at the corners of his mouth. "Especially when I'm around."

"Ah, Dirk, your parents should have named you Mr. Perfect."

"Hey, when you know you're the best, why deny—"

A bellow, full of rage and pain, shattered the air around them. Dirk and Alex pivoted, each letting out a warning snarl.

Dirk rushed down the side of the hill toward the sound. Alex pounded the earth beside him, her breath hitching in her throat as she fought the rising panic. Was that scream from an animal? Or from something, some*one* else? They'd immediately rushed in that direction, not taking the time to disrobe and shift completely, and keeping up with Dirk was proving to be difficult. She slid on the small rocks on the hillside, ignoring the branches of the brushes, breaking heedlessly through them. Dirk pulled away from her, blazing the trail ahead of her, telling her to stay behind him. They broke into the valley, bursting through the tree line. Dirk slammed to a stop in front of her and she almost rammed into his back in an effort to stop. He grabbed her, tried to turn her away, but she struggled against him.

"Alex, no. Don't look."

Fear of what she would see shot through her, but the need to see, to know what had put that shocked expression on his face, overwhelmed his warning.

"Let go of me." She flung her body away, breaking his hold on her, determined to face the worst.

"Oh, my God." Horror stunned her, making her immobile. Her gaze zeroed in on her brother, glorious in his werecat form, hunched over the body of a mutilated cow. He lifted his face to her, his bloody lips pulled into a defiant snarl. Angry golden eyes locked on to her, turning her blood to ice. His huge frame unfolded from his crouch, his tail whipping back and forth, and he cocked his head to one side as if to question what he saw.

"Bryer." The word was expelled in a harsh whisper of denial. What she had feared the most had come true. Her brother, the fun-loving playmate of her youth, was the killer. The tears came and her mind slowly accepted what her eyes showed her.

"Alex."

Dirk's gentle tone, so incongruous with the awful scene before her, drew her gaze away from her brother. She frowned at Dirk, unable to speak as the myriad of emotions tumbled through her.

"Alex, it's Conner." Dirk tipped his head toward a form lying a several feet from the dead cow. She turned, her mind reeling, and stared at the crumpled heap.

Where her body had gone numb before, pain rushed to fill those dead areas, anguishing her brain first, then her flesh. Conner lay on the ground surrounded by a growing red stain. A small cry escaped her and she moved toward the unmoving form before Dirk could stop her. "Conner!"

Falling to the ground next to him, she grabbed his shirt and pulled him onto his back. She gasped, then clutched his blood-soaked shirt, to hold on against the wave of nausea racking her. *His face. His handsome, sweet face. It's gone.* "No. Please, please, please. This isn't real."

For a brief wonderful moment she allowed a fantasy to play out. Maybe it really wasn't him. With a face that disfigured, how could she be sure? Holding her breath, she ran her hands over him, searching for some kind of identification. She had to find a clue that would tell her this lifeless body wasn't her childhood friend. Praying harder than she'd ever done, she dug into his pockets, his blood staining her fingers, her hands, her clothes. At last, however, she felt the familiar smooth object in his front pocket and knew. Slowly, she withdrew the moon-shaped stone.

"Oh, Conner." Her throat ached, her words coming out in a croak.

Her brother had murdered her best friend. Although every ounce of her wanted to deny the reality lying next to her, she couldn't ignore the horrific sight. Memories of Conner and Bryer playfully wrestling as she called encouragement to first one then the other flooded through her, battling against the stench of death filling her nostrils. More images filled her mind. Bryer hugging a laughing Conner, his arm protectively wrapped around the smaller shifter. Conner and Bryer hunting together, sensing what the other would do without signals or words. She closed her eyes, blocking out the horror. If she wished hard enough, could she make it all go away? Yet when she opened her eyes again, the terrible ugliness remained.

A low growl tore her away from her friend. She glanced at her brother, his tail still swishing, his ears laid back. "How could you? How could you do this to Conner?"

Why had her good-natured brother lost his soul and transformed into a heartless killer?

Fury swept through her. Unable to hold it back, she unleashed it, pushing all her agony out with it. She slammed her fist on the ground, her lips pulling into a snarl. "Damn you,

216

Bryer! Damn you to Hell! I stood by you through all of this, through everything the others said about you. But they were right. You are evil." She broke down, giving way to heaving sobs that racked her body. Placing her hand in the sticky mess that remained of Conner's chest, she said one last silent farewell, then rose to her feet. "No more, brother. Your killing spree ends. Here and now."

She shifted then, tearing her clothes off, allowing the transformation to rip them away.

Roaring, Bryer leapt, not giving Alex time to finish shifting. Caught in midtransformation, she did her best to get ready for the attack.

"No!"

Dirk's shout startled her seconds before his hard body rammed against her side. Bryer never reached her. Instead, she hit the ground, the jolt knocking the air from her and rattling her teeth. She shook her head, trying to make the world come into focus again and suddenly wished she hadn't. Still out of breath and aching from the blow, she could do nothing more than watch the two shifters fight.

Bryer and Dirk rolled together, the werecat clawing at the snarling werewolf. Fangs dripped saliva and blood. Claws dug into fur, puncturing the skin underneath to release flow after red flow. The two shifters tumbled over in the grass, neither one letting go of the other. Dirk sank his fangs into Bryer's shoulder, his face splattered with the werecat's blood. But Bryer barely noticed the werewolf's hold on him. He tore at Dirk's back, ripping fur and skin away in large chunks.

Alex managed to get to her front paws, but her foggy brain couldn't make her back legs work. She fell to the ground again, whining from the frustration and the searing ache in her side. She tried again to get up, and again, failed. But even if she could get to her feet, who would she help? Her brother or Dirk? Torn in body and in spirit, she lay on the ground as the battle between the two men raged on. She moaned. But what about Bryer? Should she save him and let him continue to kill? Could she watch him destroy Dirk? Or could she save both?

The two shifters broke apart, each stumbling away for a moment's rest. But the respite didn't last long. Releasing a roar that was more like a demon's howl, Bryer leapt at Dirk, fangs bared and claws flexed. Dirk, his chest heaving, attempted to sidestep the attack but couldn't move fast enough. The werecat struck him with one swipe of his massive paw, knocking the werewolf to the ground. Bryer jumped on top of him and tore at his exposed belly. Flailing now, Dirk tried to gain a hold on the impossibly quick werecat, but only managed light, nonlethal blows. Bryer let out another awful roar, this one filled with the joy of victory.

Alex's head cleared and she tried once again to regain her footing. This time her legs held and she scrambled to her feet. She wobbled a moment, fearful that her strength would give out.

Bryer jumped away from Dirk who lay gasping for air, stretched out on his side. Adopting a sly smile, he paced around the werewolf, occasionally swatting at him to elicit a groan. Making satisfied noises that sounded like chuckles, Bryer finished circling his victim and turned to face Alex.

Alex, now fully shifted, growled, lowered her head and laid her ears back. Bryer swished his tail in challenge, then lowered it between his legs, reminding her of the many times they'd wrestled as cubs. But this was no playtime. With his ears laid back, he snarled at her, daring her to attack.

Alex glanced at Dirk who lay unmoving, his gaze transfixed on her. Their eyes met and she knew, with absolute certainty, what he was thinking.

Run.

If she obeyed, Dirk would die and Bryer would continue his

killing spree. Innocent people, other friends and loved ones would die. She whimpered, torn between the two men. But how could she choose between them? She looked at Bryer who waited, giving her time to make her decision, and cringed at the hate in his face.

The urgency in Dirk's eyes grabbed her, clenching her stomach into a knot. His intense expression told her she'd have to choose.

She decided to risk everything. Shifting, she regained her human form to reach out to him. "Bryer, stop. Please. For me." Bryer's soft rumble gave her hope. "I know you can't be this cruel. You're my brother. I love you."

Bryer waved his tail back and forth, then crouched beside Dirk. His hard eyes sent chills through her. Gathering her resolve, she took a step toward them. "Please let me help him. For the sake of what we once were, do as I ask. If you do, I promise you, we won't keep tracking you. But for my sake and yours, you must leave the area and never come back."

Was that a smile on his face? She frowned, trying to understand what his smile meant. Was he agreeing with her plan? Hoping she was correct, she took another step toward the pair.

Bryer crouched and snarled at her, bringing her to an abrupt stop. Slowly, as if in a nightmare, he shook his head, vanquishing her hope. Placing his head close to Dirk's face, the werecat opened his jaws wide.

"No, Bryer! Stop!"

With a wicked chuckle, Bryer clamped down on Dirk's neck and closed his eyes. Dirk's agonized howl reverberated through her, and horror struck her in the gut, shooting bile into her mouth. Dirk's body jerked with each yank Bryer gave and she cried out, moving quickly.

Scooping up a nearby rock, she held it over her head with

both hands and raced to stand next to her brother. Her arms trembled under the weight of the stone and her body shuddered with determination. "Bryer, I won't let you kill him!"

Startled by the fury in her tone, Bryer released Dirk. Disbelief, then anger, filled his face. He let out a screech and tried to get out of the way, but it was too late.

Putting every ounce of strength she had left into the move, Alex thrust the rock down, crashing into Bryer's head. Bones cracked and blood spewed outward. Tears blurred her vision, obscuring the terrifying scene. Letting out a strangled cry, she lifted the rock one more time and repeated the blow. With her tears mixing with her brother's blood, she fell to her knees next to Bryer's unmoving body.

For a moment, the silence surrounding her was too much. Why didn't one of them make a noise? Had she lost them both? Reaching out, she touched her brother's back and ran her fingers along his soft fur, his quiet body. "Oh, Bryer." She choked, the emotion stealing her voice for a few moments before she could speak again. "Why did this happen to you? To us?" Closing her eyes, she leaned over, rested her face against him and sobbed. "I'll always love you, Bryer. Please, please forgive me."

Something stirred beside her. She was sure of it. Reaching out, she touched Dirk's shoulder. "Dirk, stay with me." A sob racked her throat, her voice sounding raw. "You can't die. I won't let you leave me, too. Do you hear me, Dirk? I won't let you go." She shook him, the rock in her gut hardening when he didn't moan, didn't move. But the rise and fall of his chest with each shallow breath gave her hope. "Dirk, you have to shift back to human form. I can't carry you by myself. I'm going to need your help." She waited, holding her breath, and almost fainted when he managed to nod. "Thank God, Dirk. Come on. You've got to try."

The first time he tried to change, he shifted part of the way, his ears growing shorter, fangs and claws retracting. But he couldn't keep the transformation going, instead giving up and allowing the change to reverse on its own. She framed his face with her hands. "Keep trying, Dirk. You have to try again. Please. Do it for me."

He groaned and tried again. His body shook, with the effort to shift again or from the pain, she didn't know. The change came slowly, much slower than it should have. She murmured encouragement to him, willing her energy, her strength into his torn body until, at last, he changed. He lay spread-eagle on the ground and she almost wished he hadn't succeeded. In his human body, the wounds appeared more brutal, deadlier. Nonetheless, she pushed on. "You did it, Dirk. That's great."

His skin was pale, his eyes closed, his breath coming in quick bursts as he pushed the air from his lungs. She pressed her lips against his forehead, closed her eyes and tried to send energy into him. "Dirk, damn it. You hang in there. Don't you dare leave me. Open your eyes, you good-for-nothing dog."

His eyes fluttered and she would've sworn he'd spoken. But the whisper was too faint for her to hear. She placed her ear to his mouth. "What did you say? Please, Dirk, tell me."

His voice, weak and breathy, tickled her ear. "I am not a dog."

Alex laughed, wiping the tears from her cheek. "Okay, okay. You're not a dog. But you're not going to be a dead werewolf, either." She took his arm and tugged him into a sitting position. Tearing the shreds of her clothes into strip bandages, she did her best to wrap his wounds. Yet, despite her efforts, the blood continued to seep through, making her cringe. But on she worked, hoping it would be enough.

"Can't." His head lolled to the side and his dull eyes closed, then blinked open.

"Yes you can. And you will." Alex called on her inner

werecat to gain extra strength, then lifted him so he could lean on her. "We have to get you help. Put your weight on me. All you have to do is keep moving your feet."

Together they stumbled forward and headed toward Bob Tally's ranch. Alex kept her arm around him to keep him upright and a hand on his chest to keep him from pitching forward. Placing one foot in front of the other, she kept up a continuous stream of encouragement. "That's it, Dirk. Keep moving. That's all you have to do. One step at a time." Alex renewed her grip on Dirk, keeping his weight on her.

"Don't think... Can't make it."

"Like hell you can't. I didn't use half of my clothes bandaging your wounds only to have you give up on me. I'm almost naked because of it." She batted her eyes at him, hoping he'd jump at her bait. Instead, he coughed and hung his head. "Come on, Dirk. We're almost to the ranch."

She eyed the blood-soaked bandages on his neck and tried to ignore the large red stain. If he weren't a strong werewolf, he'd have already died.

The badly injured man clung to her, groaning with each step they took. "Should have...werewolf...heal faster."

"We've already talked about this. I couldn't have carried you. At least this way you can help and we're less likely to get shot before we reach the ranch. Now shut up and concentrate on staying on your feet." She gritted her teeth, determined not to lose another person from her life. He needed more than his shifter's healing qualities to survive. He needed medical attention. "Don't give up on me, Dirk. It's not much longer. The ranch should be over this next rise."

Together, they shuffled onward. Alex kept her gaze fixed on the ground ahead of them, urging him to put one foot in front of the other. She didn't want to think any further than that, but her mind wouldn't listen. What if he died? Could she live with another loss? First Lara and Bryer, then Conner and now Dirk. No, she couldn't let it happen. She moaned, her heart aching as though a knife had sliced through it.

A shout brought her head up. The ranch house lay ahead, and three men ran toward them, calling to them. "Oh, thank God. Dirk, we made it. Dirk?"

His head hung listlessly against her and suddenly his full weight rested on her. Unable to keep him upright, she clutched him to her body and softened his fall. Kneeling next to him, she raised her hand in the air and waved to their rescuers. "Over here! Please help us."

Chapter Seven

"How's he doing?" Bob Tally peeked around the corner of the bedroom door. "And how are you holding up?"

Alex waved him inside and struggled to place a smile on her face. "He keeps coming in and out of sleep. I don't think he really knows where he is or who I am." Although she'd told the rancher several times since arriving, she needed to say it one more time. In fact, she could never say it enough. "Mr. Tally—"

"Bob."

"Right. Bob, I can't thank you enough for what you've done." They'd gotten lucky, finding their way to his ranch in time. Bob had carried Dirk inside the main house, then called for the doctor. He'd listened to her story and hadn't denied her anything, even when she'd begged him to retrieve Conner's and Bryer's bodies. She closed her eyes, letting the all-too-familiar grief spread through her. Letting it have its way was easier than fighting it. If only the images of their battered bodies would fade.

"Girl, I've told you often enough. You don't need to keep thanking me. I've known Dirk for a while. I'm thinking it's fitting that you two found your way to my home. That you thought to bring him here." Bob rubbed the back of his neck. "So, Ms. Grayson—"

"Now how many times have I told you to call me Alex? Fair's fair, Bob."

"Right enough." He chuckled, then sobered. "Alex, would you like me to contact your people for you? Tell them about..."

She didn't want to think of what had to be done until after Dirk healed. Then she'd deal with the pride and explain the deaths. But she couldn't let Bob handle it either. She owed it to Conner—and to Bryer—to handle their return home. "No thanks." She turned to him then, needing to see that he understood. "I'll take them home, but I can't leave right now. I can't, I won't leave until Dirk's better. Until then..." She shook her head. "Is there some way..." *To keep the bodies...safe?* She shuddered at the thought of their bodies lying in the cold storage room but pulled herself taller, forced herself to be stronger. Conner and the Bryer she'd loved would've understood her need to stay with Dirk.

"Don't you worry none." His eyes, so full of sympathy, wrenched her heart. "I'll make sure the bodies—" He coughed, clearing his throat. "I'll make sure your loved ones are taken care of until you're ready to go."

She sighed, thankful to have him helping her. "Bob?"

"Yes?"

"Do you think we could have a memorial service tonight? Nothing big or formal. If only to say a few prayers? Just something to say goodbye until they can be laid to rest properly." Her head had already said her goodbyes, but her heart needed more.

"Of course. I'll see to it."

She faced Dirk again, searching for any sign of recovery as she'd done many times since the doctor left. Was it her imagination or did he look less pale than before?

"Uh, Alex, there's one more thing. Some of Dirk's people have shown up. They're practically biting my head off to see him. I told them I had to ask you first and, frankly, they didn't take kindly to that idea."

"That's because asking a werecat for permission doesn't make a whole lot of sense."

Alex jumped, twisting toward the deep voice. Two men and one woman strode into the room. Their werewolf scents assaulted her nose, blocking out all other smells.

The tallest of the men came to stand beside her while his companions flanked the other side of the bed. The woman, tall and curvy, bent over Dirk, placing her hand on his forehead. "At least he's not running a fever." She arched an imperious eyebrow at Alex. Brilliant blue eyes locked on to hers. "What are you doing here?"

The challenge in the female's tone had Alex biting back a retort. Was she kidding? She was the one who should ask the questions. Forget the fact that they were werewolves. Who the hell were they to barge in and act like she was the intruder? "I'm Alex Grayson. I'm Dirk's...friend."

The short stocky shifter next to the female snorted. "Woo-hoo. Looks like Dirk found himself a pretty kitty to play with."

Alex inhaled sharply, then checked Bob's reaction. Or rather nonreaction. How could she expect him to take up for her? After all, what claim did she have on Dirk?

The handsome dark-haired shifter standing next to her lifted the sheet to examine Dirk's bandage-covered body. "Looks like Dirk got his butt whipped." Letting the sheet fall, he tilted his head at her. "I hear you're the one who brought him here."

Alex swallowed, suddenly feeling outnumbered. Thankfully, Bob flashed a quick smile, alleviating some of her anxiety.

"Not only that, but she killed the werecat that's been causing all the trouble." Bob's color drained from his face. "Oh, shit, Alex. I'm sorry. I didn't mean for it to come out like that."

Frowning, she struggled against the war raging inside. She'd stopped the trouble, making good on her promise to the council, but she'd lost her brother and her best friend.

"No shit?" The big male's scrutiny intensified. "Then I guess we owe you a bit of thanks. Of course, if your kind had controlled the rogue cat the way you should've in the first place, Dirk wouldn't have gotten hurt."

"I hardly think that's fair, Cannon."

Alex took a harder look at the tall shifter. This man wasn't simply one of Dirk's pack. He was a Cannon. An alpha.

"Can we get on with this?"

Cannon nodded at the other male werewolf. "Bronson's right. Let's get on with what we came to do. Sheila, go ahead when you're ready." Taking her by the arm, he tried to lead Alex to the door. "Thanks for everything you've done, but we'll take it from here."

"Hey, wait a sec." Alex struggled against Cannon, making him tighten his grip. She continued to protest, but it was no use. He thrust her into the hallway. She stepped toward him, running into his broad chest when he blocked the entrance. "Bob, would you explain to Ms. Grayson that she's no longer needed?"

Bob squeezed through the narrow opening Cannon gave him to pass. "Uh, I think she understands you well enough. Just let me know if you need anything."

"Will do. Oh, and thanks again for calling us, Bob." Cannon tipped his head at her in a curt dismissal and closed the door.

Alex scanned the yard through the front window, watching the hired hands take the coffins back to the storage room, her hand over her heart. "Thank you again, Bob, for the coffins. I can't believe I didn't think about that." Bob's carpenters had made the wooden coffins and the hired hands had joined them at the short service. The kind rancher had even taken over at the memorial when her grief had rendered her speechless, and led them in prayer.

Alex took a deep breath, attempting to settle her nerves. She'd cried so much in the past few days. But who could blame her? With both Conner and Bryer gone, she had no one. Shirking the inclination to wallow in self pity, she focused her thoughts on Dirk and the werewolves. Those damned werewolves who weren't letting her see him.

Bob's attempts to explain things hadn't made Alex feel any better. She paced the living room, then flopped onto the sofa to stare at the ceiling yet again. "This royally sucks."

"I know, Alex, but let his people help. They know what to do. The human doctor's done all he can. Dirk needs more help than he can give him."

"I was taking care of him and he was getting better." But when Bob looked away, she had to admit the truth. She'd done everything she could, sitting by his bedside constantly since they'd arrived, following the directions the doctor had given her, but Dirk was still in bad shape. "I can't take it. He has to live. He just has to." She sat up, hands clasped in front of her, and tried to resist begging Bob to make everything all right. If only he could.

"You've got it bad, don't you?"

"Bad?" She frowned, thrown off-kilter. "What do you mean?"

Bob arched one eyebrow in unmistakable body language. "Girl, anyone can see you love the big galoot. A blind man could see it. Even a stupid man. Hell, even a blind stupid man."

Did she love Dirk? Alex inhaled sharply, thrown by the lump in her throat and the thrill the idea gave her. Her breathing quickened with the memories flooding through her. Dirk's sexy grin. Dirk shielding her from the hunter's gun. Dirk taking care of her, comforting her. Dirk understanding how she felt, exactly what she needed. He'd shared a similar experience and had given her a friend when she'd needed that more than a lover.

And then she remembered his greatest gift. Dirk sacrificing himself to save her from her brother's attack. How could she have not known it? She did love him. She loved him with every ounce of her being. But what could she do about it when she couldn't even get near him?

She scowled at the ceiling again, listening to the footsteps above her, the sounds of the werewolves tending to one of their own. Dirk was a werewolf. She clenched her fists, wanting to hit something, someone. What was she thinking getting involved with a werewolf? Sure, sex was one thing. But to consider spending a lifetime with a werewolf? They didn't have a chance. Her people would never stand for it any more than his people would. Talk about Romeo and Juliet werecreature-style. Would their love have the same ending?

She froze, uncertainty taking hold, warning her to slow down. She didn't know if he cared for her other than as a friend. Wasn't that what he'd said? That they were friends? Friends with benefits, maybe. She huffed out her exasperation. But he had to care about her, right? After all, he'd saved her, jumped in between her and her brother. Would he have done that if he didn't love her?

She heard a thump above her, jolting her back into the here and now. "What the hell are they doing anyway?"

Bob followed her glance upward and shook his head. "I'm not sure. Although I've heard that when a werewolf is attacked by a werecat, they have to take action to counteract the werecat's bite. Something about the two blood types not mixing."

Their bloodlines wouldn't mix, meaning werecats and werewolves didn't belong together. No matter how much they cared for each other. She stared, trying to see through the ceiling with willpower alone. "What kind of action?"

229

"Again, I'm only telling you what I've heard, not what I know. But I think they have to bite him. You know, use their saliva to counteract the bite of the werecat."

She gaped at him and tried to understand what he meant. "You mean, those three werewolves are going to bite Dirk? When he's already so badly wounded?"

"Yeah, but that's the way of it. Although I think only one of them has to bite him."

"And then he'll get better?" She hated to think of Dirk getting bitten, but if a bite from a werewolf could save him, then it would be worth it. Still, a nagging worry wouldn't let go. "But wait. What if it's the female that bites him? Doesn't that mean they'll be mates?" Could she stand having Dirk mated to another if that saved his life? To save him, she could. But what if there was another way? "Does the female have to bite him? Or can one of the males do it?"

"Hell, I didn't think of the mating thing. I don't know, but I think it's usually the females that bite the wounded."

That bitch was going to bite her Dirk? Alex growled, confusion, jealousy and anger giving her courage. "Oh, no she won't. I have to make sure someone else does it." Alex whirled around and bolted for the stairs. Ignoring Bob's shout to stop, she took the steps two at a time, dove to the left and headed down the hallway. She flung her body at Dirk's bedroom door, bursting it wide open. The door slammed against the wall, surprising the three shifters. Alex paused to regain her balance, then dashed toward Dirk.

"What the hell are you doing?" Cannon caught her, slipping his arm around her waist and lifting her off her feet. Bronson whipped around from the window, snarling. Sheila, in wolf form, knelt over Dirk, her jaws open and fangs dripping.

"Keep your jaws off him!" Alex struggled in Cannon's arm but couldn't get free. "Put me down, you big mutt."

Cannon readjusted, lifting her higher like she was nothing more than a child in his arms. "What is your problem, little kitty?"

"She can't bite him. Don't let her touch him." Gnashing her teeth, Alex kicked out, hoping to strike a vulnerable body part. She pointed at the surprised Bronson. "You bite him. Not her!"

Sheila, a bemused look on her face, ran her tongue over her teeth. She whined, then lowered her head until her sharp fangs were less than an inch from Dirk's shoulder.

"Can we get on with this, Cannon, or do we have to wait for you and the kitty to play tag first?" Bronson plopped into a nearby armchair, boredom etched on his features.

"Cannon, damn you. Put me on my feet."

"I don't think so. Let's let Sheila finish her business first." He waved a hand at the werewolf, signaling for her to get to work. "Go on, girl."

Sheila nodded once, then opened her mouth wide.

"No!" Wrenching free at last, Alex fell to the floor, landing on her hands and knees. She scrambled away from Cannon, keeping low until she reached the end of the bed. Jumping on the comforter, Alex screamed and hurled her body at Sheila. She struck the werewolf on the side, knocking hard against the werewolf's lean body, but she was too late. Sheila's teeth sank into Dirk's shoulder.

"No." Her anguished whisper was harsh, filled with loss. Her strength left her, taking away none of the horror. Lying on her side next to Sheila, Alex took a steadying breath and faced the awful reality. Sheila was Dirk's mate now.

And still Sheila held on. Dirk's body jerked beneath Alex, thrashing, unconsciously trying to free himself from Sheila's hold. Alex, too exhausted to move, didn't resist Cannon as he lifted her off the bed and sat her in the other chair. She kept her eyes on Dirk, his body growing calm again until at last

Sheila released him. Wiping her bloodied mouth against the bed linens, the female werewolf shifted back to full human form, losing her fangs. "Umm, umm, good. Dirk is one tasty puppy."

"Damn you." Alex wanted to say more but couldn't find the energy. She'd lost him. Before she'd ever had him, she'd already lost him.

"Man, I knew werecats were weird, but this one is super freaky."

She'd had enough. All the anguish, all the horror of the past days caught up with her, sending her into a rage. She flung her body at the shifter and wound up once again squirming in Cannon's arms.

Cannon carried her to the door. "Shut up, Bronson. Something else is going on." In the hallway, he slammed the door and studied her. Moving his face nearer to Alex's, he examined her like a bug under a microscope. "Is this what I think it is, little kitty? Do you like Dirk?" He grinned, reminding her of Dirk's wicked smile. "I mean, do you likey-likey our little Dirky?"

Alex blinked, words of denial on her lips that wouldn't come out. "Will he live?" If she couldn't have Dirk, then at least she'd know he was safe. Even if that meant he was mated to that she-hound. "Will her bite heal him?"

"It will."

"Are you sure?"

His chuckle irritated her. "I'm sure. But I'm also sure that there's something going on between you two. More than fun sex, that is."

She blinked again and tried to hide her reaction. "I owe Dirk my life. That's all."

"Oh, little kitty, don't try to fool a fooler like me. You're lying. But lie away. I don't care. Still, I've never known a werecat and werewolf to fall in love."

She shook her head, afraid to admit to him that she loved Dirk. Could her love cause trouble for him?

His tone hard, he added, "It can't work, you know. It won't work." Taking hold of her, he guided her down the hall. "For your own sake, little kitty, leave and don't come back."

Alex refused to leave. The werewolves could keep her out of Dirk's room, but they couldn't run her off. Not until she was sure he would recover. Instead, she sat by the edge of the bubbling stream behind the main house and watched the window of Dirk's room. She held her head high and her back straight, determined to face the dismal future the best way she could.

Losing Conner and Bryer had torn a hole in her, a hole that might never be filled. But the fact that she'd lost Dirk, too, had destroyed her. He was mated to the she-werewolf now and she could do nothing about it. A boulder lodged in her chest, making it difficult to breathe, but she had no more tears to shed. What was done was done. Yet until she could see that Dirk was all right, she'd stay.

How had this happened? How had her brother, her friend and the man she loved been taken away from her? Didn't she deserve love? She swallowed, closing her eyes to steel herself against the sorrow. Once Dirk was healed, she'd take Conner's and Bryer's bodies back to her people, then go out on her own. How could she stay with the pride when everything reminded her of hopes now dead? The agonizing questions pounded her, leaving her shaking and cold despite the warm sun.

If only things had gone differently. If only she'd told Dirk what he meant to her before Bryer's attack. Sitting on a rock by the stream, she'd rehearsed what she wanted to tell him, but she no longer had the right. Maybe if she said the words out loud, she'd get them out of her system, freeing her to move on.

"Dirk, we need to talk." She shook her head, hating the cliché phrase. Gathering her thoughts, she tried again. "Dirk, I need to tell you something." She could almost see his mischievous grin and feigned a halfhearted giggle. "Dirk, for once, stay quiet and listen, okay?"

"But I haven't said anything yet."

"Oh, shit." She spun toward Dirk and placed her hand on her chest. "Damn it. Are you trying to scare me to death?"

Dirk, pale and unsteady on his feet, chuckled, then winced at the pain. "I think I'm the one closest to death."

She couldn't help returning his grin. "You can say that again." Hurrying to him, she led him to a nearby rock. She wanted to slip her arms around him but settled for taking his hands. "Hey, it's good to have you back."

"It's good to be back." Dirk glanced around the area. "We made it to Bob's place. Although I don't remember too much after getting my ass kicked by your—"

He slammed his mouth shut and gave her an apologetic look. "I'm sorry about Conner, Alex. And Bryer, too. Look, if there had been any other way... If you'd had any other choice... He would've killed you, too, you know."

She pressed a palm to his cheek. "I know. It's all right. Or at least it will be. Besides, you're not the one who..."

"I can't begin to imagine how hard that must've been for you."

She choked back a sob and her throat closed up. Would she ever get over having to kill her brother? Even if she'd done it to save Dirk? "Are the others gone?"

"You mean Cannon and the rest?" Dirk glanced toward the house. "Yeah. They weren't too happy about my asking them to leave, but I couldn't stand another minute in that room. I had to find you. I had to make sure you were all right. Especially after what happened."

The silence that filled the space between them wasn't strained. Instead, she remained quiet, letting his nearness soothe her, taking comfort by laying her head on his shoulder. Nothing else mattered except him.

"Alex, you said you needed to tell me something. What is it?"

Her tranquility shattered and she took a deep breath, hopefully bringing in courage along with the air. She sat up and wiped away a tear. "Yes. I did." She wanted to go on, but her mouth wasn't listening to her head.

"And?"

Suddenly, she could no longer meet his gaze. Instead she turned to the creek and fervently wished she'd kept her mouth closed. What made her think he cared for her? Just because she loved him didn't mean he had to love her back. In fact, she wouldn't have blamed him if he didn't. A werecat falling for a werewolf. Talk about delusional.

"I repeat. And?" He bent lower so he could see her face. "If you know nothing else about me, Alex, you know you can trust me. Tell me what's on your mind."

She did trust him, trusted him with her life. But could she trust him with her love? She searched his face and wanted to reach out to touch the stubble on his cheek. "I wanted to tell you that..." Again, her tongue stopped working even as her brain shouted at her to get it over with.

"Yeah, we've established that you wanted to tell me something." He chuckled, then winced again. "I don't suppose you were going to tell me the doc left more pain pills. I sure could use a couple right now."

"I don't know, but I'll check with Bob." Saved by the pills. "So you're feeling better? And Sheila's bite helped?" The female werewolf's face came to her, but she shoved the image away.

"Alex, you're driving me crazy. Speak your mind so I can say what I need to say."

Did he want to tell her that he'd taken a mate? Anger coursed through her, fueled by the cruel blows life had given her. She steeled her resolve and prepared for the pain he might cause her. All she had to do was tell him that she loved him and then she could leave, hopefully without her tail between her legs. "Fine. I'm going to say what I have to say. But don't think you have to say anything back. In fact, it might be a good thing if you don't."

"O-kay. If that's what you want."

She shot him a glare. He quickly pantomimed zipping his lips. "Good. So I'm just going to blurt this out. Dirk Claxton, I love you." With the words spoken, she stood and paced away from him. She stopped with her back to him, unable to maintain eye contact yet unable to leave.

"Alex."

"No. Don't say anything. I know what I said is ridiculous. I mean, we haven't known each other very long. And the idea of a werecat and werewolf becoming romantically involved is ludicrous. Sex is one thing, but love? Pff. What a joke."

"Alex."

"All I wanted was to let you know. That's all. I don't expect you to have the same feelings for me that I have for you. So now that I've said what I wanted to say, I'll get out of your hair. I'm happy you're doing better, Dirk. Have a great life." She was halfway to the main house when he called for her, his tone gruff and commanding.

"Come back here, Alex. Don't make me chase after you."

She ground her teeth, fought back a retort and got ready to face him. Holding her head high, she slowly turned toward him and thrust out her chin. "What do you want?" What more could he want from her when she'd already given him her heart? His face, however, was unreadable.

"Would you come back here, please? I haven't had my say yet."

She groaned to release a lot of pent-up anxiety, stuck her chin higher and trudged over to him. "Do you need something other than pills? Do you want me to get Bob?"

He took her hand and she smothered back a gasp. She'd had her life turned upside down, but would he say something to make it worse?

"You're a fool, Alex Grayson."

Chapter Eight

Alex may have spilled her guts to a man who didn't love her back, but that didn't mean she'd let him put her down. "Okay, I gotta admit it. That wasn't what I was expecting. But gee, thanks for your opinion." She jerked her hand away. "I'm sure you'll understand if I don't stick around to listen to you call me names. Let's pretend this little confession of mine never happened."

"Will you stop flapping your yap for a second? I think you're a fool because anyone who would want me has to be a fool."

What? Alex studied him, unsure what he meant. A glimmer of hope flickered in her heart. "I don't understand."

"It's a good thing you're beautiful, Alex, because at the moment you're acting pretty dumb."

"Hey, watch it." The fact that he'd called her beautiful kept the anger from rising. Instead, she tried to move away, but he grabbed her, pulling her close. He took both her wrists and held her in place.

"I'm kidding. Sheesh, how can you love a man and not know he's a kidder? All I can say is that it's a good thing I love you, too. Otherwise, you'd be in a shitload of embarrassment right now."

"Let go— Wait. What did you say?" She took a couple of deep breaths, trying to slow down her pounding heart. "Did you say you love me, too?" Although his eyes sparkled with humor, the sincerity she saw made her hold her breath. Could it be true? Did he really love her? She narrowed her eyes. "Are you serious? Or is this one of your jokes?"

"Let me give you an answer you'll understand better than words." Placing his palms on her cheeks, he brought her lips to his. The kiss, soft and yet possessive, lingered, mixing his breath with hers. Alex leaned against him and the kiss deepened, his tongue skimming the inside of her mouth. She sucked, drawing in the special flavor that was all Dirk. He groaned and held her tighter, one hand locked onto the small of her back, the other cupping her buttocks. She clasped the back of his neck, rejoicing in the love they shared. She believed the love in his kiss and sighed.

"Dirk, take me. Make me yours."

He panted, his breathing labored and made a face. "Damn, I can't. But God knows I want to."

She brushed her tongue lightly across his lips. "Then do what you want to do." Running her hands gently along his shoulders, she reveled in her man's physique. "Don't you want to show me how much you love me? To prove it to me?

"I do. I really do."

Following the path of her hands skimming down his chest with her kisses, she murmured against the hollow of his neck. "Then do it."

He tensed, breaking their kiss and, although he tried to hide it, she saw the wince he made. She broke away from him. "Oh, hell, I'm sorry. I wasn't thinking. I got so horny that I forgot about everything else except wanting you." She gingerly placed her hands on his chest.

"You're horny and I can't do anything about it. Aw, hell, now I'm going to die for sure."

Alex laughed, then put on a sexy expression. "Hey, I have

an idea. Maybe you can't do much, but I can." Taking his hand, she led him into the house and up the stairs to the bedroom she'd slept in.

Standing by the bed, she patted the comforter, welcoming him to sit. "You lie back, enjoy and let me handle everything."

He licked his lips and glanced toward his private parts. "Handle away, sugar." Alex walked enticingly to the end of the bed and he grinned at her, the expectation in his face lighting his features. "Take it off, Alex. I want to see your smokin' body while you do whatever it is you're going to do."

She tugged her T-shirt out of her jeans and smiled coquettishly. "Like you don't know what I'm about to do." Swaying to unheard music, she continued to move her shirt over her stomach, gliding it over her breasts, taking her time with each movement.

"Damn, girl, but you are hot."

"Yeah? How hot?" She whipped the shirt over her head and tossed it at him. Taking her breasts, she rubbed her thumbs over her nipples, peaking them.

"Blazing hot." He raised his gaze from her breasts to her face. "Hot enough to be my mate."

She froze. "Mate?" She crossed her arms over her breasts, suddenly feeling vulnerable. "Oh, no. I forgot about that. About her."

"Hey, don't cover up. What's wrong? You forgot about who?"

"Your mate, of course."

Dirk's jaw dropped and he gaped at her. "My what?"

"Your mate. Sheila." Why did he look so confused? "You remember Sheila, don't you? The she-werewolf that bit you? Come on. You know what I'm talking about. She bit you, thus saving your life and making you her mate." Repeating what she said wasn't helping but she couldn't find the right words to make him understand.

"I remember Sheila, all right. And I know she bit me." Dirk placed his hand on the teeth marks already healing on his shoulder. "But she's not my mate. No way."

Alex dropped her arms, exposing herself, but she was too excited to care. "Sheila's not your mate?"

"I don't know what else I can say, Alex. She's not my mate." He leaned back, his eyes growing bigger. "Oh, I get it now. You thought her biting me made us mates."

"Well, yeah. I mean, that's what I've always heard." She moved to sit next to him and he took her hand. Her heart beat wildly, but she kept the hope she felt from her face.

"And you're an expert on werewolves and their mating customs, right?" He grinned at her, at once making her feel better and mocking her.

"Isn't that how it works?"

"It can. But that kind of bite is a different kind of bite. Sheila bit me to give me some of her energy, not to make me her mate." He narrowed his eyes, searching her. "Do you understand?"

"I think so." Alex relaxed next to him, relief flooding through body. "If I had any more tears in me, I'd cry."

He slipped an arm around her. "Why would you cry?"

She brought her head up to stare into his amazing blue eyes. "For once, I'd cry out of happiness. Because you not mated to Sheila means that maybe, just maybe, I haven't lost you, too."

"Ain't no maybe about it, sugar. I'm all yours." His gaze bored into her. "If you'll have me, that is. And more than as a lover and friend. As a mate."

Alex bit her lip and squeezed his hand, bringing his gaze to hers. "I'd like that. But with you being a werewolf and me being a werecat... You know it won't be easy."

"I know. But I don't care, Alex. As long as you're beside me, I don't care what the rest of them think." His brow furrowed as a cloud passed over his features. "Of course, if you don't want to go down that road, I'll understand. I won't like it, but I'll accept your decision."

Alex let a soft smile play on her lips. "We'll need to talk it through to figure out how to handle everything." She lowered her gaze to the bulge under the sheet. "But let's talk after."

His sexy grin returned. "Agreed. After."

She helped him undress, taking care not to hurt him. Swallowing her nervousness, she struggled to keep the slice of ache in her stomach from showing on her face. Although she'd seen most of his wounds, had dressed them, the amount of bandages covering his body still rattled her. Bruises covered what few areas weren't covered in bandages.

"Oh, Dirk." She closed her eyes, then opened them and hoped he'd see the plea for forgiveness in them. "My brother did this to you and I couldn't stop it soon enough. I am so sorry."

"No, Alex, it's not your fault. And it looks worse than it feels. Besides, let's not talk about what happened. The time for all that is later. Right now I don't want to think about anything except you."

Slipping onto the bed, she kissed the bruises on his legs and traveled toward the hard pole looming ahead. "Let me help heal your wounds." Until he healed, she'd be the one to show him how much she loved him. They had time enough for the other way round.

"Anything you say, Nurse Kitty."

For once she didn't laugh. She was too focused on taking care not to press against his injuries. Gently, she took his shaft and laid the tip of his mushroomed cap against her cheek.

"Who knew someone so tough could have such a soft spot. And I'm not talking about your heart."

"Ooh, pretty lady, you are one big tease."

"Am I? Or am I merely enjoying the moment of anticipation?" He moaned and spread his legs farther apart. Squeezing him with care, she wrapped her hand around his cock and curved the palm of her other hand to cup his balls. He moaned and lifted his head to watch.

"Alex, if you don't put me inside your mouth soon, I'm going to go crazy."

"Man, you werewolves don't have much control, do you?"

"I'll show you who has control."

He reached for her, but she batted his hands away. "Cut it out or I'll have to stop."

"No, for the love of shifters everywhere, don't stop."

Sliding her hand down, she massaged him from tip to base. His huge shaft, curved for a woman's pleasure, twitched in response.

"Easy, boy." A crashing roll of desire shot through her, wetting her pussy. Cautioning herself to go slowly, she flicked her tongue over his oozing cap and struggled not to deep-throat him. "I love you, Dirk. Every inch of you. From the very first moment I saw you, I wanted to have you."

His agonized moan thrilled her. Not only did it make her feel powerful, she delighted in the pleasure she gave him. With a sigh, she circled her tongue around the weeping tip, then slowly inched him inside her mouth. A multitude of flavors touched her tongue and she sucked, bringing them to the back of her throat.

"Ummm." He tasted like the forest wind. Like the hot sun on the back of her neck. If she could have him for the rest of her life, she'd never tire of his taste.

He took her hair in his hands, holding her to him. She moved up and down, sliding her tongue along his shaft, then back again. She lapped him up, released him and started over. Dirk groaned and let go of her hair to grip the sheet. His cock grew impossibly larger, longer. His life's essence pulsated in her palm, warming, wetting her skin.

"Get on top of me."

She refused, letting her "no" flow warm air over his dick. No way would she risk hurting him. Instead, she bounced his balls between her fingers and renewed her attack on his shaft. At first he protested, but his complaints soon turned to appreciative moans that made her even wetter, hotter. His shaft was a hot brand against her palm, a brand she wanted to burn into her skin. Inhaling, she took in his raw masculine scent and committed it to memory. This was her mate. No matter what anyone said about the two of them, he was the one for her.

She fingered her pulsing nub, rubbing harder and harder until the engorged nub throbbed mercilessly. Continuing to work her finger, she matched one hand's movement with the other, massaging herself as she pumped him. She blew on him and he jerked, giving her the gratification of knowing she thrilled him. Licking his tip, she lazily slid her tongue down his rod, slurping in the slick mix of his pre-come and her saliva.

"You're driving me crazy, Alex."

She chuckled, using her breath to flush warm air over him and loving the way his shaft answered. "I seriously doubt that." His growl sent shivers of lust through her.

"Please get on top before I explode in your hand."

She closed her eyes, the image of him shooting hot milk sending her over the edge. She came, her body's river flushing over her fingers. Trembling with the cascading climax, she dived back onto him, relentless in her determination to bring him to the brink.

"Holy shit, woman."

Yes, she was his woman and he was her man. Sucking, she bobbed up and down, working him with her hand and her mouth. Her tongue lashed at him, pressing against the rise of the veins, licking every taste from him.

"Oooh, I'm going to come. Damn, Alex, get on top."

She ignored his request again and readied for his climax. He groaned, tensed and then let out a savage cry, gripping her hair harder, holding her in place. Enjoying his possession of her, she took him in. His body shook, quaking under her command until at last he let out a long sigh and relaxed.

"I wish you'd done as I asked."

She slid over his leg to crawl into the curve of his arm. Resting a hand to ride with the fall and rise of his chest, she played with his nipples. "Are you telling me you didn't enjoy what I did?"

He laughed and kissed her forehead. "Hardly. But I wanted to do so much more to you."

"Don't worry. Once you're healed and back to your studly self, I'll let you make it up to me."

"Hey, is everything all right in there?"

Alex grabbed the sheet and tugged it over their bodies. She hoped Bob wouldn't open the door. "Uh-oh. We must've gotten too loud."

"Yeah, Bob, we're good." Dirk wiggled his eyebrows at her and whispered, "Damn good in fact."

"Oh, okay. Good to know. I heard someone yell and... Oh, uh, never mind. Sorry to have disturbed you."

"No problem, Bob. We'll see you in bit."

Alex snuggled against Dirk. "I can't tell you how great Bob's been."

"Yeah, he's a good friend to the pack. To most

werecreatures." Dirk fingered a strand of her hair. "Speaking of the pack, what are we going to do about us?"

Suddenly, the fantasy spell she'd been under broke loose. "Boy, who knew later would come so soon? But you're right. We need to talk and now's as good a time as any." She twined her fingers with his, needing to feel his skin against hers. "Have you ever heard of a werecat and a werewolf mating before?"

"No. I've heard of them having sex of course. But actually mating? Can't say I have."

She sighed, hating to think about the problems that their union presented. "My pride will never accept you as my mate." There. She'd said it.

"I figured as much. And I don't know what my pack will do. Oh, sure, they've accepted humans before but that was because they became pack soon enough. Unfortunately, I can't change you into a werewolf."

"And I can't change you into a werecat."

They lay together for a while, each deep in thought, until Alex broached another problem. "Even if our people could learn to accept us, we still have the problem of children. Is it possible for us to have children? Would you want children?" Dirk stroked her hair and she relaxed a little with the comforting touch.

"Yeah, I think I'd like to have a child or two. But we definitely can't do it in our animal forms. That'd be like a dog mating with a housecat. Still, I don't know about the other way round. Maybe if you stayed in your human form after conceiving? I'm sorry, but I don't have a clue."

She lifted onto her elbow to study him. "Then what are we going to do?"

Chapter Nine

"Alex, stop fussing over me. I'm fine." Dirk repositioned the backpack over his shoulder. "I'll be damned if I'll let you carry the load."

She rolled her eyes but allowed him to have his way. "Fine, Mr. Macho Wolfie, take it. I always wanted a pack mule, but I guess you'll have to do." They'd left the pride two hours earlier, hefting the backpack filled with the provisions her friends had given her, and were making good progress. Returning Conner's and Bryer's bodies to her people had reopened the wounds their deaths had left her, but she'd wanted to see them home and laid to rest. After a week of scornful glances, muttered remarks and even blatant rudeness, she'd accepted what she'd known all along: Dirk would never be fully welcomed to live with her people. To Dirk's credit, he'd handled it all with his usual brand of humor, but she'd seen the relief on his face the moment they'd left.

His scowl turned into his sexy grin. "Good. I'm glad you understand your place, woman."

"Uh-oh. Do not tell me you dared to use that term."

He sidestepped her jab at his arm. "Hey, you didn't mind it when I called you that during sex."

She picked up the pace and took the lead. "That's different."

"Right. Different. Not."

Alex had gone half a mile before he finally called out to her, telling her to hold up. She pivoted to face him, checking him for any signs of fatigue although he'd recuperated from his injuries and had no lingering problems. "Yeah. Why are we stopping?"

"Because, my sweet little pussy—" his grin grew bigger, "—do you know where you're going?"

She blinked at him, suddenly aware of her mistake. Not thinking, she'd started in the direction that led to his pack. "Oh. I, uh..."

He ran his hand behind her neck to pull her in for a quick kiss. "I thought we decided that the city was the only place we could go. Are you changing your mind about living with the humans? Because you know my pack isn't going to welcome you—hell, me—with open arms."

She shook her head and couldn't meet his eyes. She'd gladly given up her family, her people for him, but it still hurt to think they wouldn't have a home with either of their kind. "Not at all. I guess I thought that maybe..." She eyed him. "Are you still certain of your choice?"

"Definitely. I happen to like humans." In a flash, his cockiness was gone. "Besides, I would go anywhere, live anywhere with you. You're my life, my family now, Alex."

The knot in her throat was filled with the emotion she saw in his eyes. Damn, but he was great with words. Great at sex, too. "What do you think the pack will say when they find out? Because you know they'll find out eventually."

"I think Cannon knew my decision back at Bob's when I ignored his command to stay in bed." He slipped the burden to the ground and rolled his shoulders. "But I don't care what they'll say. If I know the Cannon brothers, they'll come around. In time and especially if we have kids."

"We don't know that we can have kids, remember?" She

ignored the twinge in her abdomen at the mention of children. Why keep bringing up the subject when there was no way for them to have children?

"Sure, I remember. But we don't know if we can have kids as humans, do we? I've been thinking. I know a doctor in the city who might be able to help us answer that question. In the meantime..."

A flare of heat replaced the twinge. "In the meantime, what?"

He lifted her off her feet, gently taking her to the ground. "In the meantime, we can sure as hell practice making one."

Her clothes were off seconds after his lay strewn on the ground around them. He kissed her neck, then skimmed his way along the slope of her shoulder to the valley between her breasts. She tunneled her fingers through his hair and moved his tongue over her aching nipples. "Tease them, Dirk. Make them hard."

He complied, sucking then nipping them. She squirmed, already feeling the warmth of her wetness moistening the cleft between her legs. Pushing her breasts together, she held him, enjoying the way his moans tickled her skin.

He lifted his gaze, showering her with unspoken love, then thrust his tongue into her mouth. She cupped his neck, capturing him, and sighed, reveling in his touch. Sucking, he rolled his tongue around hers, causing a shudder of delight to course through her. He was the one she'd waited for. From the moment their eyes met, her body had known, giving her brain and heart time to catch up.

Their bodies moved together, melting together under the hot sun. He pressed his leg between hers, opening her wider, and she happily responded. Using his leg, he rubbed against her, spreading her juices. She pushed back and rocked, needing more. Sighing, she ran her hands down his hard back, his flexing muscles moving her hands up and down.

She looked skyward, squinted against the bright light and longed for a shooting star to make a wish on, hoping to stay as they were at that moment forever. Too soon, they would have to find their way in the human world. Conner and Bryer were gone, but she still had friends, people she cared about in the pride. Could she face never seeing them again? Would she make friends among the humans?

Fear of what lay ahead churned at her gut, but she refused to let it take hold. Somehow with Dirk's help, she'd make a new home in the city. If they could survive everything they'd been through, then they could handle whatever came next. Skating her fingers down his arms, she concentrated on thrusting her hips against his groin. His kisses blazed a trail down her skin and into the hollow of her neck. She tilted her head, showing her throat, and he answered with a low rumble against her skin. The sound, so wild, pulled at the animal within her. She clutched him, suddenly afraid of losing him.

"Dirk. My Dirk." She hoped those simple words would relay the depth of her emotions. Emotions too strong for her to find the right thing to say.

He lashed at her breasts, lessening the force of his leg against her. Moaning, he slid his fingers between her folds. He stroked her, using her movements to increase the pressure on her nub, catching her between his fingers. Exquisite pain exploded within her.

"Uhhh." She dug her fingernails into his back, raking into him, drawing blood. Although she knew the wounds would heal, they'd leave a faint scar, warning others to stay clear of her mate. Another climax erupted, leaving her breathless. "Please, Dirk, now."

Ignoring her, he slipped two fingers inside her, then out, bringing her sweet moistness with them. Continuing the exquisite torment, he rubbed his thumb against her hot nub and plunged his other fingers into her. She cried out as yet another release swept over her and she clung to him for support. His chuckle drifted over her.

"Stop laughing and put your mouth where your fingers are."

"You are such a bossy little kitty, aren't you? Good thing I like bossy women." He feathered kisses in between her breasts, stopping for a quick lick at each nipple, then down the soft mound of her stomach. He took his time, teasing her, working her until she had to grit her teeth to keep from shouting at him to hurry.

"Now it's my turn to order you around. Spread 'em wider."

She did, eager to have his tongue on the most sensitive part of her body. Tormenting her again, he took his time, moving slowly over the ticklish skin on the inside of her leg. Biting, sucking, he inched closer to his goal.

She growled her frustration.

Giving her one of those grins that made her insides turn to hot lava, he ran his hands up her legs and stopped, pressing his thumbs at the creases. "Ready?"

"Are you frickin' kidding me? Dirk, I swear, if you don't— Oh, hell, yes!"

He parted her lips and raked his tongue over her sensitive nub. She inhaled sharply, instinctively shifting to bring out her claws, and dug into him. He yelped, then plunged down again, licking her harder and faster. Her cries flowed into loud moans, encouraging him. "Dirk, damn, please. Take me now."

Instead, he buried his face between her legs and intensified his sucking. He tugged her aching clit inside, then let it go, following the brief reprieve with a lash of his tongue. She tensed, every fiber in her readying for her climax. She screamed as it pummeled outward, spreading into her arms and legs, tremors shaking her from head to toe.

And still he took her. Faster, harder, he attacked her swollen nub, bringing her to an even higher height.

When she could breath evenly again, she commanded, "My turn, Dirk."

He lifted his gaze to hers and, catching her off guard, scrambled around, keeping his face at her pussy and putting his dick directly above her head. She reached out with her tongue and touched the tip of his cock. Sweet pre-come dripped off the end onto her mouth. She licked her lips, enjoying the taste of him. He tasted so right. But she wanted more.

She grabbed his buttocks, lowering him, and blew on the mushroomed top. He moaned and answered by taking her sweet nub and surrounding skin into his mouth. She opened her mouth and took in the top of him.

"Oh, shit, Alex. Take more."

Fondling his balls with one hand, she took his shaft in the other and started stroking him. His shaft twitched, throbbing his pleasure. She swallowed him in with one quick motion and heard his delighted shout. Running her tongue first one way, then the other, she dragged him in and out, wanting to give him every ounce of passion she had inside her. Panting, he let her pussy go and groaned.

"I'm coming, Alex." He pushed his cock farther into her mouth. "Argh!"

She almost choked, but took a deep breath and kept him, taking as much as she could.

"Alex, no. I don't want to come. Not yet."

She changed to a different rhythm, pulling on him, then letting him slowly slide out. Slowly, she inched him into her mouth until his cock's tip pushed at the back of her throat.

He lifted his ass, taking his cock away, and spun around to face her. Capturing her mouth, his tongue wrestled with hers, challenging her, playing with her. She tasted her juices mixed

252

with his and pulled on his tongue, taking every drop. He lifted away and she clutched at him, trying to bring him back.

"I want you, Alex." His voice was heavy with need.

She held back a tear. "You have me. And I want you just as much."

Dirk licked her shoulder, nibbling at the soft flesh of her throat. "If you were human, I'd bite you to make you mine."

"Then bite me."

He lifted away from her, studied her face and asked, "But what good would it do? You'd still be a werecat. Our blood doesn't mix."

"I know. Still, one day, I'd love it if you could bite me." She flattened her hand over her heart. "But it's okay. You've already marked me where it really counts."

He touched her face, then added a quick lick to her earlobe. "And you're already my mate in my heart. That's all that matters."

A strange expression filled his features, one combining love, desire and something more she couldn't identify. Roaring, he shoved inside her, sliding her body upward. Her body rocked with the pounding of his dick and she wrapped her legs around him. Together their bodies moved, their sweat slicking them together as though they were one, the heat of their bodies matching that of the sun overhead.

"Oh, Dirk, yes!"

He gripped her butt, sped up and pumped into her faster, deeper, longer. Her vaginal walls wrapped around him, clenching and unclenching with each of his moves. He filled her completely, tightly as though they'd been made for each other. Her legs shook, weakened by her efforts to keep up and the many orgasms thundering through her. Her panting breaths kept time with his. When his body tensed, she was ready and tightened the muscles of her cave, seizing him, possessing him completely.

Shockwaves of climax rippled through her, traveling into him, calling for his own climax. Answering, he roared his release, earthquakes of desire shaking his strong frame.

He collapsed next to her, breathing heavily. Gathering her into his arms, he placed a quick kiss on her forehead. "That was incredible."

"Yeah. I think I'm going to need to rest a bit before we get moving again."

"Agreed."

They lay quiet for several minutes, each lost in thought and the comfort of the other's arms. At last, as the sun started its descent, Alex turned on her side and searched his face. "So we're really going to do this?" She touched his mouth, then looked into his eyes.

"Do you mean living in the city? Or being mates?"

"Both, of course. Why would we do one without the other?"

"Never mind. I guess my brain's not quite recovered from the sex yet. You know. As in mind-blowing sex." He sat up, taking her with him. "Tell me again, Alex. Are you really ready to leave everything behind? Are you ready to take the chance that we won't be accepted anywhere, even in the city among the humans?"

She took his hands and pulled them against her heart. "With you, I'm ready for anything."

The relief on his face almost broke her heart. Had he really doubted her? "Then I guess we'd better get to town. We've got a whole new life ahead of us. And, sugar, I can't wait to get started."

She nodded, keenly aware of the dangers that lay ahead, and gathered her clothes. Once dressed, he took her hand and turned toward the setting sun.

About the Author

To learn more about Beverly Rae, please visit www.beverlyrae.com. Send an email to Beverly at info@beverlyrae.com or join her Yahoo! group to join in the fun with other readers as well as Beverly! http://groups.yahoo.com/group/Beverly_Rae_Fantasies/.

Wanted: One wild man. Domesticated males need not apply.

Dance on the Wilde Side
© *2009 Beverly Rae*
Cannon Pack, Book 2

Veterinarian Tala Wilde has always had a fascination for wolves—and a secret longing for a wild man. Her fantasies are so powerful she finds herself howling at the moon and dancing in its light.

Still, when she catches just such a man breaking into her clinic to free the canines, she wonders if finding the man of her dreams is a little too much reality for comfort. Is he half animal...or just half crazy? Should she howl along with him? Or howl for help?

Devlin Cannon never wanted a mate—until he answers Tala's innocent call. Even when he wakes up trapped in one of her dog runs with a rump full of buckshot, he knows the shapely vet is destined to be his. Trouble is, not only is she not a shifter, she doesn't even know they exist. Luckily, the sexual sparks they strike together soon lure her into his arms—and entice her inner animal out to play.

But before he can claim her for his own, they'll have to survive the hunters already hot on his trail, who are ready to skin them both alive...

Warning: Definitely not for the tame at heart. Do you like your sex missionary style and predictable? Then don't read this book. However, if you like hot sex with bites and licks all over, release the animal within yourself and read on.

Available now in ebook and print from Samhain Publishing.

Enjoy the following excerpt for Dance on the Wilde Side:

He struggled to keep the animal inside from showing in his eyes, on his face. But oh, how the animal wanted his mate. "Don't worry. I'm going to make you scream, Tala." He gently brushed a strand of hair away from her face. "I want you to scream my name."

A raw rumble rolled in his throat and he moved to lie on top of her again, to rub against her and luxuriate in the feel of her. The heat in her expression drove him wild and he thrust his hands into her long hair, securing her head in place. His tongue attacked her mouth, wanting to possess all her tastes, all her essence. As he rubbed, she whimpered, a whimper of need and urgency, pushing him to the edge of reason. "Are you ready to scream, Tala?"

Her eyes narrowed, but she nodded, her panted breaths making her breasts bounce to their rhythm. "We'll see who screams first."

Ah, a challenge. And just the type of challenge I love. Grabbing her hands, he pulled her arms above her head and held them with one hand. She paused, motionless, as a flicker of alarm crossed her face. He ignored the hurt her look gave him. "Tala. You know you can trust me. Still, if you want me to stop..." *Don't make me stop.*

"Yeah, I know. But can you trust me?" An answering determination sparkled in her eyes and she bucked, trying to break free of his hold. The harder she fought, the tighter he held her, the brighter the shine in her eyes became.

An amused delight pumped his blood faster. "So you want to play rough, huh?"

She gritted her teeth and bucked, trying to throw him from her, a grin spreading over her beautiful face. At the sight of her sweating and fighting against him, the power of the animal within him rose, threatening his tenuous hold. Fangs grew and he battled to keep from shifting. "Damn, woman, you're strong."

"Not sure you can handle me? Come on, Devlin. Show me what you've got."

He renewed his hold on her and, using his other hand, guided his shaft between her folds, just far enough to torment her. "Do you want me, Tala?"

She giggled. "Do you want me, Devlin?"

They laughed together this time and he knew he'd met his match in more than one way. His lips came down on hers and he tasted the muskiness of his pre-come. His abdomen tightened with the taste and the smell, and the wolf inside roared his need. Holding himself, he moved his cock against her clit, working it around her, over her.

She tensed, the passion showing on her face.

"Scream for me, Tala."

"No." She panted the word, adding evidence to what he already knew. The corners of her mouth tipped upward, beckoning him to kiss them. "Make—" *pant,* "—me."

He dragged his tongue over those taunting lips, nibbling and sucking. He rubbed his dick against her, harder, enjoying the wetness spreading between her legs and onto him. "Don't mind if I do."

Pushing her legs farther apart with his own, he moved onto his knees and braced against her. Her face lit up with anticipation. God, how he loved her expressions. He lifted her legs, positioned his dick and slammed into her. She grunted from the impact and wrapped her legs around him.

"Oh, damn, Devlin. Fuck me." Wild eyes met his, demanding more from him.

He found her nipple and sucked, matching his sucks to the

pounding he gave her, his hips lunging faster with each thrust. She arched to meet him, urging him to take her, possess her. Her pussy enclosed him, wrapping her hot wetness around him, tightening every time he drove into her, releasing when he slid back out.

She's so tight. So wet. She feels so good, so hot, so...mine. He closed his eyes, fighting against the inevitable, trying to make the sweet ecstasy last.

At least until he won the challenge. "Scream my name, Tala. Scream it so everyone will hear you."

She squirmed, trying to break free of his hand holding hers. Soft mews of lust murmured from her, thrilling him more than he could have imagined.

"Scream my name."

Just as he was sure he couldn't hold on much longer, he heard her whisper. "Devlin."

He opened his eyes and almost lost his grip on what little control he had left. The look of desire, want, need...of love...in her eyes stirred him to the core. He couldn't imagine his life without her. "Louder. Don't just say my name. Shout it like you mean it."

She panted, gasping with each lunge as they rocked together on the bed. "Devlin." She said it louder, with meaning.

"More." He let go of her arms and parted her folds to pinch her clit. She jerked, another orgasm racking her body. "Scream."

Throwing her head back, she flattened her hands on his chest. "Devlin!"

He rammed into her stronger than ever before and she cried out at the force of his thrust. They scooted to the headboard, bumping her head against the wood. But she didn't complain.

He bent over her and took a breast in his hand, still inside her, never wanting to leave her. "God, that's a beautiful sound. Do it again, Tala."

"Devlin!" She screamed his name louder, longer, digging her nails into his back, fixing his body to hers. "Devlin!"

The exhilaration flowing through him found its way to his heart and he couldn't resist any longer. His physical control was no match for the emotions bursting inside him. At last he climaxed with a howl ripping from his throat. Fighting the animal within him no longer, he lowered his head, opened his jaws and sank his fangs into her shoulder.

"Ow! Shit!"

The strength she'd shown earlier was nothing in comparison to the strength she now used to toss him off her. Scrambling from the bed, she stumbled backwards until she struck the dresser. She sank to the floor and leaned her throbbing shoulder against the solid oak. "Ow! Damn it all to hell and back. You bit me!"

Devlin rose up on one elbow, blinked at her as if trying to focus, and swung off the bed. "Tala, let me explain." His amber eyes slowly gained more brown.

Tala gripped her shoulder, blood oozing onto her hand. "Are you nuts? What do you think you are? Some kind of animal? You bit me!" She grabbed an old T-shirt from the dresser and stuck it on top of the wound.

"You said that twice already."

She scowled at him, his remark stoking the volcano threatening to erupt from within her. *If he thinks I'm angry now...*

He winced. "I know. I'm sorry. I should've prepared—"

"Get away from me." She attempted to calm the mix of

pain, shock and—God help her—lust trying to overwhelm her brain, but couldn't. "Why the hell did you bite me?" *Does it really matter?* She gave it a moment's thought. *Yeah, the why does matter.*

"I didn't mean to. I just got carried away in the moment." Pushing his hair away from his remorseful face, he beseeched her. "Tala, please, listen to me."

He inched nearer until she stuck out a hand to stop him. "Please listen? What next? 'Please let me go for the jugular this time?' Would you like me to lie still while you finish the job?" Keeping her eyes glued on him, she grasped the furniture and hauled herself to her feet. *I can't believe it. This guy bit me!* Gritting at the pain, she snatched up her robe in the process, and headed for the bathroom.

Devlin started to follow her. "Oh, no you don't. You stay where you are. Or get the hell out. But don't you dare follow me." She thrust her finger at him in a threatening jab and stalked into the bathroom, slamming the door behind her.

Tala fell against the door and tried to catch both her breath and her sanity. *What the hell just happened? One minute I'm getting laid and laid good. Okay, laid great. And in the next, I've got teeth in me. Had their rough play gotten out of hand?* She crossed over to the sink to stare into the small oval mirror above the basin and frowned at her white complexion. *Sure, I've had rough sex before and even a little biting, but this is wild. Too wild.* With two fingers, she gently removed the robe and blood-reddened shirt to examine the injured area. Two major holes flanked a row of smaller indentations with similar marks in another semi-circle below. *Looks like an animal bit me.*

Reaching for a washcloth, she wet the soft cotton under the faucet and gingerly dabbed at the gashes. The sting shot down her shoulder and into her arm. *I will not cry. I will not cry.*

"Tala? Are you all right? Do you need my help?"

Is he kidding? "Never mind. I'll take care of myself."

Tala continued cleaning the area until the bleeding finally slowed down. She fumbled through her medicine cabinet, located the rubbing alcohol and poured some onto the cloth. Inhaling a long one, she held her breath and placed the alcohol-soaked material on her shoulder. A quick yelp escaped her before she could stop it.

"Tala, please. Let me help you."

She ignored Devlin's knock on the door as well as his words. Tears came to her eyes, and she stuffed the bathrobe's collar into her mouth to stifle her cry. Gripping her robe with all her strength, she waited for the pain to lessen.

"Tala, are you all right? Answer me or I'm going to break down the door."

Oh no, he didn't! She'd thought she was angry before. But the fury boiling over in her now put her previous ire to shame. *How dare he threaten me! First, he tears up my car, then he bites me like some caveman—or more like a sabertooth tiger—and now he has the nerve to threaten to break down my door?*

"Devlin, back off or I'm going to bite your balls off." *Crap, would he think that sounds as sexy as I do?* Her mind was on kinky sex when she'd just been bitten. Was she as crazy as he was? She threw the blood-soaked cloth to the floor, grabbed the bandages from the medicine cabinet and plastered on a quick bandage.

"I'm worried about you, babe."

A red stain spread across the bandage. Enough was enough. She'd put herself in danger with this stranger long enough. Determined, she swung open the door.

She registered Devlin's surprised expression as she charged at him, relishing the fact that he moved as fast as he could to get away from her. He'd gotten dressed in the meantime, and his shirt flew open in his attempt to get out of her way. But she kept at him, punching her finger into the middle of his solid chest.

"I told you to back off and I meant what I said. And don't call me babe. I'm no one's babe. Especially not yours."